FLASHING YELLOW

•

Flashing Yellow

a novel by

Mary Burns

TURNSTONE PRESS

Turnstone Press
607-100 Arthur Street
Artspace Building
Winnipeg, Manitoba
Canada R3B 1H3
www.TurnstonePress.com

Printed in Canada by Friesens for Turnstone Press.

Turnstone Press gratefully acknowledges the assistance of the Canada Council for the Arts, the Manitoba Arts Council and the Government of Canada through the Book Publishing Industry Development Program.

Canadä

The Canada Council | Le Conseil des Arts
for the Arts | du Canada

Acknowledgements

Thanks to Dave Robertson for his faith and continuing support, to Joy Olson for her advice on botanicals, and to the staff of Turnstone Press for their courteous and prompt attention to process.

Canadian Cataloguing in Publication Data
Burns, Mary, 1944-
Flashing yellow
ISBN 0-88801-258-6
I. Title.
PS8553.U68F52 2001   C813'.54   C2001-910051-5
PR9199.3.B7923F52 2001

For the other ten of the eleven of us
Bev, Donna, Kay, Tim, Judy, Mike, Pat, Tom, Jerry, Molly

The older I get the more secrets I have, never to be revealed, and this, I know, is a common condition of people my age. And why all this emphasis on kissing and telling? Kisses are the least of it.

—Doris Lessing, *Under My Skin*

[one]

The convention and trade centre on the harbourfront in downtown Vancouver resembles a ship frozen to shore: its make-believe canvasses are stuck in one position, as if the wind always blew the same way, and its prow points confidently in a direction it will never sail. Shinny had toured the building with her girls during Expo '86 and had returned occasionally for movies at the Omnimax—a feature on sharks her youngest, Elfie, wanted to see and, another time, *The Wonders of the Serengeti*. She could still remember the heavy lope of the lionesses, their faces bloody from the last kill, herds of elephants, galloping giraffes whose necks swayed so wildly she thought they must hurt, but she could not remember where she had parked her car. It could not have been this hard to find a space. She would have remembered that, and should also have kept in mind the spot she finally found, because to thrive in this city you needed your own trails, places where you knew you could get what you needed, like the animals with their water holes on the Serengeti. The hotel provided the only easy place to park, in the basement of the ship—did they call it a hold? she wondered—which cost two dollars for each half hour. People who had more money than time could zip in and ride an elevator directly upstairs, which was what Shinny thought she should do because even though she had devoted more or less the entire afternoon to preparing for this, she was going to be late if she did not find a spot soon.

"Like right now," she said out loud. Lately she had developed the habit of speaking her opinion to an empty car, an empty room. Occasionally, when the strands of the day emerged in a pleasingly even fringe, even breathed "Thank you" to a shadowy presence the general size and shape of her late mother. "Because I'll be damned if I'll pay four dollars an hour to park my car," she continued, now vaguely addressing her oldest daughter Lawreen.

"Lighten up a bit, Mom. You can afford it. Grandma would have wanted you to make a nicer life for yourself."

"Well, she wouldn't have wanted me throwing it away on an overpriced parking lot," Shinny replied to her absent offspring as the light turned green and she crawled around the corner onto Cordova, beginning her third circuit of the block. "There!" She spotted a car about to free up a space the perfect size for her Pony. Only a block from the main entrance and plenty of streetlights and traffic between here and there. She patted the back of her hair, still missing the mane she had worn for so many years, but liking the feel of her neck. She stroked more than patted it, as she would a cat. Thought of that movie again, those bloody-faced lionesses. Brushed off the front of her coat—her mother's good coat—threw her shoulders back and started toward the brilliant entrance of the frozen ship resolutely as if she were about to step on a gangplank rather than the sensor that caused the doors to snap open at her approach.

She had clipped out the newspaper ad that attracted her and folded it into the change section of her wallet so that she wouldn't lose it, but she didn't need to dig it out because here, not ten steps into the lobby, stood a notice board listing all the activities taking place in the hotel and convention centre that evening. Antique toy collectors. A retirement party for Air Canada employees. The name she wanted, *VISTAGRANDE*, came right after North American Mountaineering Society banquet, the reference to food reminding her that she had not eaten a proper dinner again tonight but snacked on crackers and cheese while she waited for her hair to dry. The ad had mentioned refreshments.

A long corridor and wide, with glass walls on the left displaying the lights of the harbour, the charcoal silhouettes of Stanley Park trees in the near distance. On her right, the vinyl pleats of doors that can be quickly folded in or out to make a room larger or smaller. She followed a middle-aged man and woman, good striders in sensible footgear, who no doubt took their finances seriously, just as people had been telling Shinny that she ought to do. As specifically Lawreen and her husband Ken had been saying since Shinny's mother died and her house in Meadowvale sold and the proceeds were split between Shinny and her older sister Carol, who lived in Charlottetown. A hundred and fifty thousand dollars each.

Now, when she did not particularly need money, Shinny was rich. And she should not just let the money sit in the bank, nor spend it all, blow it—again according to Lawreen and Ken—but put it to work so that when she retired—little more than ten years before Shinny became an official senior—she could live in fine fashion, travel, bestow generous gifts on her grandchildren, and have something left to pass on without ever having to worry about the state of the Canada Pension Plan.

"You've got your whole life ahead of you, Mom. You want to be independent." Lawreen again. Shinny resisted the impulse to argue back aloud, as she had in the car, because she was nearing a welcome sign with *Vistagrande* spelled out in the company's distinctive script, long tables draped with royal blue cloths anchored by silver coffee urns and stacks of white china cups and saucers, perky attendants holding piles of printed material—but the volume of her mental response increased to a shout: INDEPENDENT? JUST WHAT DO YOU THINK I'VE BEEN ALL MY LIFE?

"Good evening! Welcome to Vistagrande!" said a girl who had to be younger than Elfie, a girl with the big dark eyes and thick black hair of an East Indian, who spoke perfect, un-accented English, just as Elfie's boyfriend Brendan did.

The pleated vinyl partitions had been arranged to accommodate perhaps a thousand chairs, most occupied already, which forced Shinny to ditch the plan she had of lighting on a chair near the back, so that she could slip out unobtrusively if the information proved to be too puzzling or boring. She had to take a seat three rows back from the platform set up for the speaker.

"Excuse me, thanks." She shrank past the knees of a couple in what she guessed to be their late sixties, and, if you could tell anything at all about books from their covers, comfortably well off, both in light-coloured, light-weight wools, both with heads of snowy hair expertly cut. Unless they had dressed to look the part, as Shinny had, polishing the black pumps she last wore at the funeral, spot-cleaning the coat. She could safely adopt whatever identity she liked because she would never see any of these people again. Opening the folder the girl outside had given her, she settled into the upholstered seat of her straight-backed chair and assumed the role of the serious investor, frowning at the printed page she held in an effort to appear knowledgeable, even cynical, and not as ignorant as she felt. "Five Steps to Building a Successful Investment Portfolio." She inhaled deeply and began to read just as a squall of anticipation stirred the crowd, the white light intensified at the podium, and a small bearded man in a coffee-brown suit jogged into view, smiling and waving as if he were the host of a late-night TV show.

"You're probably wondering why I called you all here . . ." he started, and the audience joined in laughter. Grateful on one hand that the tension she felt had been broken, Shinny otherwise wondered what was so funny. The man, Carter Biggs, had paused to adjust the microphone downwards and the audience waited, many smiling as if this actually were a TV show and the next joke would come along in a minute.

"Now," he continued. "There is no reason business cannot also be pleasure. Is everyone comfortable? Good, because if you're not comfortable your attention is going to wander and I don't want you to miss anything. So . . ." The couple on Shinny's right had removed the yellow pads and yellow pencils from their Vistagrande folders, so she took hers out too and wrote the date at the top of the page. February 9, 1999. Nines. If her middle daughter Annette were here she would make something of that, Shinny knew.

"Every day we get prospective clients phoning and asking the most basic question: what kind of return can I expect if I turn over my life savings to you? Will I do better with Vistagrande than the bank? I can't answer that question because mutual funds are not like bank deposits, your money is not going to paddle along like a good little duck until he gets to the pond where all the big ducks play."

More laughter. It was how he said what he said. In the know, a wise guy. About thirty-five, like Lawreen and Ken: the younger ones knew more about everything worldly, they had better radar for navigating life's shoals. Shinny still operated by senses, which would inevitably weaken and finally fail. Even now she had trouble reading fine print. With her mother gone, her father long gone, her aunt, even Mr. Gillespie, the old man she had befriended in her co-op—with the old ones gone or about to go, the people her age now stood in the front lines, like the figures that flip up on a carnival shooting range. Whereas Carter Biggs, with his expertly trimmed, deeply gleaming cinnamon hair, clothes that fit like a second, more fashionable, skin, and his knowledgeable patter, clearly thought he would live forever. But this was no place to be dwelling on death: she had come to learn about money. A screen had dropped down to the platform and a projector in the back of the room beamed a graph onto it.

"And that's why, even with the political uncertainties, and recent corrections in the market, equities are still a wise choice. Let me show you what you'd be looking at today if you'd invested just $10,000 with us ten years ago. Let's say 1988."

She dutifully copied down the numbers on the screen, but her mind weighed anchor instantly. 1988. Annette left home that year, Lawreen got pregnant. Lawreen didn't have a hundred thousand dollars but she had Mattie, so you had to consider: there are investments and then there are investments and maybe life offers a bargain, people or money. That seemed to be the deal in her case: empty apartment, full bank account.

Shinny's stomach growled and she wished again that she had eaten dinner. There was no sign of refreshments, even though Carter Biggs, the fund manager, announced he was close to the end of his presentation and would soon be taking questions. Young men and women, all in royal blue jackets, all with lapel pins shaped like a rising—though it could be a setting—sun, with the word *Vistagrande* scrolled across them, stood in the aisles ready to take the questions people had written on their yellow pads. The attendant nearest her clutched a handful of paper, meaning the question period would be a long one. She couldn't leave yet, and it might be some time before she could. Yellow papers fluttered like disabled canaries from hand to hand. She should get in the spirit, write a question of her own. If this fund is such a good thing, why isn't everyone buying it? Too suspicious? Maybe, but it was the question she really wanted to ask, for her mother, in an effort to persuade Shinny to curb her impulsiveness, had wearily reminded her years ago that if something looks too good to be true, it probably is.

She felt hot, but it could be the coat she had kept on for comfort despite the crowded room and all the bodies giving off heat, the fire that is kindled by greed. Because wasn't it greedy to want to make more money when she already had more than she'd ever had, or ever expected to have, in her life? No, it wasn't, Ken explained, it was just good sense. So maybe good sense produced the same kind of energy greed produced, maybe that was why it felt so hot to her, or maybe her hormones were flickering like the light on the dash when the oil is running out. She slipped her arms out of her coat sleeves and let the coat rest on her shoulders, which helped enough so that she could return her attention to the speaker, who was reading a question off one of the little canaries: "Are you bullish or bearish on gold?"

"I'm glad you asked that question, because metals are always one of the more controversial elements in a fund mix. And gold, unlike, say, iron ore or copper, is not as closely tied to the business cycle. With gold you need a little knowledge, and a lot of nerve. Now I've been bullish on principle, but a cautious bull. I want to make sure that that flag I'm about to charge is red, not pink, not orange, but truly red. Yet there are some interesting cases . . ."

Crazy to have chosen tonight's seminar when there had been one this afternoon and another was scheduled for tomorrow afternoon. It would be a rare Saturday night out, she had reasoned, but at eight-thirty she could barely concentrate for hunger. She fingered the pockets of her coat for something— gum, a mint; found wadded-up Kleenex, a few coins. She realized that she had never worn this coat before, that the Kleenex, the coins, and yes, there was something edible, a butterscotch wrapped in cellophane—had all been deposited in these pockets by Mom.

The muscles around her mouth involuntarily pulled down and her Eustachian tubes began to fill. She had to stop thinking of how much she missed her mother and listen to the man on the podium. It was Mom's money, after all. Doing something smart with it would honour her memory, like a statue, or a plaque mounted on a park bench. Come to think of it, maybe she should do that: donate money for a bench somewhere. She wrestled the long-stuck cellophane off the disc of candy and slipped it into her mouth.

All at once the corner of a curtain blew back, exposing the scene within the scene—the smell of cleaning fluid that seeped from seat cushions; cleaning fluid merging with hair gel, muffled farts, cigarette breath, cologne. Oh yes, and the air blowing discreetly through grates in the ceiling to ventilate all the offensive odours, at least dilute them. The woman on her left, who had slipped off her shoe. That smell, and the look of a foot deformed by bunions. The grey dribbling through the ponytail of the person in front of her. The neat little man at the front talking about gold as if he were the chief and they his tribespeople and he could deliver not only great wealth but immortality. She slumped beneath the padded shoulders of her mother's coat, not a crone chewing betel nut, but a modern grandmother who lived alone in a government-sponsored co-op apartment and worked at a hardware store, who had let her daughter convince her that there was some point to this. The amplified voice of Carter Biggs pinged off walls that were not really walls, only curtains—curtains that couldn't blow back like the one in her mind because they were made of stiff vinyl that masked the gaping room with all its empty chairs just on the other side. Fullness hiding emptiness. She stared at a brown spot on the back of her hand. Carter Biggs was describing a prospector he had met when he was a boy. All the heads in the room tilted up attentively. Through tears that had not spilled nor wholly evaporated she saw the speaker surrounded by a mandorla, what she thought of as a halo except that it surrounded his entire body. A steady blue oval misting to red on the inside.

She sniffed and blinked and tossed her head and looked again. It was less like a halo, she decided, than the ring that forms around the moon before a rain. Mesmerizing. And he, the practiced speaker, who had been rotating his head to make eye contact with potential clients in every part of the room, seemed now to be beaming his headlights directly at her.

"Next question? Hmm. Oh yes." He smiled and raised his hand to his beard, which he stroked as he continued. Lifted eyebrows so blond they appeared as slashes of silver in the spotlight trained on the podium. "If I didn't get this one at every seminar, ladies and gentlemen, I'd make it up, because the question might sound frivolous to you, but the answer—and I mean this—the answer is serious. Big time. So here it is: if your fund is as good as you say it is, how come everybody doesn't buy into it?"

The remaining butterscotch slipped into Shinny's larynx, provoking a cough which she could not keep sufficiently discreet to escape the attention of Carter Biggs, who paused.

"Are you all right?"

She managed to nod, though the tendons in her shoulders had atrophied. The man in the row in front of her craned around to see who she was. I'm sorry, she wanted to say, I'm nobody!

"Okay, then. The answer is as simple as it is profound, ladies and gentlemen. The answer is . . . fear." He let the word sink in. "Get outta here, you're saying. People afraid to get rich? You bet! It takes courage to move up a step, two steps. While the air isn't exactly rarified, it's different stuff. You move in circles closer to the centre. You have nothing to gripe about. And we love our gripes. You betcha."

Laughter like the tentative edge of rainfall.

"Sure we do. They're comfortable, right? Like the old sofa. Yeah, the springs are worn out and the cat scratched the upholstery all to hell, but at least we know we're not going to get sick from any new synthetic fibres. Better the devil you know? Am I right? Hmm?"

Shinny considered: When she looked at her bank statement, saliva gathered in her mouth and she felt vaguely uncomfortable, as if she were wearing oversized shoes; troubled, as after a holiday meal when the fridge was stuffed with food she could never consume before it spoiled.

"Hmm?"

He seemed to be waiting for her reply. Better the devil you know? She shrugged. He sealed the exchange with a dip of his brown-bearded chin. Later she wondered if the company had intended to plant someone in her chair. Someone who would nod at appropriate times, ask the right questions. There had been that one empty chair, close to the front. Mutual funds. Carlo, one of her bosses at the hardware store, had suggested she look into them. "You know, Shinny, comfort in numbers." She would not be in this alone, there was that.

Carter Biggs's voice issued through the microphone like velvet ribbon through a buttonhole. "Okay. I see you're following me. So let's let that one lie for now." A beat, then static as he unfolded another of the paper canaries.

"Next question?"

Cara mama. Elfie repeated the words silently, long-bowing them in her mind. She loved this language. The simplest phrases spoke the passion of the people. She would learn to speak Italian fluently and then she and Brendan could stay, marry, find permanent jobs here. And Mama could come and visit. And Papa, Smokey, if he'd come by himself. There wouldn't be room for Oona and the baby.

"*Grazie,*" she said.

The counterman's eyes boiled with suggestion. She held her breath. If she smiled he would think she was encouraging him so she turned away and walked back to her table, and only then did she glance behind to see if he was still watching.

"*Cara mama.*" She sipped, studying her pad of blue airmail paper.

We finally got to go to La Scala last night!

Her small, backslanting script often forced Shinny to resort to a magnifying glass. She had asked Elfie to write larger, straighter letters and while Elfie had promised to try, she thought the better solution would be for Shinny to consult an optometrist. Vision could be corrected but handwriting came naturally, an extension of the self, and Elfie doubted that she could she transform her entire being.

It was Il Trovatore *by Verdi, the story of two brothers, the Count di Luna and Manrico, who's the troubadour, and the gypsy woman who tried to throw Manrico into a fire when he was a little child to avenge her mother because the Count's father burned her at the stake. I know it's complicated. I wish you could have seen it. Anyway, it's a revenge story. Azucena meant to throw the Count's son into a fire, but she was so upset she mistakenly threw in her own child. Hard to believe, but that's the thing, Mama: Verdi makes you believe it. Anyway, Azucena took Manrico home to raise as her own.*

When the Count and Manrico grew up, both of them fell in love with the same woman. Leonora. She loved Manrico and the Count was so angry about it he put Manrico and Azucena in prison and condemned them to death. Leonora promised to marry the count if he would spare Manrico's life and he agreed, but Leonora couldn't really do it. Before she visited Manrico in prison for the last time, she swallowed poison. Oh, Mama. The prison scene was just devastating. People were actually sobbing. She died in Manrico's arms. Count di Luna was so angry that he ordered his soliders to kill Manrico immediately. This is when Azucena got her revenge on her mother at last, because she told the count that Manrico was really his brother.

God, Mama. I couldn't even sleep. I don't see how Brendan could because he gets just as excited as I do and also a little depressed, because he always compares himself, and I know what he means, but we can't all be Verdi.

She finished her coffee and stared at the scarred tabletop until the scratches and cigarette burns began to morph into images of the righteous gypsy woman, skirts tossing as she strolled through the gyspy camp in full control of the stage. Fabulous. But Leonora's arias won the memory competition in Elfie's mind. *D'amor sull' ali rosee.* Let my love fly to him on rosy wings of love.

Workers and students at the other tables sipped dreamily, or smoked, chatted in speech too rapid for her to follow. Their breath and the smoke from their cigarettes made the inside of this coffee bar as foggy as the outside. The timbre of many voices crowded her mind. She had forgotten to write that Leonora was going to become a nun to avoid the Count. But it was getting too complicated. She wanted to finish the page and mail the letter.

How are you, Mom? I think of Grandma so much. But Canada seems like another planet from here. Everybody assumes we're Americans. It's hard to explain, especially when I get mail from California. Did Annette tell you about her new goats? I finally got Smokey's Christmas present, so you can tell him if you're talking to him. I wrote, but nobody knows what happens to the mail. It's worse even than in Canada. How are Mattie and Mariah? Tell Mattie I still expect a letter. Thank Lawreen for her card. I could stand another. The bad postal service means that it's even more exciting to actually get a letter.

I miss you, Mom, and everyone else too, but we feel we belong here. At least for now. I'm going to find you a tape of the opera and send it. Maybe I can get an English copy of the libretto, too, because the story is really too complex to write. It won't be La Scala, but you'll get an idea at least. And then you'll know what I mean.

Con amore, sua figlia,
Elfie.

It was just seven-thirty: she had time to sleep before her class that afternoon, but the music still chimed in her. *Mi vendica!* She couldn't practise until Brendan awoke. Or she could wake him. Slip into their apartment, take off her clothes, slide her cool body up against his warm one, though he might resent being woken, even in this way, when he'd had so little sleep. This energy, part coffee, part passion. What to do with it? She left the café and stepped into the not much fresher air of the street. Two blocks north, cars sped along a major thoroughfare. If there were a beach, like in Vancouver . . . But there was only the Po, and canal fragments. She walked towards the Duomo; if it was open she could climb to the roof and gaze out over the dirty, noisy city. *"Cara mama."* She said the words aloud this time, trilling the *r*. She could shop in Italian, understand directions—if people did not talk as fast as they were inclined to. When she could speak the language like a native, she might be able to feel more Italian, experience the big emotions that had inspired Verdi. *Mi vendica!* Avenge me, the gypsy woman cried. Elfie threw off the hood of her jacket and lifted her narrow face to the drizzle: *"Mi vendica!"* Here in the wet streets, with cars spitting past, it was okay to sing it aloud: no one could hear her anyway.

The March A and C Hardware flyer featured seeders and dibbles, trowels and hand cultivators, electric hedge trimmers, weed eaters, dormant spray, lopping shears, potting mix. Rushing the season, Shinny thought, it not being Easter yet, but Anthony and Carlo, when they did consult her, seldom let her opinion affect their decisions. She tacked the flyer to the wall behind her cash register, for easy price reference, and slipped off the brown apron Anthony had decided the staff should wear to compete with the personnel that manned the hardware superstores. In Anthony's mind, Revy and Home Depot were contemporary dragons he must outsmart or slay.

"Like it or not, they're settin' the tone. We gotta look just as sharp as they do. This is nice. Simple. What do you say, Shinny? You like the colour, eh? Matches your eyes?"

Anthony, the older brother, heavier set than Carlo and distinguished by a scar that sectioned his right cheek into plump, shiny-skinned portions, like a scored orange, punctuated his question with a wink. Unlike Carlo, the quieter of the two,

Anthony flirted instinctively. Yet he had no intention of straying from the bed, and especially the table, of his wife Adriana. Once Shinny understood this, she had been able to settle comfortably into the job, her first outside the grocery trade in a decade.

Seven years later she knew how to mix paint, measure lengths of cord and wire, chain; she knew which caulking compounds worked best on which materials; she could stock and price and deal with customer complaints and balance her cash every day. Not that there was much cash to balance. Tonight, and most nights, the tray she carried back to the office contained more charge and debit slips than cash. She had come into money when it was going out of style.

"What do you think, Shinny? A good day? Better than yesterday?" Carlo spoke without looking up from the computer screen that glowed blue on his side of the double desk.

"Not too bad when you add up the charges. Better than yesterday for sure."

"Tomorrow will be better still. People are hot to get into the gardens, eh? Seeds. And we're getting lotsa flats this year."

"Enough flats to plant Queen Elizabeth Park. Too many flats. Tell him, Shinny," Carlo pleaded. "Remind him how many leggy, brown-leafed snapdragons we ended up with last year."

"I tell ya, we gotta look like we have everything they have." Anthony waved a wholesale catalogue that featured a line of garden ornaments.

Occasionally they brought out a jug of homemade wine and offered her a glass. On especially slow winter days, Carlo would set up the TV they kept in the office to follow international soccer, and they would tune into "Home Improvement," a situation comedy featuring the star of a make-believe television show about tools, which they considered their theme show, and Shinny would hang around to watch with them. But this was rare because they both had wives who wanted them home after work. Rarer still since Carlo had started working out at the community centre gym.

Carlo slid Shinny's cash tray to the centre of his desk. "Hear from Elfie lately?"

Shinny placed her big hand over her heart and widened her eyes. "They went to La Scala. She's in love."

"Didn't I say?" Carlo and his wife Joan, who had no children of their own, had taken a special interest in Shinny's youngest, become like godparents to her. Aware of her passion for music, they had introduced her to opera by taking her to see *The Magic Flute* in Vancouver years before. In fact, their frequent stories of opera in Milan had inspired Elfie and Brendan to apply for graduate studies in Italy. Carlo had given her the names of Emmanuele family members to call on when she and Brendan left last summer.

"Not much time for letters, I guess. I told her to write you, though, Carlo."

"Doesn't matter. We'll call her. Such a busy girl. What a life, eh?

"So I'm off. Say hi to Joan for me. Have fun at the gym. You ready, Anth?"

He followed her to the door and locked it behind her. "Now don't get into any trouble, blondie."

"I'm not making any promises."

Six fifteen, just twilight, rush-hour traffic slowed to normal congestion so that the occasional gap opened between vehicles heading south, and the crowds at the bus stops had thinned. At the confectionary on the corner, displays of hyacinths, daffodils and tulips, primrose and primula brightened the sidewalk stands. Shinny could actually smell the flowers over the car fumes and the scents of various neighbourhood restaurants that drifted into the street from the long-established pasta places, the newer Salvadoran and Thai cafés. Purple and white crocuses bloomed in some of the yards of the few remaining houses on the side street she turned into, Robertson Street, but there were not many private homes on this street any more, nor any other in the neighbourhood. Those that had not been bulldozed to make room for modern condo developments had been divided into suites—three, sometimes four, sometimes five to a house. The washed-out, green-shingled, three-story derelict on the corner of Robertson and Bennett was a fine example of its type when the Grandview-Woodlands section of the city actually had offered grand views of the north shore mountains from land on which tall trees stood. The landlord had repaired the front steps on the old house not three years ago, but he had used bargain wood and the treads were already sagging. Still, an unpruned forsythia in wild yellow bloom brightened the entrance, drawing attention away from the steps and the particle-board stand-in for the oval glass window that originally graced the front door. Potential buyers, halted by the For Sale sign poking up from long silky spring grass, might be cheered into thinking of possibilities.

In the lobby of the co-op building across the street from the old house, Shinny's mailbox was jammed again. Most of it junk mail: prospectuses from various mutual fund companies, holiday tour-package catalogues, Vancouver School Board's schedule of continuing education classes. She scanned return address corners for the rising sun logo of Vistagrande, in vain. Nothing in the business section of the paper today, either. She did not expect to see news of profits already. No. Carter Biggs had emphasized repeatedly that investors should consider Vistagrande a long-term proposition. Nevertheless, the business news reporters regularly sought his opinion on the rising or falling Canadian dollar, corporate profits, changes in the consumer price index, bond market prospects, assay results of various up and coming mining properties. When she found his name, she clipped out the article in which he was quoted and slipped it into the Vistagrande folder she had saved from the seminar.

After his talk that night at the convention centre, he lingered in the corridor near the long tables where plates of cookies had finally been placed, answering a few more questions, no longer the tribal chief but a regular fellow prospective clients could trust to make them rich. Shinny nibbled on an oversized chocolate cookie and watched from the shelter of a potted fig. A man about her height of five and a half feet without shoes—in her high heels she stood taller so that when he caught her staring he had to raise his eyes to meet hers. The woman from the audience, the cougher. He reached into his trouser pocket. She wiped her lips with her palm. As he walked towards her the floor of the convention centre pounded and the window giving out on the harbour rippled, flashing reflections of the lights outside. She could have sworn it.

"Thank you for coming," he said and handed her a Vistagrande lapel pin like the ones the young attendants sported.

"Thank *you*," she replied, much as she did to customers at A and C. Was he coming on to her? No, he couldn't be, a man his age, in the know. A business man.

Her first package from Vistagrande contained a profile of Carter Biggs, *Canadian Business Magazine*'s Mutual Fund Manager of the Year. She learned that he was thirty-eight, that he had majored in geology at the University of Toronto. MBA from McGill, in Montreal. Never married. Known for his grasp of market trends and the accuracy of his hunches. One picture showed the conservatively dressed, blond-browed, brown-bearded man whose face had remained fixed in her mind from the meeting; a second picture suggested there was more than business to Carter Biggs. Cowboy boot resting on a rail fence, plaid shirt unbuttoned at the throat, jeans, his short-fingered hand on the head of the Irish setter at his side. Shinny would have found the image of him stepping off one of the space shuttles more credible. Carter on the range?

She made it down the hall without running into any of her co-op neighbours and then she was home. 6:33, according to the kitchen clock. She dumped the mail, her purse and a loaf of bread on the counter and went through to the living room, where she picked up the remote control and clicked on TV. She used to hate it when the girls left the television blaring for no reason, but since Elfie had left for Europe in the fall the apartment had screamed EMPTY when she got home from work; there was no music, none of the deliberate stopping and shifting that signified Elfie was practising and wouldn't want to be disturbed. Luckily, re-runs of "Home Improvement" played every night at six-thirty. Back into the kitchen for a banana and the mail. She turned the electric heat to twenty and settled on the couch without taking off her trench coat. She would wait until the room warmed up.

Tim and his wife were arguing about Tim's addiction to sports. They were sitting in a fancy restaurant and a football game was being telecast over a TV in the restaurant's kitchen. Shinny knew exactly how it would turn out because she had seen this particular episode before, but the familiar jokes and voices created a comforting backdrop as she attacked the mail.

A hydro bill, a sale notice from a department store. No letter from Elfie, but something that was not bulk mail or a bill. This she ripped open first.

"GIFTS FOR PARKS: The Vancouver Park Board Gifts Program provides a means for individuals, businesses or organizations to donate funds to the Park Board to enhance the park system. Popular donations include benches, trees, picnic tables and water fountains . . ."

She scanned the page until she saw a figure: $2000–3000.

The attached page listed locations where bench sites would not be available for years. All of them waterfront, which was where she wanted her mother's memorial bench to be situated. Were all the best spots taken already? She picked up the phone to call the Parks Board, forgetting the office would be closed at this hour.

"Mom?"

"Oh Lawry, I was just going to call out. What's up?"

"Have you opened your mail yet?"

"I was just doing that. What should I be looking for?" Three lines to a plaque, forty spaces per line. She looked around for a pencil. How many spaces did *Elfriede Shinnan* take up? Would *(nee Vanderclag)* fit too?

"I gave your name to the Regional District Parks. The spring program is just out and I thought you and Matthew could do something together. Canoeing maybe."

"Canoeing!" Shinny had never tried a canoe or sailed on a boat of any kind, unless she counted the Sea Bus and the big ferries that travelled between the mainland and Vancouver Island.

"It's fun. Matthew tried it at camp last year and he loved it, and Ken's taken him out in a rental a couple of days since then. But with work and Mariah's schedule we hardly have time to get away. Anyway, it would be good for you, and good for the two of you to do something together."

"Mmm." Water. She bent down to pick up a pencil that had rolled beneath the couch.

"What's wrong? Are you watching something? Do you want me to call you back?"

"Not really, no." A show called "Cops" had just begun. Policemen breaking down doors, chasing criminals in cars and on foot. Burglars and drug addicts and car thieves lay on the ground or stood up against buildings, clothes torn, hair ratty. Some sick or bloody. She reached across the coffee table for the remote and clicked the TV off. Wrote *Elfriede Shinnan* on the back of the Parks Board envelope. "So what do I have to do? Does Mattie know about this?"

"I told you he likes canoeing. And Mom . . ." Potential agreement had won Shinny the less judgmental, more affectionate *Mom*. "We got Mariah's new photos back today. If she doesn't get called for at least a cereal commercial something's wrong somewhere."

"Cute, are they? Well, the photographer would have to be a real klutz not to get a cute picture of Mariah." She couldn't think and listen at the same time but she could write numbers above each letter.

"I know. That's what everybody says. She's such a little doll, not that I tell her that. Anyway, with this new agent and these new pictures it's just a matter of time before she starts getting real jobs."

"Mariah, on TV." Only sixteen letters! She wrote *nee Vanderclag*, added parentheses. "Does she know what she's in for?"

"Oh mother. She's always been such a ham. You know. Mom?"

"Sorry Lawry, I hardly got my coat off." Thirty-three!

"Anyway, look at your mail, see if the brochure came. Greater Vancouver Regional District Parks. Canoeing at Deer Lake. The sessions are on Sundays, early. Mattie could spend the night with you so you didn't have to come pick him up. Should I tell Mattie yes?"

"Aren't canoes kind of tippy, Lawreen? I mean, is this for beginners? Don't forget your father drowned."

"Oh, mother. It's Deer Lake we're talking about. You'll be fine, and I told you Mattie has done it before. They don't tip unless you do something you're not supposed to do. It says no experience necessary."

Shinny reached for the banana skin and held it to her seeping forehead. "I suppose I could try it and see if I like it."

"Sure you can. You'll probably love it. I'll tell Matthew. How are you anyway, Mom? Feeling good? Work going okay?"

"Fine, fine. Let me look at this brochure and I'll call you later, or tomorrow." It was typical of Lawreen to have planned all this out before asking, knowing Shinny couldn't do a thing to disappoint Mattie.

"I'll tell him. Just look for that brochure, okay? And call them? I'll talk to you tomorrow."

The banana peel fell to the carpet as she stood and when she stooped to pick it up she realized she would probably have to kneel. Didn't canoeists kneel to paddle? She should have been paying more attention.

Mattie kept his eyes on the wave of milk sloshing up the sides of the bowl he was carrying to the dining room table, where Mariah sat on Lawreen's lap while Lawreen clipped her nails. Snip. Matt chewed his own nails down. Snip.

"Ow!"

"Mariah, this doesn't hurt. Your nails are like your hair, not like skin. It doesn't hurt to cut hair, does it? Matthew, I hope you didn't use too much sugar."

"Ow!"

A new box of Cheerios, plenty of crunch, even though he'd filled the bowl almost to the top with milk. When he had spooned all the o's into his mouth he would drink the remaining milk right out of the bowl. Cheerio crumbs and partially dissolved sugar would stream into his mouth. In the living room around the corner, Ken watched the TV game show "Jeopardy." Matthew chewed in time with the music that played while the contestants were thinking of the answer to the jackpot question.

"Grandma's going to do the canoe class with you, Matthew."

"Cool."

"Ow!"

"Did you ask her about my project?"

"I thought you asked her." Snip, snip. Matthew blurred his eyes and the blades of the tiny scissors glanced like swords. "There. We're finished. I told you it wouldn't hurt, honey." Lawreen's puckered lips came round Mariah's little ear and squeezed into her dimpled pink cheek.

"We're supposed to give a progress report on Thursday."

"Oh, Matthew. You know what my days are like. You were going to do this with Grandma. What can I tell you? She's lived more than half the century. Don't you have anything to turn in?"

He circled the inside bottom of the bowl with his index finger, collecting sugar. "We just have to talk."

Mariah slid off her mother's lap and headed for the kitchen. "If you want some cereal, wait for me, Mar. Well, you have that picture I gave you of Grandma and me, the look-alike one. And that ad for Meadowvale Farms where my dad's parents raised horses. That's family history."

January, February. This was March. The teacher wanted them to collect one item for each month of the last year of the twentieth century. "What about that picture of your dad that was in the newspaper?"

Now a car commercial played on TV. Some car zoomed down an open road while in the kitchen Cheerios bulletted into Mariah's bowl. "More," Mariah demanded.

"Mom?"

Lawreen reappeared, frowning. "Sit here, and don't spill."

Mattie telescoped back, saw them small, in a circle. Mother pouring milk out of a big plastic jug, that dent between her eyebrows. A chorus of girls sang: "You better drive one." From back here he would have to shout. "MOM?"

"You don't have to raise your voice, Matthew. I don't know if I still have that. I guess I can check."

"Good. Leave the milk, okay Mom? I'm going to get another bowl." He could pretend to be sick, but then he would probably have to go to Mariah's old daycare. Or he could pretend to be small, to disappear, and then the teacher wouldn't call on him.

Here was a plaque at the base of a tree, a tall evergreen, maybe a fir. Shinny could never remember the names of trees, though people's names stuck in her mind. "In memory of Adolph Felbinger." Maybe she should forget the bench and choose a tree. While the Parks Board had found her a spot on the east-side waterfront, they would guarantee the location and the bench for only ten years.

The earliest flowering trees were past peak bloom now, later cherries and apple, wild lilac and elderberry just coming into bud. Morning grey sky above and between the dark and medium greens of the conifers around the Nature House. She breathed in the rich, wet smell of earth and cedar. "It's great to be in the woods, eh Mattie?"

"This isn't real woods, Grandma. You should see where I went to camp last summer. Not even electricity lines, like this. No phone lines. Nothing but trees."

"I bet that smelled good."

He was ten and a half and the top of his head reached his

grandmother's shoulder. As Mattie grew, Shinny shrank. According to an article she had read in a magazine at her dentist's office, yoga could help stall the process. The force of gravity apparently caused the vertebrae to slump together as a person aged and if you reversed the load, by standing on your head each day, the vertebrae should loosen up again. Shinny meant to give it a try.

The couple closest to them dreamily sipped coffee they had poured from their personal thermos. Shinny wished she had some. Predicting then experiencing a restless sleep marked by anxious images of herself as a voyageur heading for a waterfall none of the scouts had warned her of, she had set the clock ahead for daylight savings, then forgot to adjust the alarm button. She and Mattie had to leave the co-op in such a hurry there was time only to grab bananas and Granola bars to eat on the way.

"The lake's down here, Grandma."

"But I think we should wait, Mattie, like all these people." She stepped closer to the couple with the coffee, who were either childless or had teenagers who couldn't be bothered to join their parents on Sunday morning excursions. "Are you here for canoeing?"

The man answered, a pleasant-looking man with a tweedy brown-grey beard, a snap brim cap. Coffee fumes whiffed towards her with his words. "This is it. The instructor said to wait here for the rest of the people while she checked the equipment down at the lake."

"Thanks. Hear that, Matt?"

She smiled at the man and, turning away, inhaled deeply again. Rain in the night had infused the morning air with moisture, leaving it thick but fresh, and now that she had got them safely here she could relax. She tuned out the human voices and heard birds, many different kinds of birds they must be, from the variety of twitters and whistles and songs that busied the air, but she could see only crows. Always crows.

Dancing down to the edge of the group to see if there was anything to eat, flapping back up to a branch or a wire and squawking their triumph or disappointment.

As usual—as if the earth itself were Noah's ark—everyone had come in pairs, but a more motley collection of pairs today, not just husbands and wives. Two sets of women, one other duo consisting of an adult and a child. The child half of this other pair, a boy roughly Mattie's age, followed Mattie around the Nature House, moving closer when Mattie bent down to poke at a corpulent banana slug, watching as he edged the slimy creature onto a piece of bark and scuffed carefully over to where Shinny stood.

"Look at this!"

"Ugh. Should you be picking that thing up, Mattie?"

A pleading glance from eyes green as Elfie's.

"Show this guy what you have, Matt."

The boy's father nodded his permission. His wife might be waiting at home, or they might be divorced and this was visiting day. Shinny could not tell by the expression on the man's face, which fell into absolute neutral after their brief eye contact. Early forties, she guessed, wiry ginger brows, smooth, pinkish, just-shaved cheeks, a nose that bulbed out slightly at the tip, as hers did, taller than the coffee drinker, faded blue jeans, a forest green cap with a tan corduroy bill.

The Parks Board instructor strode up from the lake with her clipboard.

"Hi, I'm Kathy and I'll be your guide this morning."

She signalled for everyone to follow her to the lakeshore where red canoes bobbed on the dark water like chili peppers in broth. A canoe for each party. Kathy told everyone to grab a personal flotation device from the pile on the dock and choose their craft.

"I thought we'd be with somebody experienced, Matt. Are you sure we can do this? I've seen people canoeing before but I have never done it myself." Barely a ripple marked the lake's smooth surface. No one else seemed worried.

"You can go in the bow, Gran. Not right in the front, but just ahead of the middle thwart. I'll take the stern." The excitement and the cool air had reddened his child-plump cheeks, and his mouth hung open slightly as it tended to do when he concentrated. He held the craft steady against the shore. Shinny climbed in the back, which sat safely in the mud.

"Come on, Gran. Up there. I won't push off until you're settled. Okay? Just hang on to the gunwales."

She could see weeds poking through the water, which meant it must not be too deep, and she was wearing a personal flotation device. Larry had not been wearing a life vest, a life preserver, as they called them back then. Of course, Larry had not been planning to make contact with the river. "Sure, Mattie. You just tell me what to do."

The canoe rocked from side to side as Matthew thrust it into the lake. The water received it smoothly and held it. Amazing. She rested her bum against the thwart, thankful there was a pad to kneel on, gripped the paddle with her right hand. At least this way Matthew would not be able to see her frowning and biting her lip. This was supposed to be fun. A few of the other couples remained on shore with Kathy, practising strokes in the air, so it seemed she and Matthew were not vastly more inexperienced than most of the group. When everyone was properly outfitted and launched Kathy paddled off in the lead canoe, in which the single father and his son had taken the middle and front positions.

"Maybe we should have gone with her."

"That kid has have never even been in a canoe, Grandma. We've got experience."

"Yeah, right. Just take it easy, okay, Mattie? Don't rock the boat!"

He laughed. "Hold the paddle like this." He lifted his to demonstrate. "No, Gran. Keep your hands further apart. I'll steer, you just go from side to side, get the feel of it. Okay?"

Worried about leaning too far over, Shinny cautiously dipped in the tip of the paddle and it skittered across the water, forcing her arm up and back.

"Whoa!"

"Stick it in deeper, Gran. Then pull straight back. Look how they're doing it."

A pair of women moved slowly and surely towards the centre of the lake, counting. "One," said the paddler in front. "One," echoed her mate.

"We don't need to count, unless you want to Grandma. Counting's more for rowers. See? You're doing it now."

She felt muscles she hadn't felt before in her upper arms, which were already strong from lifting cartons and sacks in the storeroom, even though Ted, the part-time warehouseman, was supposed to take care of all the heavy lifting. Now she understood the importance of kneeling; it helped her to thrust the paddle into the water cleanly, a knife slicing water she would never have thought so dense, murky though it was. They were not the last canoe in the flotilla, but neither were they near enough the leader that Shinny could gauge the progress of the man and his son. Not that she had time to look if she was going to match Matthew's impressively even strokes.

"You are good at this, Mattie. Your mom was right."

He grinned, pleased, the comical grin of a kid whose mouth is filled with teeth that need the discipline of an orthodontist to line up in the conventional way. She loved him passionately, and she trusted him. Yet she couldn't help wondering: was it just inexperience that had determined the leader invite the single man and his son into her canoe? Or had she too admired the masculine look of those newly scraped cheeks that suggested the scent of aftershave lotion whether he used any or not. Spice. Musk. Of course they would be a much better match, Kathy, this robust girl of, probably, twenty-five, with her easy air of authority, and this devoted single father.

"Look, Grandma. Ducks."

"Yeah, neat, Mattie." Brown ducks. She didn't know ducks

any better than she knew trees or birds but the coffee drinkers had paused and the man raised his binoculars.

"Only mallards," he announced. "You can always count on mallards, and Canada geese." "And crows," the wife added.

Shinny aimed carelessly every few strokes and irritated the surface so that the paddle chattered and pushed back at her, as it had in response to her first attempt, but the more she paddled the more she fell into the rhythm and the easier the paddling became. There was a flow and she did seem to be going with it. The sound of the water slicking off the blade. Delicious.

"I can just imagine what my arms are going to feel like tonight," she said aloud.

"You'll be fine, Grandma." Mattie ignored the canoes floating around them and imagined the lake empty, himself the scout from a ship of Hudson's Bay adventurers. Just ahead, Kathy swung around to face the group.

"If you can pause for a minute . . ." she began. "Look up there and you'll see the nest of a bald eagle. We have two bald eagles' nests on the lake. Whoop! There he goes. See him? The male. Hunting."

Next she pointed to a mound of mud and brush sticking up from the lake shore: "We have beaver lodges, too. This is the older one and we have a feeling it's been abandoned."

"Wouldn't it be neat if we saw a beaver, Matt?"

"Yeah, it would. I saw one at camp. They're cool."

"Any questions?" the leader asked.

Shinny thought of the yellow papers at the Vistagrande seminar. She had not gotten home until after eleven, and had ended up eating the usual peanut butter sandwich she resorted to on nights when will and imagination failed her, drinking a glass of milk and gazing at the house across the street where rims of light glowed through cracks around the chipboard-covered windows. Carter Biggs. That circle around him, had everyone else seen it?

He spoke her thoughts almost as they sprang into her mind. But his real genius might be that he could trick people into believing they had a personal connection with him; his hazel eyes the eerie kind that appear to follow a person, as do the eyes of saints in certain pictures and statues which draw crowds of devout people hungry for a share in the miracle. She had handed her application form to one of the young attendants and was promised a call, so she panicked when the phone rang. Could it be him, already?

"I know it's late, but I couldn't wait to find out how it went. I won't be sleeping much tonight anyway: the baby's got a cold. Were you in bed?"

"Tina! No, I only just got home a half hour ago. A long meeting."

"So?"

"It was okay. I learned something. The fund manager..." How could she explain? "The fund manager was quite a character. Convincing. So I signed up. I'll invest a little, see what happens, see what it looks like in a year or so, though they tell you not to count on much in the short term."

"Did you meet anybody?"

Although Tina had been adamantly feminist for years, committed to raising her older son Scottie by herself, her politics had softened as time went by and alone turned to lonely. Then she and George, who had been working for years at the liquor store just down the block from Tina's father's plumbing supply store, suddenly discovered each other. Having finally finished his degree, George was ready to move on. Now they had Homey, a second son for Tina, and Tina could only think of matching Shinny up too.

"I didn't go there to meet anybody, Tina."

"Come on, businessmen must go to these things, and guys around your age, who are saving for retirement. Didn't you notice any singles?"

She had hunched inside her mother's coat, sucking on a

butterscotch that could have been years old, shuddering at the dismal scene in which she played an extra. Those bursts of bleak depression exposed a world without the shine hope puts on it. Then the manager, Carter Biggs, had singled her out of the audience, and later, in the corridor outside, that weird connection had pulsated between them. But she would never tell Tina about that. How could she, when she didn't understand it herself?

"That wasn't the point, Tina. I was there to learn about money."

"Well, don't let money distract you from love. You don't get out enough. You'll never meet anybody unless you do some serious looking around when you do get out."

"I get out every day."

"Just a sec." Shinny heard Homey whimper.

"Poor thing. I should let you go. Did you give him anything?"

"Dimetapp. He's sleeping now and I guess I should go, my arm's about to drop."

Shinny stared at the circles the droplets of water from the paddle made on the lake surface, dreaming, as Matthew propelled them smoothly forward.

"I could do this every day, couldn't you, Grandma?"

"It's not as scary as I thought it would be."

"You're doing great, Gran."

The flotilla stopped again near the lake's eastern outflow, where waterlilies in fragrant creamy bloom bordered the shore.

"This is as far as we're going to go today, so you can turn your canoes around. Take your time heading back and feel free to ask any questions." Once again, though the time was now, Shinny couldn't think of anything to ask. "Do you have any questions, Mattie?"

He was peering over the side of the canoe, dangling his hand in the water. "What kind of fish are these down here?"

"Probably bullheads. Sometimes we get the odd brown trout."

The sky brightened to a thin even white the insistent sun would presently burn into separate shreds of cloud. Kathy skimmed by with the single father and son, who were both paddling expertly now, though Kathy and the man were also engaged in some talk about vegetation. Shinny waved to the boy.

"So can I take that article for my project, Grandma?"

That article, about Larry. The truth about her father so troubled Lawreen, she had made Shinny promise never to tell Mattie that his grandfather had died as a result of a drunken stunt. Lawreen also wanted her to tear out the last paragraph of the newspaper article, in which Larry's survivors were listed, because the list did not include a wife carrying the dead boy's unborn child. Lawreen had let Mattie assume that Shinny and Larry were teenaged newlyweds when the accident occurred. "It's kind of ripped, Matt. Are you sure you want it?"

"He was my grandfather, right? And even though it must have been way sad for you, Grandma, it's kind of interesting for the people who didn't know him."

Way sad. Larry, you dope. You could have known this boy! We could have had a life! His voice had echoed off the railway trestle, across the river, down to the beach where she sat drinking beer with the rest of the kids. A thundering "Hey!" from between the two hands that cupped his mouth. Creating such thunder at such a height, no hands, threw him off balance so that another "Hey!" of surprise came to them seconds before the splash. Not a loud splash, the other kids claimed. Hardly a splash at all, except in Shinny's memory, where quicksilver water spouted higher and higher around his plunging body, as though he were exiting life through a fountain.

"Well, I guess it's all right, Mattie. But we should photocopy it. It's the only picture I have."

"Do we have a family tree or anything?"

That's what they should have. A tree commemorating her mother, the family's tree, with everyone's names on separate plaques to hang from the main branches. An actual family tree.

"Not yet. Maybe we could do that together too. Make a family tree."

"A girl in our class has one. I don't think she made it. I don't think you make them, Grandma. They just sort of are." He was thinking of the chart as it appeared complete, names in neat boxes, relationships illustrated with firm black lines, as if they had all been planned.

Shinny's simple inquiry to the Vancouver Parks Board had linked her to a web of environmental groups, all of which needed money, to magazines, book clubs, and mail-order businesses, all with some slant on the environment. Greenpeace, the Sierra Club, Lands End, L.L. Bean. She liked the look of the people in the catalogues, the straight-teethed women in long skirts and dresses and handsome, rubber-soled shoes. A blur of teal, purple, forest-green and navy pleasured her eyes as she fanned through the pages before putting the catalogue on the throwaway pile. And this, on brown paper, like the unbleached paper towels and coffee filters Anthony stocked in housewares: Take Charge! scrawled in green across a picture of women rafting through a spray of white water, all of them laughing. Inside the brochure more aggressive language: "Take charge of your future, take charge of your life, develop your potential. Adventure excursions for women. Rafting. Camping. Climbing." Though the pictures were printed in brown and beige, Shinny imagined that the women in the raft, hanging from ropes on the cliff, hiking a trail near the snowy top of some mountain, had all purchased their clothes from one of the catalogues she had just discarded. The mailing lists had to be connected. How else did these companies latch on to people so quickly? Except this, the Xandria Collection. Perfumed paper. A different universe—courtesy of, it could only be, Tina.

She picked up the phone.

"Are you busy, Tina?"

"George is giving Homey his bath. What's up?"

"You and Lawreen, you keep trying to change my life. The Xandria Collection?"

"What?"

"My mail, I get so much mail. I can tell what comes from Lawreen because it's all connected somehow, outdoor activities, courses, mutual funds. But Lawreen would never sign me up for the Xandria Collection. You're the one who's always trying to fix me up."

"I swear it wasn't me. I never heard of the Xandria Collection. What about Annette, Elfie? What about some secret admirer who's trying to turn you on?"

"Mmm." Shinny didn't believe her. If Tina had never heard of the Xandria Collection, how did she know the catalogue offered racy underwear and sex tools?

She had slid the glass doors open because it was a warm evening, despite the rain. Spring rain. From where she stood enduring Tina's protestations she could see the boxes she had packed with potting soil and planted with geraniums, marigolds, purple and white petunias. By midsummer her balcony would resemble those lush and cheerful balconies she had always admired on the west side of town. Except for the summers she had, with Smokey's help, dug up a small backyard patch in which the girls could grow radishes and tomatoes, Shinny had never had time for gardening. So this delighted her, a little balcony glade, just the right scale. With a little luck the flowers would block her view of the derelict house.

Tina, who had veered off topic to report Homey's new tooth, returned with an ascending voice level: "Xandria Collection? For God's sakes, Shinny! Give me some credit!"

"Okay, okay. Just checking. I'll talk to you later."

She put the phone down and picked up the catalogue. There were lubricants in different flavours, scented candles, lace teddies. Satin cords. Dildoes. Shinny turned the glossy pages and the blatant appeal to her libido worked. She shifted on the couch. Was someone trying to make fun of her? Could it be Len, her last friend? She called him a friend because it was silly to call them boyfriends at this age and she had never felt comfortable with the word lover. Lovers operated in a different world where women wore satin to bed and men used movie words, *darling*. Carter Biggs would have a lover. A lover taller than he was and slender, with a voice silky as her swinging blonde hair, who would meet him in elegant hotel rooms after meetings such as the one Shinny had attended at the trade and convention centre.

Len had worked as a transit supervisor, travelling one Sky Train to the next, checking to see if people had paid their fares. Divorced, unhappy on his own and obviously attracted to Shinny, he began stopping at A and C every day on his walk down the Drive home from work. When he walked up to the counter of the hardware store, dressed in his blue uniform with the Sky Train badge over the chest pocket, Shinny would joke: "Here's the sky guy." He might purchase a package of batteries or ask if some item or another were in stock.

Len wanted a wife to replace the one who had left him. He told Shinny this on their first date, and his honesty impressed her.

"Yeah, living alone can be tough," she agreed in an understanding way. She had never lived alone herself but appreciated how it might feel. In her last year of high school then, Elfie was busy with the orchestra, her friends. How would Shinny bear it when Elfie moved out?

For six weeks Shinny met Len every Saturday night, for a movie, for dinner. A good-enough-looking man, dark hair still, sideburns that grew to the jawbone joint below his ear, a moustache, hands with unusually long nails which he kept scrupulously clean. They had sex the first time at his place, an orderly bachelor apartment off Venables. Kissing first, on the couch, ravenous kissing on Len's part. Before he flipped the couch open to make a bed, he pushed her an arm's length away. "Okay?"

Which was considerate, of course, but couldn't he tell? Then, lights off, clothes off, the shiver of skin on skin. She traced the bumps on his spine with her finger while he rolled on a condom. An interruption, but a sensible one: they weren't teenagers. Then more of the ravenous kissing, her throat, her face, her mouth as he climbed on. Fast, but he promised to control himself the next time—it's just that it had been a while, he explained—and held her tight. "I know," she said. "For me, too," and wriggled against him, hoping it was not over yet. It was. He slept while she lay wondering if need could turn into love. She remembered the old Elvis song, "I want you, I need you, I love you." It seemed there might be a progression. But she had not been able to talk herself into loving Len despite his need, his admiration for her, the paucity of other men, attractive or not.

Five years later she didn't like those fires breaking out down there, reminding her of the dry spots in her life. Len couldn't have sent her the catalogue: if he wasn't married now he'd have likely pitched off a Sky Train platform into the path of one of the computer-controlled units he used to travel, suicide the only possible cure for the loneliness that had so terrified him. Weeks, entire months passed when Shinny did not think of sex. Another effect of aging, she supposed, gratefully, for what was the point of wanting something you couldn't have, or at least couldn't have the way you wanted it—the way you used to have it. She walked out to the balcony, pinched withered petunias off their stems, as the woman at the nursery had advised her to do.

The warmish rain freshened her bare feet. Still light, a soft grey light, with a band of white in the west where the sun would soon dissolve in the ocean. A siren screamed through the intersection of Robertson and Commercial.

She tossed the dead petunias into the garbage and piled the junk mail into a bag for the co-op recycling box. Then she reconsidered—you never knew who had volunteered for recycling and would see the contents of the box. She took the Xandria Collection catalogue out, then rummaged through the rest of the paper until she found the Take Charge! brochure. Xandria went into the garbage but she attached the brochure to her fridge with one of the fruit-shaped fridge magnets the kids had given her. An inspiring picture, those happy women, flying on white spray.

But look at this! Caught up in the paper recyclables, a letter from Elfie that could have been here for days!

Cara Mama, Sorry I haven't written this month.

A photo slipped out from between the blue folds. Elfie and Brendan, both of them dressed in black, Elfie in a short skirt, black stockings, looking cool, international. A cathedral behind them, or a palace. Yes, it was a palace, in Venice. *Pallazo.* Arched doorways and little angels carved into the frames around the numerous windows. It couldn't be made of gold yet it looked golden, like Elfie's hair, which Shinny remembered not as golden so much as the colour of unwatered grass in the summer. It had to be sunlight gilding the scene.

The pallazo in the picture is near the orphanage where Vivaldi used to lead the orchestra. Remember that tape you got for me, the story tape about Vivaldi's life? I thought of it when I saw that orphanage.

I know I told you we were coming back in the summer, but we could get a fabulous job. Sort of musical camp counsellors on the

*Ligurian coast, near Portofino where all the rich people go.
Apparently they send their children to this music camp and it's
supposed to be amazing. One of the best parts of the coast. Hard
to turn down, Mom. Sorry. I know you miss me (us), and we were
going to drive down to see Smokey and Annette. But...*

"Damn!" Driving down to California with Elfie and Brendan
was going be Shinny's summer holiday, her justification for
buying a new car, a station wagon or even one of those minivans
that had become so popular. An excuse to trade in her Pony.

But alarm overwhelmed her disappointment. That tape! She
should have listened to it before she snatched it up so enthusi-
astically and brought it home as a surprise for Elfie. The music
was beautiful, but the story concerned a violin student of
Vivaldi's who turned out to be the lost granddaughter of the
Duke of Cremona! Only Smokey knew the truth, but what if
something alerted Elfie and Elfie asked? Shinny had never been
a good liar. She had been rehearsing for twenty-three years and
none of the phrases she had practised rolled smoothly off her
tongue but still staggered out in obvious need of support, which
is why she didn't want Elfie romanticizing over stories of mysterious parentage. Orphans. Long-lost relatives.

What was it with that country? First the opera about the
gypsy and the son she stole from his rightful father, now a
reminder of that long-lost granddaughter.

What if Smokey had told his wife Oona and Oona—for
whatever reason—had told Annette? Annette seemed fine now,
but there was a time when she craved singularity: the news that
she was the only one of the three girls to have a living biological
father who not only knew of her existence but rejoiced in it
would have given her precious ammunition with which to
wound both Lawrie and Elfie.

The sky had cleared as it darkened and the pink neon sign
over the consignment clothes shop at the corner, plus the traffic
control light, reflected dimly on Shinny's sliding glass door. The

rhythmic interplay of the lights reminded Shinny of jazz songs by singers who don't use words but doodle with their voices, and the thought of music led directly back to Elfie. She went without thinking into Elfie's old room, which she no longer visited every day, and pressed the play button on Elfie's sound system. A Brandenburg concerto immediately ravished the room. It was music Shinny might never have come to know had Elfie not decided when she was eleven that she wanted to play the violin. Frightened at first, because what did she know? What could she do if Elfie needed help, for example? Shinny gave in, as with most things Elfie wanted, and scraped up the extra dollars to lease an instrument she could use for lessons. Elfie practised every day without being reminded and moved through her books with an alacrity that amazed her teachers. At fifteen, she and a girlfriend were busking at the Granville Island Market. She needed better teachers, a better instrument, summers at music camp. Smokey helped, intrigued by Elfie's obvious talent, not knowing, because Shinny had not told him, about the grand piano in the apartment where Elfie was conceived. Shinny pretended that Elfie's musical talent had come from her maternal grandfather, who hummed Beethoven symphonies as he milked his cows. That was the story her mother had told, at any rate, and there was no reason not to believe it. By the time Shinny grew old enough to pay attention, her grandfather had turned as deaf as Beethoven and she was too young to recognize what he muttered and crooned as he puttered about his soggy acres. Her own father liked radio music: the pop songs of Perry Como, Giselle McKenzie, big bands. Her mother was a fan of Lawrence Welk. There was little chance Elfie's talent had come from them.

She turned off the lights in the living and dining room, slid the balcony door closed, locked it and lay down on her bed fully clothed. At least she knew better now. Despite the yearning the Xandria Collection had stimulated, she would never go out looking for sex the way she had that night. Not that she had admitted to herself that's what she was looking for. A man, yes.

The beginning of a new relationship. Nothing wrong with that. More than twenty years later the scene leapt from memory like a mugger from undergrowth along a path she had meant to avoid: foggy dawn light, the upraised lid of that grand piano. Quiet, quiet. She slipped on her white pants, buttoned her white sweater tight against her throat. Winced at the toenail polish that glared so gaudily in daylight. Bright, but not the carroty brightness curling over the white sheet. Oh, that hair. What if Brendan and Elfie had a baby with carrot-coloured hair? A red-headed Singh? What if Elfie tried to trace the source of those genes? Impossible. Shinny had never even learned his name.

In the cone of light from his desk lamp, Mattie sucked on a Tootsie Pop and studied a photograph of his mom and his grandma dressed to look alike. His mom loved this picture. Date: 1969. He placed the picture on top of his Spiderman paperback and picked up an ad she had cut out of some paper from the 1970s for Meadowvale Stables. Her dad's parents, the Blakes, used to keep horses at Meadowvale Stables. Lawreen never talked about the Blakes—Mattie figured they were dead—but she had cut this ad out of whatever paper long ago. Next he considered a grey and white snapshot showing Grandma Shinny on top of a spotted cow. Some time in 1945. A girl baby in a dress, a pair of arms holding her steady. Her mother's arms, she said. This too went on the pile to his left. His second newspaper clipping reported Grandpa Larry's death. It was not the actual clipping but a photocopy of the picture with its caption, and the headline that ran over the story. Grandma Shinny wanted to keep the original for her own memory box. Mattie liked the picture of his grandfather better than the picture of his mom and his grandma dressed alike, and both dated from the 1960s. He needed items for the 1910s, the '20s, the '30s. The '50s would be covered if Grandma found the book of her father's she said she had kept, about coping with the effects of polio. So Mattie was keeping up with the project, as he kept up with all his school obligations.

Although he shrugged as if he didn't care, or outright denied it when asked, Mattie liked school. He liked having somewhere to go in the morning, someplace he was supposed to sit, something he was supposed to do.

He was keeping up with the project but some kids were doing better. The girl who had impressed the heck out of the teacher by bringing in a family tree added a picture to one of the branches of her tree and told a story about one of her ancestors every time the teacher asked his students to report on their projects. An interesting story, too. Mattie wondered if the people she talked about were really so interesting or if it was just how she talked about them. Another kid in the class had a grandfather who was an explorer and had discovered some big copper mine in Chile.

While Matthew had been able to gather only the odd document and a few photographs, some kids had brought in their own family history books with crests on the covers and pictures and news about each of the family members inside. Matthew had never thought objectively about his family before this assignment. He understood now that some families took more pride in their existence, seemed surer than his of their place in the human scheme.

Now the teacher wanted the kids to write explanatory paragraphs about each item they'd collected. Mattie had written one so far: *This is my grandmother sitting on top of one of her grandfather's dairy cows in Meadowvale, B.C.* Boring. He spread out his pile of paper scraps to review them yet again. The only picture that held his interest was his grandfather's. Larry, Grandma called him, as if he would always be the same age he was here;

short, light hair slicked nicely back, shirt sleeves cuffed high on his arms to show off his biceps. Mattie had examined this image often. He thought he saw a private kind of message on the boy's face, the glint that comes into a person's eyes when he is trying not to say: *I know something you don't know.* But he might be imagining that expression because he knows the boy died less than six months after the picture was taken.

Lying in his bed at night, staring at the curtains of black-watch plaid Lawreen hung over the windows to subdue the morning light, Mattie had lately considered whether Grandpa Larry really knew he was going to die. If he did, couldn't he have changed things? Not walked on that railroad trestle? Did he feel helpless to stop the plan, to change it? And whose plan was it, anyway?

On the eve of the date his assignment was due, Mattie cut out the picture of his teenaged grandfather and glued it to a clean piece of paper. Then he cut out the headline that ran over the story: "Teenager Falls to Death," but he crumpled what was left of the newspaper story itself and tossed it into his wastepaper basket. Underneath he printed his description of the artifact. "My grandfather Larry Blake six months before he died trying to rescue..." he thought for a moment "his pet dog... Sky from a railway trestle over the Fraser River." He slid the page into his millennium project folder and filed it in his backpack.

A virtual pasture now grew on the corner of Robertson and Bennett, grass with seed heads resembling ripe wheat, big healthy dandelions. A "price reduced" sticker blazed across the "For Sale" sign. Shinny veered to the edge of the sidewalk to evade the skateboarder rolling down the street and gathering speed as the slope steepened. It sounded as if he was travelling on pavement, but skateboarders could hop boulevards and curbstones, eyes on the next obstacle: direction determined by the thrill potential of the terrain.

Saturday night barbque smoke puffed up from various backyards and from the balconies hanging off her co-op building. Oh, it smelled good and wouldn't she like to be sitting in someone's backyard, sipping a glass of wine, listening to chicken or burgers sizzle on the waves of heat from burning charcoal, chatting intently with a new acquaintance, trading the best stories of their lives, the most dramatic and interesting, the safest.

"Long day?" Her neighbour Jackie stepped off the elevator with a Hibachi.

"Too long," Shinny complained, pressing the close button to hurry the conveyance to the second floor. Jackie obviously had plans for tonight despite her chain-smoking and letting her grown-up son Deke not only live with her but insult her. Their curses frequently pierced the inadequate walls that divided their suite from Shinny's.

She didn't think of weekends until they were upon her and it was not unusual for her to have nothing to do on a Saturday night. A beautiful Saturday tonight, the sun still high enough to pole through her sliding glass doors, which she shut to muffle the tantalizing smell of grilling meat and the sound of happy voices. Life was a kite whose string had shied out of her grasp. She closed the drapes, clicked on the TV.

Before Archie Gillespie died last fall, she used to visit him in his apartment below her on nights like this. If anyone had time on his hands it was Archie. No time now, no hands, and Shinny had not yet befriended the elderly woman who had replaced him. She surfed through a rerun of "Seinfeld," a re-run of "Home Improvement," the news, the last half of "Star Trek." A show about insects on Channel 9, a cartoon, a talk show of some kind. She held this for a moment, her empty stomach billowy with anticipation. It was Carter Biggs. She pressed the volume arrow. He was talking about financial planning, which was odd in itself, because the big investment season had passed. Could this be a rerun, too?

"You have to know what you want, where you want to be in ten years."

The videographer zoomed in. While he listened to the next question Carter rested his tongue on his lower lip, then nodded in understanding and responded immediately, as if he had the answer to everything. He sat perfectly still, the picture of knowledge, self-assurance. Eyebrows silvery above eyes that appeared amber on her screen, an unwrinkled forehead. How did people become so sure of themselves?

The interviewer wanted to know the same thing.

"Carter, if there's anything that has set you apart from other fund managers, it's the accuracy of your hunches. Is this something you were born with? A sixth sense?"

The camera pulled back to reveal that Carter's apparent stillness did not extend to his hands, which he held in loose fists, forefingers pointed out and describing circles as he spoke.

"There's nothing mysterious about it, Robert. I study the market, I research the history of the company I select and consider its performance potential in light of present political and economic realities. Then, too, you have to remember that I've been at the game for well over a decade."

"And you're still a kid!"

Carter cocked his head to the side dismissively. "This last month, for example, I investigated emerging markets in South America. Brazil is looking especially good and we're acquiring equities in some forward-looking companies in that fascinating country. To those who say that Brazil is still a developing country, I say we may not have to wait as long for some countries to develop the way we used to, because technology is changing everything. Of course I saw all that in the numbers, from my office in Toronto, but I like to know what it's like for the local Brazilians. Do they tend to be easygoing, or, if they were put through hardship, would they rise up and revolt? Do they tend to be motivated to make a lot of money? Are they very materialistic? Do they like borrowing money or do they like to save it?"

The theme music began and the host of the show asked Carter for a final word of wisdom.

"The important thing is to know your territory, whether it's Canada or Brazil. And by the way, we don't have to look to foreign markets exclusively, not with the potential we have right at home. Just so you don't let yourself drift into any backwaters, financially speaking. Be the captain, pay attention. Take charge."

The camera had moved in to fill the screen with the head and shoulders of Carter Biggs. He spoke directly to the lens. Then the theme music began to play more loudly and the camera pulled back to frame the host of the show and Carter Biggs, standing, shaking hands. Shinny stood, too. *Take charge*, he'd advised, as if he could see through the TV set all the way into her living room, to her, poised on the couch. *Don't let yourself drift; be the captain.* Then past Shinny to the brochure magnetted to her fridge. Those laughing women. If they could do it, why couldn't she?

On Monday evening the rain-puddled walk along False Creek was quiet except for the occasional jogger or cyclist and the Canada geese that honked and hissed at any threat they sensed to their broods. Shimmery water reflected lights, shapes that wavered in narrow ruffles. Tina had agreed to meet Shinny at the community centre after Scottie's ball game and she wasn't making any promises. She would come to the introductory meeting, but a five-day raft trip?

"You should get somebody else to go with you, Shinny. I'd love to, but I don't know." Tina wore her dirty blonde hair long, with bangs that flopped down to her eyebrows. Turtlenecks no matter what the season. In warm weather, a sleeveless turtleneck tucked into cotton shorts. When she was seven she had fallen on a live soldering iron and a large lumpy scar disfigured the skin on her chest, just above her breasts.

"You said George wouldn't mind."

"He wouldn't, theoretically, but he's never spent five days alone with Homey. I'd worry."

"Scottie would help, and your mother. Just try it, will you, Tina? I don't have anyone else to ask." Her daughters were no longer available for company and she had lost touch with the women she had known when the girls were young; other mothers, parents of the girls' friends. Besides, Tina would fit in. Taller than Shinny and larger-boned, more athletic-looking, only their

hands were the same size, and that's because Shinny had dispro-
portionately large ones.

She could see the community centre across False Creek,
which isn't really a creek but an inlet of the ocean bounded by a
stone and cement wall, more a city pond. Elfie had played a concert here once. The Vancouver Youth Orchestra set up in the
outdoor amphitheatre on the point, proud parents and friends
arranged on grass humps landscaped to resemble steps or
benches. If plaques could be attached to grass benches, Shinny
would have liked her mother's memorial to be situated here.

George pulled into the parking lot at seven exactly and
Scottie stuck his head out the window.

"I guess you weren't rained out, Scottie."

"We won, Aunt Shinny!" Tina kissed him through the open
back window, and patted Homey's head. "Come on, we're late."
They hurried inside to the lounge and joined the group of
women sitting on the carpeted floor, on cushions and on
couches all more or less facing Heather, the Take Charge! rafting
leader, who stood in front of the pull-down screen on which she
intended to project slides.

Fifteen women, Shinny guessed. Heather confirmed it.

"I have to tell you that we have only eight spots per trip.
Assuming you're all going to sign up, I'd have to schedule
another trip. Just so you know.

"The rafting itself is easy," she promised. "I steer and you
help by paddling. I show you how and after the first day you get
the idea. We provide wetsuits and helmets and any other safety
gear that may be necessary. If the river is too high we have the
option of portaging any sections we feel might be unsuitable for
rafting. Okay? This first slide is an aerial shot of the northern
Cascades in Washington. Our river is that green line to the bottom left of the screen. Do you see it?"

She used a pointer to help those who couldn't find the gleaming ribbon in the darker green tree cover. The river narrowed as
it curled through canyons, then spilled out broader, plunging

west. Heather stepped right up to the screen and her black silhouette dominated the image as she poked her finger at a section where the river was most narrow, the water wildest. She stepped back, clicked the button on the slide carousel and a new image took the place of the overview. The first in a series of action shots: a head-on angle of women with their oars in the heaving green water, sun slanting through the treetops. Then the one Shinny knew so well from the brochure: heads thrown back, laughter, white spray showering them, sparkling. In this full colour shot there were actually rainbows.

"Wow!"

"Didn't I tell you, Tina?"

The day before they were due to leave Vancouver, Shinny drove over to Main Street, across the railway overpass guarded by the grey marble lions donated to the city by Chinese immigrants, down to the waterfront park. The old canning shed to the right of the tugboat dock flamed scarlet, as it did every evening when the sun beamed directly onto it. At this time of day there were no trains clanking into one another on the tracks behind the park, no forward beepers as giant forklifts moved containers around the docks beyond the canning shed. No helicopters lifting off the pad beside the cruise ship terminal to the west. The Sea Bus maneuvered easily past ships waiting to load sulfur, lumber, wheat, towards the North Vancouver quay. Back and forth twice an hour, as night fell and the lights of the city outshone more distant starlight.

The benches here were not the classic type with slats for the rain to run through, but thick slabs of cedar, one for the seat, one for the backrest, joined by metal pipe; the whole assemblage rested on a concrete base. Solid rather than graceful, an appropriate design for the working waterfront. The plaque, set too deeply into the wood slab for anyone to be able to easily pry it loose, read simply: "Take a Load Off, in memory of Elfriede (nee Vanderclag) Shinnan." Shinny had not even used her full letter allowance.

The day the bench was to be installed, Shinny made a picnic and invited Lawreen and Ken and the children to come to the park.

" 'Take a load off,' Mother? Shouldn't we have talked about this?" Lawreen's eyelashes fluttered.

"What, you don't like it? It sounds like my mother."

"Okay, but this is public. How much did you have to pay for it? Do they give you a discount for the east side?"

Shinny reached for Matthew, massaged his shoulders. Elfie and Annette would not have criticized her choice of words. Elfie would have hugged her, cried. There it was, Grandma's name, in a place thousands, maybe millions of people could read it during the ten years the city would allow it to exist here.

"This is a cool park, Grandma. Look at that! Another helicopter!"

"It is cool, isn't it, Matt. Why don't you go spread out that blanket? I picked up a barbqued chicken and I've got a cake."

When he had dragged the picnic blanket up the rise near the playground, where Ken pushed Mariah on a swing, Shinny sat down on the new bench and waited. Lawreen, arms folded across her chest, joined her, but with a sigh loud and long enough that Shinny would not mistake resignation for pleasure.

"This is for my mother, Lawreen, not for you."

A sea bus steamed over from North Vancouver; the whistle blew on a tug. Shinny stared straight ahead, though if she were to turn just slightly to the left she could see the best view the city had to offer of the Lions Range peaks.

"Sorry, Mom." Lawreen put her arm around Shinny's shoulder and squeezed. "It is a good idea. I was just thinking something more dignified . . ."

Shinny supposed Lawreen would never come here again. Lawreen had never been particularly close to her grandmother, despite being Elfriede's first grandchild. Whenever they visited

Meadowvale, Lawreen tried to persuade Shinny to drive over to the Stables, to try again with the Blakes, who had never acknowledged her. She took after the Blakes more than the Shinnans, Lawreen believed. It didn't matter. There were no more Blakes, no more Shinnans. Only Shinny, a nurse tree fostering unpredictable growth, the girls, the grandkids.

She visited the bench this evening to say goodbye, for though the raft trip seemed fated, she had never attempted anything so adventurous. Speaking softly, hardly moving her lips, in case anyone was watching and took her for one of the street people who habituated this park, she tried to explain. "I feel I ought to try some things before I die, Mom. Lots of people do this and I've never heard of any accidents. It was like a message, you know? That man on TV. I think it will be all right. I did okay in the canoe, better than I thought, but if anything happens, do what you can for the girls and Mattie and Mariah, will you?"

A couple sprawled on the driftwood-strewn beach, hunched together, maybe necking, maybe shooting up: it was that kind of neighbourhood. Ports Police in a blocky epaulet on the park's shoulder, Waterfront Social Services on the other side of the overpass. Nothing she did here would be considered odd.

Then a cyclist wheeled towards her, helmeted head down; ginger brows, smooth cheeks pink as if just shaved. Having worked in the retail trade for most of her life, Shinny had a good memory for faces. She knew the man instantly as the single father canoeist from Deer Lake Park. She intended to smile when he looked up, but he never looked up, just pumped his knees and rolled straight down the centre of the cinder path.

When she got home Tina called with the bad news.

[two]

June 25, 1999

Cara Mama,

I am writing from my bella prison. It is so beautiful here and the sea makes me homesick, even though the Golfo di Genova is not English Bay. It's hard to be separated from Brendano. That's what the little girls call him here. He's a big hit with them. Did you hear Smokey's news? Another baby! It's getting so that he's losing count. He said number three, but if he's talking about his new family it would be number two, and if he counts Annette and me, it's number four. If he counts Lawreen, which he ought to, it's number five. I guess it's cool. It's not going to make things any different than they've been since he got married. Annette says that Oona reminds her of one of her goats—a long face and a kid sucking on her all the time. It is kind of weird to have a dad who is sort of a grandad—if you count Mattie and Mar—starting all over again.

Brendan and I have found a cove where we can meet for some privacy after we're finished with the kids for the night. Not that we ever really are! We have to sleep with them. Make sure no one hurts themselves and comfort bad dreams away. These kids are spoiled, Mom! But anyway, last night just after dark I took my fiddle and made my way down this path that is really kind of treacherous unless you know where you're going. Everything is so steep here! You wouldn't believe the kind of land people farm on. Brendan has this idea for a suite based on the cycles of the tide— Liguria. He swears the tide has a different sound here and now he's convinced me. I think it's because of all these little coves. I miss you Mama. A whole year! Will you really come this fall?

Shinny stood back from the edge of the cliff and studied the river that frothed through the gorge below. Green, but mostly white, bubbling, spraying up. The green was not a clear but a milky green because the water originated in a glacier. Old ice gave the river its milky cast, and so maybe its sense of thickness too. Until she canoed with Mattie, Shinny had thought of water as slippery rather than thick. Larry had slipped into it conclusively, a stone that missed a skip.

The river spoke like thousands of people arguing in voices too soft for her to understand the subject of their disagreement. Low sun burned through the long graceful bristles of a ponderosa pine. She pushed at a piece of lichen with her running shoe. To her left, slightly upriver, water forced through a small natural arch. Pretty. Had she not become so uncomfortably intimate with the river today, she would have softened with pleasure and snapped a picture with the camera Lawreen and Ken and the kids gave her for Christmas. In fact, she should go back to her tent and get it right now, before the sun set, so she could share this beauty with everyone, tape a snapshot to her cash register at the hardware store. Yes, I was right there, right on that wild river. You, Shinny? I thought you were afraid of water. She would show Tina and Lawreen and the kids and Ken. She would make copies and send them to Annette in California, who would undoubtedly show her dad, Smokey, who would be surprised. Shinny? Another copy for Elfie, in Italy.

Thoughts of her girls added to her worries. She squatted, then sat, picked a stem of dry grass and poked it between her bottom teeth. Lawreen would not think much of her if she left the group at this point. Even if she took pictures of this stretch and described the rapids in the technical terms Heather used, even then Lawreen would be disappointed, Shinny knew, and maybe Annette too, or maybe not. Annette had never been as naturally bossy as Lawreen. Elfie would be forgiving, at least now, though the time might come when Elfie found it hard to forgive her mother anything.

Take charge, he said. She saw his face on the small screen, the tip of his tongue lightly resting on his plump lower lip, his eyes, brown like hers, yet clearer and a concentrated golden brown, those silvery-blond eyebrows above them. But he was discussing financial planning and in that area she had taken charge by turning first twenty-five thousand, and just before she left, another ten thousand over to him—to the Vistagrande fund. *Be the captain*, he had said, but he was talking about money, not about risking her life to prove that it was still worth something. One way of taking charge was to decide what she could do and what she couldn't, and act on it. She was afraid of water, this stretch of it anyway, and it had cost her a thousand dollars to try to convince herself otherwise. Well, she was stronger and the rind of skin around her waist had firmed and she had not noticed the heart hurry that so frightened her when she first felt it, just before her periods stopped for good. Although the Vitamin E capsules she swallowed every day might be responsible, exercise strengthened the heart muscle too.

Muscle. The part of her body she associated with emotions, where hate came from, love, fear, sorrow, was a muscle, same as the back muscles that had ached so after the first day on the river. A muscle with revolving door valves that cycled emotions just as it cycled the blood that kept her alive. "Not for the faint of heart," read one of the lines on the brochure.

She had strengthened her heart muscle with vitamins and all this exercise but here she stood, practically sunset on only the third day, nothing if not faint of heart. She didn't think she could do it. She didn't think she wanted to do it. Correction. She knew she didn't want to do it. And she was just as disappointed in herself as everyone else was bound to be. Heather, the group leader, the other women on the excursion. What would Carter Biggs say? Cut your losses? Buy low, sell high? If she left now, would she more or less come out even? Carter Biggs could be difficult to read. He spoke forthrightly enough but in phrases as cryptic as those Smokey used to read to her from the *I Ching*. "The perception of risk is very, very important in finding bargains. We often look at the discrepancy between reality and the outlook."—Biggs. "Perseverance furthers."—*I Ching*.

A small flight of Oregon juncos converged on the oak scrub along the cliff top. Shinny caught movement out of the corner of her eye but hadn't the leisure of mind to look closely enough to try to determine what species of birds they were. Diane and Lynette, the lesbian couple in the rafting group, knew everything about nature. Diane and Lynette, along with Heather, who also knew everything, had discovered several edible weeds and flowers to supplement tonight's meal. They were the ones who belonged out here, Shinny knew. If the raft overturned, they would confidently swim or float downstream until they reached an outtake where they could clamber onto land, dry themselves off and survive on whatever wild foods they found until rescued.

The river pushed along, sluicing its banks and carving more finely the arch it had sculpted over hundreds of thousands of years. Back at camp, someone laughed; Lynette, she thought, because Lynette had that hardy ho-ho way about her. Mixed in with the aroma, fading now with daylight, of sun-heated pine and volcanic rock, Shinny could smell frying onion and garlic.

Heather knew what she was doing. She had taken this mostly green group through some stretches that were almost as wild as the one below, and instead of swallowing the women, the river had given them an exhilarating ride. To Shinny it felt as if the raft were jointed, like a snake, and could undulate over rocks she thought should break it. Tomorrow would be the most fun. They were all excited.

Above the roar of the river came a clanging sound, someone's idea of a dinner bell.

"Coming!" Shinny called, turning onto her knees to stand. Part of her liked it that someone else was taking responsibility for accomplishing the basics; part of her wanted to say—to hell with your bells, I'll eat when I want to. That same part was trying to muster the courage to tell the group she wanted to leave, so she did not intend to make a point over the meal.

Diane crouched beside the fire, stirring a pot of something while Lynette forked salad onto plates.

"Sure starts to cool off when the sun goes down," Shinny said as she joined the group. "I'm going to get my jacket."

Heather bobbed her head as she chewed. It wasn't a matter of giving permission so much as acknowledgement, Shinny knew, but she hated having to account for her every minute. That part of group camping they could keep. After the first night out, she had got into the habit of pegging her little red dome at the edge of the cluster of tents, foreseeing a need for occasional privacy. For later that night, around their first campfire, when river stories ran out and the women turned to talk of relationships, Shinny had crept away, pleading tiredness. How she could ever explain her history with men? Should she even try? Well, I have a sort of thing going with my mutual fund manager. He sends me messages through the TV and I get letters from him every month.

"Hey Shinny, get over here! You're going to miss out."

"It smells good, what is it?"

"Stinging nettles. It tastes like spinach, but if you don't like it plain you can add it to your stew."

"Can't wait to try it," she said, and it was true. She had signed on for new experiences and this one she could handle. We ate right off the land, she would tell Tina and Lawreen, who would be skeptical but proud, and Annette, who would approve, country girl that she had become.

"Sit with us," Diane invited. Her morning-glory eyes widened as if Shinny were the light of dawn. Lynette patted the stump alongside the blanket they were sitting on.

"Thanks."

Part of it was this, being the extra. Everyone so kind, applauding her for coming along even though her intended partner—Tina—had to cancel at the last minute because Homey developed an ear infection.

"Fabulous or what?" Lynette smacked her lips.

"No or what about it. It is fabulous. Let's look for more nettles tomorrow. Like it, Shinny?"

She pointed to her mouth, which was engaged in chewing the stringy stuff. It didn't taste bad, but the texture! Leaves gone slimy under a flower pot or a saucer forgotten outside. All the same, a good sport, she raised her eyebrows and smiled encouragingly.

"What's amazing is that it loses its sting completely."

"Thank God for that." She swallowed.

Heather sat across the clearing with Phoebe and her nose-studded friend Cynthia, and the sisters from North Vancouver, Nancy and Nicole. Nancy, who had some experience with wild rivers, was comparing the relative merits of rafts and kayaks. Blonde, lean Nancy, who might have stepped right off the pages of the L.L. Bean catalogue, thought she'd get a more challenging ride in a kayak.

"Sure, if you know what you're doing. But for inexperienced river runners a raft is definitely the safer bet."

Safer. So what am I afraid of?

"Okay, we've been good, right?" This was Nicole, the oldest of the group, Nancy's shorter, stouter sister. She called herself a fish economist and though Shinny knew she was referring to a job more plebian, she could not dismiss the image of Nicole as a biblical character, handing out the fishes Jesus mysteriously multiplied.

As if she too saw herself as a distributor of food, Nicole held up a large tin-foil square, which she opened when she reached Heather.

"We've eaten our veggies, now it's time for some real food!" She ripped open the foil, revealing a couple of dozen chocolate brownies which she had managed to keep intact for three full days.

"Nicole, you're an angel!"

"An angel bearing devil's food. Thanks sis, just like you to come through."

It was good, it helped. Shinny finished her square too quickly, then extended the pleasure by licking her fingers.

The star-spattered blackness of night had finally eroded the shapes of the mountains across the river. Phoebe placed more wood on the fire. Soon she would suggest that they sing. Shinny knew the routine now, their third night together. The first night, eager to make a good impression, she stayed for the singing and the stories. It had been a good day; the powerful sweep of the current had thrilled her, and rafting proved to be easier than she had anticipated. Beyond keeping her warm and dry, the wetsuit provided a kind of padded security. Heather steered, shouting instructions, her strong arms glistening with the water that splashed off her oar. They rounded a bend, bumped cheerily through a riffle. Cynthia whooped. A narrow, slightly elevated chute tested Shinny's stomach but they were in it, shooting through, before fear could fully blossom.

This morning started easily enough, with a two-hour meander where the river widened as it passed through farmland. They relaxed and enjoyed the scenery along the banks until the river narrowed again. The chutes dropped more steeply and skirted some huge boulders. Cynthia whooped half the afternoon. If yesterday was a three on a one to ten scale, and today a five in some places, tomorrow was going to be a six or a seven. Today Shinny had not had time to recover from one thrilling ride before Heather called "chute" again and they had to prepare for the next. Her stomach muscles ached as much as the muscles in her shoulders. She didn't want to go through this again tomorrow, but tomorrow was the apex, the part they'd all signed up for. The deepest canyon, the wildest water.

So what am I afraid of, she asked herself, tonguing chocolate off the crevices in her teeth as she stared into the fire. Death? This was Heather's ninth trip on the river. No one in her charge had died or even hurt themselves seriously. Besides, if Shinny should die, it wouldn't matter so much now that the girls were raised, on their own. Even the Elf. Of course they would miss her, she thought, as she missed her own mother. Mattie too. Her nose stung. Silly.

"Well, that was great," she said, getting up with her plate and stretching.

"You okay, Shinny?" Heather called after her.

"Aside from my seized-up arms and legs you mean?" Shinny purposely shuffled heavily off. Let exhaustion explain why she was turning in earlier than anybody else.

"Goodnight, then."

" 'Night."

Away from the fire the black night loomed and the river shushed insistently. Instead of ducking into her tent, she flicked on her flashlight and retraced the trail to the cliff. Heather ordered the women to dig a latrine at each campsite, but Shinny preferred to pee in the bush. There was something erotic about it, forbidden; cool air on her skin, the drill of her urine on the ground. Wild animals no longer frightened her as they had the first night, when the reverberating growl she thought must be coming from the throat of a bear or a wolf interrupted her sleep and she flipped onto her back to keep wary vigil until the growl began again, from the pit of her own stomach.

"Don't you wish there were some," Heather replied when Shinny asked her about wildlife. "Wolves got wiped out years ago, and if there are any bears around, they'd be up in the mountains this time of year. You'll hear coyotes but seldom see one. Porcupines and possums, raccoons. Nothing bigger than you are."

Porcupines. From what Shinny knew, they could fire their quills at predators. The thought caused her to yank up her jeans so quickly she lost her balance and dropped her flashlight, which rolled away over what she had thought was even terrain. She stood carefully, stealthily, as if something were out here pursuing her, as though she should make no false moves, and slowly rotated her body in a complete circle, focussed on the ground, searching for the yellow eye of light at the end of the plastic cylinder.

It would be stupid to lose a flashlight. How was the trip, Mom? Great, except I lost my flashlight the third night. Was that going to be the big news?

The campfire leapt like the flame of a fat candle; she could see it through the tree trunks, but she wasn't sure she could make it from here to there without tripping over a root or a stump. Was it possible to get lost within sight of her group? She could call, but that would be even more embarrassing. They would come, find fear pinning her to this patch of earth, dry but for the blot where she had wet it. They would see she had not been using the latrine.

"I lost my flashlight," she would have to confess. And though Phoebe and Cynthia, who could be sharp-tongued, might laugh at first, a laugh of relief perhaps, because she had not broken a leg or been pierced by porcupine quills, or bitten by some rabid creature of the night, most of the women would be solicitous and probably find the damn thing for her in seconds. Still, it would be easier on her ego to simply disappear into the darkness, like cartoon characters that dematerialize as a survival strategy. If only she knew the magic word.

"Stupid," she whispered, addressing herself. Then she saw it, under a low shrub, it seemed, stopped by the trunk or the stem of whatever it was, its eye staring away from her. A few steps, which she took, carefully, just in case she had not remembered the true lay of the land here, which was possible, since she had been more concerned tonight with interior landscapes. She reached through the bush, lost her balance, regained it, moved closer, using both hands, as if the flashlight were a wriggling fish that might escape her. Then she had it.

"Thank you," she said aloud to whomever might have helped, likely her mother, modestly pulling whatever strings she could.

Shinny moved no closer to the river that night but she could hear it distinctly from her tent, competing with the voices of the women and usually winning, though the clear soprano of one of the women—probably Phoebe—lifted above it now and then, superior, aspiring, beautiful. A reminder of Elfie. The tape of the opera she had sent. You'll love it, Mom, she had promised. Well, Shinny didn't love it yet. Betrayal, revenge. It would be better if Brendan led Elfie away from the dangerous world of opera into the orderly confines of chamber music, such as they used to play together.

Okay. She probably would not die. Heather did not want to die any more than she did, nor did she want anyone in her care to die. Heather wanted them all to have fun. The clenching in Shinny's stomach should go away if she gave in. There was a flow, she could go with it, as she had at Deer Lake, as she had the first days of this excursion. If she relaxed she would be a better oarswoman, upsets would be even less likely.

They were singing "Kum-ba-yah, my lord." Everyone knew

at least the chorus to that one. "Kum-ba-yah, my lord, kum-ba-yah." She toed her socks off into the bottom of the bag, unzipped her jeans and wriggled out of them, folded them into a square and placed them under her head for a pillow. She would sleep on it. If she was going to leave the group, she could tell Heather in the morning.

Turning onto her side Shinny tucked her hands under her cheek. She always lay on her side, with her hands beneath her cheek or folded between her knees. Tonight she briefly noticed the heat in the connection before she fell into sleep. Maybe it really is just tiredness, she considered—her next to last conscious thought. Maybe that's why I lost my nerve.

She woke burning, angrily hot; kicked off her sleeping bag. This was no malfunctioning internal furnace such as used to wake her, but something branding her skin in selected areas, her hands, arms, her face, her thighs. Such fire! She reached for her flashlight, thinking she might discover insect bites, but the plastic cylinder that was so excruciatingly painful to hold instead illuminated spreading redness, skin swollen, blisters forming on the stretched skin. Maddeningly, dizzyingly itchy! Just the thing she knew she shouldn't scratch. Forcing herself alert, her entire body screaming, she aimed the light down. More torture. A searing crimson pond on the inside of her right thigh, also the left.

"Help!" It had to be the middle of the night, still dark, the river pressing on. But something had got her—an insect? A snake? Maybe she was allergic to the stinging nettles she'd eaten for supper. So why break out in such random spots? Or maybe it was chicken pox. Maybe Mariah had picked them up at school and infected her. Could you get them twice?

"Help! Someone!" If she had to get up . . . Tears started. The pain! Sucking whiteness. Room enough in it only for self-recrimination. But of course I had to put my tent way back here, away from everybody. And the river, plashing, roaring. Doesn't the damn thing ever turn off? I have to get up!

"Help!"

Carefully, unzip the tent with swollen fingers. Swing out the legs. Grab the jeans. But no! Because whatever it was had attacked the softest skin on the inside of her thighs. What if she pulled up the torment with the jeans? What if it went any higher? Please!

"Heather! Somebody! Help!

The teeth of three zippers engaged almost immediately. Heather rolled out her tent flap and pressed on her light in a single motion.

"Shinny!" What's the problem? Oh my god, what did you do to your face!"

"I didn't do anything. Something bit me, I think. My hands too, my knees. I'm burning up!"

Nicole recognized it instantly. "Don't touch her, Heather, or anybody else. It's poison oak. I didn't see any around here. Where were you, Shinny?"

"Just—around—over there, by the river." She didn't mean to allow the whimper into her voice, but more of them had emerged from their tents and shone their flashlights at her so that she stood in the hub of a wheel of beams. No one was coming any closer either. Punishment. She should have used the latrine everyone else used. She should not have been thinking of ditching. "I dropped my flashlight and I had to crawl around on the ground to find it. Maybe that's when it happened. I didn't think of poison oak. What am I going to do?"

"Aw, Shinny." Nice Lynette. "I have some calamine lotion. That might help."

"If we had a bathtub we could give her a soda bath and put chickweed in." Lynette's partner, Diane.

"Here." Heather had disappeared into her tent momentarily and now reappeared with a plastic bottle she extended to Shinny. Calamine would be about as serviceable in the situation as peeing on a house fire, but she had to do something. In her shirt and undies, parts of her shivered while other parts raged. She squirted the lotion at her knees, missed, whimpered again involuntarily.

"How long does it last?" Her nose dripped although she was not crying. She didn't think she was crying. Dizzy. Light headed.

Nicole sighed. "The news isn't good, I'm afraid, Shinny. It can last for weeks."

"You know in all my trips down this stretch, I've never had another case of poison oak."

"I'm sorry. I've never even seen poison oak! And this stuff isn't doing any good." She sniffed. "And my nose is running."

"Maybe you should give her one of your antihistamines, Nic. Sounds like she's having an allergic reaction." This obviousness from Nancy.

"We've got to get her comfortable while we decide what to do. Heather, do you have any gloves?"

"We have some, Lyn. Remember? In case we got callouses?"

"Dear Di. I knew somebody would have gloves. Would you look for them, hon? Shinny, can you make it back to your tent? When I get the gloves I'll help you get settled."

"You'll have to burn the gloves then, Lynette. This is really contagious." Nicole, who knew so much and had seemed so human when she distributed the brownies, kept her distance.

"You mean if I even touch myself it's going to spread?"

"Too bad you got it on your hands," said Phoebe.

"It's too bad to have it anywhere. Reason Nicole knows about it is she got it one time as a kid, at our cottage in Ontario." Nancy again.

"Yeah, I actually had to stay in bed for a few days."

"It was a week."

"Oh great. I'm hundreds of miles from my bed."

Lynette, gloves in place, laid a comforting hand on her shoulder. "Come on, Shinnny. We'll make a nice bed for you here, while we think of the best thing to do."

"Anyway, it's hardly hundreds of miles," Heather called after them. Shit. What were they going to do? "Let me think."

Sharp Phoebe, the lawyer who loved to sing in the dark, reminded Heather of the farmhouse they had passed earlier that day. With Shinny and Lynette limping off, the other women automatically moved to the fire pit, though they had doused the embers thoroughly before retiring to their tents.

"What time is it?" Cynthia asked.

Diane examined the illuminated face of her wristwatch. "One in the morning."

"And tomorrow's the biggest day."

"We won't be doing the river tomorrow with Shinny like she is, will we, Heather?"

"I'm just trying to think. I've never had this happen before. You know, I've actually never had any serious injuries or illnesses." One of her rafters contracting poison oak? Bizarre! "Phoebe's right, we can't do the river with Shinny in the condition she is, and we can't leave her here alone."

"Man . . ."

"It's not her fault, Cynthia."

"I know that. But we were working up to this. The best part. It's like coitus interruptus."

"I think we should check out that farmhouse. There's probably a nice farm wife who would take her in," Phoebe suggested.

"And then what?" Heather wondered if they would demand refunds.

"We only have another day after today. Anyway, we should get the fire going if we're going to stay out here. Nancy, can I share your blanket?"

"I suppose I could get Donna Lee to pick her up on the way to get us."

"Or maybe she could come early? Take Shinny back?"

Heather thought of the extra expenses involved. "Maybe. I don't know."

"Damn!"

"Shh. She might hear you. And it wasn't her fault." Paranoia gone with Shinny safely away, Nicole recaptured control, her position as the oldest in the group.

In Shinny's three-person tent, Lynettte took up most of the space, blocking and unblocking the limited light, a manic cloud. She used one tissue to daub Shinny's face with calamine, another for her hands, another for her thighs, above her knees. Talking gently as she worked. Motherly, although she had never, would never bear children.

When was the last time someone had taken care of her? That question skipped through the fog before Shinny could answer it.

"Thank you for being so nice to me, Lynette."

"Poor Shinny, but you'll be okay."

"You'll have to go without me."

"We won't leave you here alone. I promise. I'm going to get rid of this garbage. Can I bring you anything?"

She shook her head, an odd sensation. The fog moved with her, thinning for only the second it took to remember that hours ago she would have been glad of an excuse to leave the rafting group. "Sorry," she breathed, to Mom, who saw all these things.

"Hey, you don't have to be sorry, Shinny. It's not your fault. I'll be back in a minute to check on you. Just rest for a while."

At the fire pit, a pennant of flame fluttered up from the dry twigs Phoebe and Cynthia had collected for the morning. Heather snapped larger branches off a dry limb to feed it. The worst of it was that she couldn't let any of the women see her indecision. She was supposed to be prepared for anything.

"Move over, ladies. I've got some contaminated Kleenex to get rid of," said Lynette.

"Don't come anywhere near me!"

"Nicole!"

"Don't be so judgmental, Diane. You never had it. Nikki was just one big red ball, and the summers in Ontario are so humid." Nancy defended her sister.

"All right, all right. But we have to do something with her. She can't raft down the river and we can't just wait here."

"You're right, Lynette." Heather had considered bringing a cellular phone but back in the city, in Vancouver, integrity had won over convenience. If women were going to take charge, they had to do so under any circumstances. This was the perfect challenge.

"Who wants to hike back with me to the farmhouse? If we hit the road early, we might catch a ride with some farmer. We could start as soon as it starts getting light. Lynette?"

"Sure, I'll go."

"No. Not you, Lynette. You have to take care of her. You've already come into contact. Phoebe, let's both go with Heather." The two youngest, ready for another adventure.

"Better check the place out to see that it isn't some white supremacist outpost," Diane warned.

"Why? We're all white."

Lynette knocked Diane with her shoulder. There was Cynthia's brittleness again. Age, they supposed.

Shinny lay in the darkness, better dark than that whitish-yellow disc that had drawn her towards the poison oak. Oh sure, blame the flashlight. She tried to swallow the nausea back. Too many pots on the boil, a line-up of customers, somebody needing help finding something, somebody else needing to return something that didn't work, didn't fit, that was broken. Fire in the infected spots, fuzz in the brain, shivery yet hot. Sick to her stomach.

"Here, Shinny. Open your mouth. I'm just going to drop this in. Don't choke, okay?"

Lynette. Tufts of grey hair, overweight and shapeless in her grey sweat pants and shirt, eyebrows that curved up at the inside edges, deep shadows beneath her eyes as if she never got enough sleep. She should have been a nurse, but she had defied her natural talent and gone to work in the school system; a vice-principal now.

"Can you hold this bottle of water? Drink whenever you can. Diane says the infection will subside if you flush it out. Diane has many good ideas."

Wherever the water spilled it doused the fire at least for a few seconds.

"It might feel good now, but you'll get cold when it evaporates. It's still several more hours until the sun comes up, then you won't be cold anymore. Heather and Phoebe and Cynthia are going to catch a few more hours sleep then hike back to that farmhouse we noticed today. Remember? That old-fashioned one? They'll phone for help. I brought my bag over. I'll be sleeping right outside."

"Oh . . ."

"It's okay. I want to hear you if you call. Diane's going to look for some plants in the morning. A special kind of mint that grows around here, yerba buena. To make a poultice. Everything's going to be all right. Just try to rest."

As if she could do anything else. No more voices now except the river's streaming below. White water, white noise.

The furious light the sun ignited on the red nylon of her tent woke Shinny from the drowse she had fallen into when the anti-histamine began taking effect. Bright light, clamouring river, and something else, out of place here. An engine?

"Lynette?"

"I hear you, hon. Help has arrived! How're you feeling?"

She was feeling slowed down. Just answering would take too much energy. Mouth dry. She willed her forearm to rise so that she could examine the effect of the poison. Ugly. Fingers the pink of underdone meat, swollen so that her hand resembled a mitt more than a glove.

"Shinny?" The whine of a carefully disengaged zipper. Lynette's round face, salt and pepper bang wisps. "Are you okay? Did you hear me?"

It was like this when the starter motor went on the Pony. Click, but nothing happened. The long habit of self-sufficiency clicked, but her muscles refused to turn over. "Strong medicine."

Lynette understood. "I know. I was wishing they were the non-drowsy type. And I gave you two pills. But it's helping, isn't it? With the pain?"

Shinny blinked in reply, noticed a tightness around her eyes. Lynette's eyebrows curved into upward-turned sickles. Concern. Do I look so dangerous? she wondered.

"And they're back, with the farmer I think. I'm going to see what's up. We've got help, hon. You just be still."

Shinny's eyelids dropped and she entered a bright brown place sense struggled to penetrate. Voices. A man's and the women's. The river river river.

Outside, around the fire, Heather, Phoebe and Cynthia stood in a clot by Glen, the man who had driven them back to the campsite from his farm. Nicole brushed her hair and slipped jeans and a sweatshirt over the long underwear she slept in. Lynette alerted Diane, who was a deep sleeper and wore earplugs to ensure silence.

Nancy filled a pot with water. "Coffee?" she asked, particularly of the man, who was a guest here. Pleasant-looking, she thought; too pleasant looking to be a white supremacist, though looks should not count. He seemed uneasy, his head bobbing as Heather introduced each of the women. Crinkling his eyes behind the lenses of his glasses as each woman shook his hand.

"Glen grows herbs on his place. He's a contract herb grower."

"Cool." Lynette was relieved, Diane would approve. But were they going to turn Shinny over to him just like that? "Did you phone Vancouver, Heather?"

"I tried. No answer. Glen offered to look after Shinny until Donna Lee comes for us day after tomorrow."

Lynette stiffened.

"Don't worry, Lynette. He's got a whole family there, a woman with kids. She'll be safe. And he's got stuff to help her." Phoebe poked Diane. "Herbal cures. Did we luck out?"

A man in his fifties with a kindly face, dark blue jeans, worn white sneakers. Tan windbreaker over his t-shirt. A red cap with the initials CHF above the bill. The red cap appealed to Lynette. Still.

"Your wife wouldn't mind? You know how contagious poison oak is. How old are your kids?"

Heather answered for him. "He's a widower, Lynette. It's his housekeeper who will do the looking after. She and her husband live next door. So the kids won't get it."

"We've been workin' on a medicinal salve that should help your friend although I can't say for sure because I haven't seen her yet so I have no idea how bad she might be." The rural Washington twang in his voice, syllables stretched and flattened some, the *g* dropped from his *-ing*'s.

"We'll get her. Come on, Diane."

Several steps away, when they were out of hearing range, Lynette asked Diane what she thought.

"It's probably okay, Lyn. He'd have to be really sick to do anything to her in her condition. Anyway, he'd get it himself if he came too close. Hey, there's an idea for rape prevention. Tell the attacker you've got poison oak on your thighs!"

"And Heather seems to think he's okay."

Their voices disturbed the pixillated-bronze blanket under which Shinny did not quite sleep, yet was not quite conscious.

The ascending whine of the zipper, like an air-raid siren in an old war movie.

"Can you stand?"

Somehow she did, and stepped into baggy cotton shorts that belonged to Lynette—nice Lynette. Propped by Lynette's gloved hand, she walked bow-legged to the clearing where Glen waited with the rafters.

"Oh, yes, I'd say here's a woman needs some help."

"The antihistamine she took zonked her, which is probably good until she gets more comfortable. Do you want her on your front seat?"

"Set her down in the back. I made a bed."

Later she would remember how dead she felt. She could hear, she could see through the slits in her puffy face. She had, apparently, moved under her own steam, but her personality, who she was, had shut off while these people decided things for her, moved her around, squirted lotion on her body, helped arrange her on the blanket over the air mattress in the back of Glen's pick-up truck, which smelled flowery. The puffiness of the air mattress and the sweet scent enhanced the impression that she was on another plane. Would death, in fact, be like this? Consciousness independent of the body but existing somewhere in space?

His head appeared over her. The red cap, sun-faded. Spectacle frames clear around the bottom, darker around the top half. A neutral face with a forehead like an ivory-striped washboard. The women were shipping her off, and he was the mailman. Urgent pain forced through the drugs. Okay, she would go; they could send her express.

"Lynette?" The nicest. Not afraid to touch.

"She's calling you, Lynette." More faces filling in the layer below the branches of fir and pine which gleamed as sunlight poured onto them from the eastern sky. Really morning now. Phoebe, wincing. Cynthia, curious, but leaning back. Nicole and Nancy together. Heather. And finally Lynette, hair still uncombed, broad face oily now. Sickle eyebrows.

"You're going to be okay, Shin. I'll see you day after tomorrow. Glen is going to take good care of you. He's got just the stuff."

Diane took Lynette's arm, pulled her back.

"Just wanted to say thank you." Puffy cheeks prevented her from enunciating clearly.

"What?"

"THANK you." And tears, that stung as they dribbled down her temples into her hair.

"Poor Shinny."

The truck engine started, her head wobbled against pillows of air. She concentrated on the irregular blue stream above. Now what?

At camp, on an island in Howe Sound, north of Vancouver, Matthew trudged up a rock-and-root clotted trail with a group of boys. Striker, a thirteen-year-old, hiked just ahead. Every ten steps or so he whipped around and made a face, showing lots of teeth, stretching his cheeks, trying to mimic the actor Jim Carrey. Striker's parents had signed him up for the two-week session too. Most of the other kids attended for one week only. At the end of the first week, Mattie and Striker, the camp counsellors, Robert, the leader, who was a deacon in the church that sponsored this camp, stood on the dock waving goodbye. Striker blew kisses.

His third year here, Mattie knew which bunk to choose in the cabin he was assigned to, same as the one he slept in last year. Striker took the top bunk, lay on his stomach and talked down to Mattie, whispering until late at night. Mattie usually fell asleep to the rasp of Striker's breathy voice. Last night he had detailed his family's plans for New Year's. They intended to fly to New York and stand in Times Square to watch video coverage of the new millennium beginning in every country of the world.

"Lots of people aren't going to celebrate 'til next year. The new millennium doesn't really start until 2001."

"Only nerds think that and nerds are gonna miss out. I'll be on television."

"So? My sister's on television all the time. Cat food commercial."

"That's your sister? In the hat?"

"Yeah. She's been in a movie, too."

"Cool."

Striker wanted to be on TV, he wanted to meet Mariah. Mattie would rather be a counsellor like the guys who got to live here all summer, swim every day if they wanted, take the boats out, shoot arrows with the bow. He narrowed his eyes, as he did when he was taking aim, visualized the target.

Striker stopped without warning and Mattie bumped into him, and the kid behind Mattie bumped into him. Striker laughed as the kids behind the kid behind Mattie lost their footing and tumbled down the trail. Mattie knew Striker imagined himself in a summer movie, *Camp Loco* or something.

He tuned Striker out and returned to the idea he had for getting a picture of one of the old-time gangsters, a black and white he could photocopy so that it looked like the other pictures in his millennium collection.

Towards the end of the school year he had become more interested in the project, but because he still lagged behind some of the other students, his teacher had instructed him to use the summer to fill in the decades missing from his file. He thought it was the '30s when gangsters ruled, '20s or '30s, something. He would have to look that up in the encyclopedia, but the story was coming along. Maybe he could even get a picture out of a library book, then copy it on recycled paper, which looked old, so that it would look like a personal family picture. From his dad's side, because he had almost nothing from them. Ken kept saying he would help, then it would slip his mind. "Write to your grandmother, son. I think she saved everything."

"Dear Grandma Webster . . ." Mattie started, picturing the ironed blouses and the smiling round face of his dad's mother, the wattles beneath her jawbone, the solid feel of her body when she hugged him. She bowled and she curled and she sewed quilts with a group of ladies in the Saskatchewan town where his dad grew up, Swift Current. Mattie had visited once: he remembered blue skies hot and flat as one of the shirts she ironed for Grandpa Webster, and processed cheese slices, in individual wrappers, that his Grandma gave him for lunch. Lawreen never bought that kind of cheese. He reached into his pocket for one of the Sour Patch candies he had smuggled into camp and so far kept secret.

"You look just like your daddy, Matthew, when he was your age." Grandma Shinny predicted she would say just that, but he didn't let on. "She'll tell you you look just like your daddy, Matt, just like I tell you you look like your mom. It's what grandparents do . . . look for resemblances, you know, to see if they're being carried on. So you be polite about it, and don't correct her, okay?"

He licked the sugar off the palm of his hand, forgetting that he had lathered on insect repellant with the same hand. Yuk. He spat. Striker took it as a challenge, laboured deep in his throat for a gob, turned and spat further.

Mattie kept his head down. Grandma Shinny didn't seem as old as Grandma Webster and she took him to the hardware store every now and then, let him stand behind the counter, push buttons on the register, and fool around with the bins of nails and hooks and screws. He would fill one of the small brown bags and weigh it on the scale at the checkout counter as if it were a bag of lemons or a bunch of bananas. Grandma Shinny felt more like a pole than a truck, a warm bending pole. He used to think she was saying antsy when she talked about her job. It was the fast way she talked: A and C—Antsy.

Too bad she had not had a more interesting life. That picture of her on a cow, that booklet she gave him on living with polio survivors. "This will give you an idea of what it was like for my dad, honey, and lots of people like him who got hit with polio. Gives tips on just how to do the most simple things."

He slapped a mosquito. Yeah, right. My great-grandfather got polio in the 1950s and had to wear a leg brace, walk on crutches for the rest of his life. Matthew had read some of the book. Embarrassing. Check your cane and crutch tips before you go outside in cold weather. He didn't want that to go in any millennium box. Family history, sure, but what would people in the future think? People now? He hadn't even told anybody about his great-grandfather's polio because what if they thought it could be passed down and that he was destined to be a cripple, too?

He needed more from his father's side of the family: the gangster had to come from them. Or maybe he should be a cop. A G man. Somebody who busted gangsters. No, a gangster. A gangster who fled to South America. Then he would have something foreign like that kid whose great-grandfather explored mountains. An uncle gangster who escaped to South America, and then . . . he stepped high over a particularly gnarled mass of thick fir and cedar roots, then into a patch of deer fern by the side of the trail, as this was just the sort of place Striker would stop. The kid behind him stepped to the side as well. Striker kept going. Mattie followed carefully, keeping some attention on Striker, trying to anticipate his next move, but most conscious thought on the story of his paternal uncle, who, he decided, went straight after he made it safely to South America. Maybe started an orphanage. Yeah. This could be the family story for the '30s. The former gangster who moved to South America and opened an orphanage for street kids. Now all he had to do was the '10s and '20s, and the '90s. But the '90s would be easy. If Striker thought Mariah was cool, everybody would think so. He could put a video copy of the cat commercial in the millennium box. The description: My sister Mariah Webster at the start of her TV career.

The grainy screen Shinny drowsed beneath rippled with the bumps in the road. Glen took it slow, keeping to third gear, although he usually tore along this stretch of park frontage between his place and the state highway that led to the village. As he geared down to turn, he pressed the brakes carefully, so as not to send her sliding head-first into the cab.

He had not seen a case as bad as hers since his son Evan and the Mexican kids from the orchard up the mountain got into it hunting rabbits. Careless kids, running around in shorts and T-shirts, carrying BB-guns. Jumping into irrigation ditches to cool off. Individuals who could not bear the affliction—as Evan could not, moaning up there in the bedroom where Glen intended to put his passenger—people who suffered so intensely could get a cortisone injection to speed the natural healing process. Evan almost thirty this year, so it had to be going on twenty years ago that Louise pleaded with Dr. Fredericks to come out to the house. Glen had not seen a case so bad since because around here people knew the plant and avoided it to the point of actually pruning it back each spring or killing it with powerful herbicides. Glen had not a herbicide on the place.

Push the gearshift down into second, let the clutch off slowly. One more turn, down his own lane and they would be home. A surprise for Nita. Well, he could hardly have refused the trio that showed up before his coffee had finished brewing, women needing help. Young. Not all of them young, he found out. The tall brunette, the leader, described it as a rafting adventure for women. It was not the first time the river had driven someone up to his doorstep. Kayakers in particular the last few years; more kayakers than fish in the river.

Here was Dixie barking to beat all hell. The dog liked visitors and if Nita had failed to find his note on the counter, she would know about company now. He eased down the long gravel driveway, wagging his hand outside his window to quiet the dog; rolled alongside an irrigation ditch past a field purple with echinacea augustofolia. The driveway led to a settlement of buildings, his own white clapboard off to the right and, in the opposite direction, to the left of the barn, a cottage greyer in colour, needing paint this year. Bikes propped along the side of it. A big cottonwood shading the barn. He coasted over a plank bridge right up to his back door.

"You okay back there, ma'am?" Her name was Shinny Shinnan, they said. The swollen-closed eyes opened to the size of goat pupils. The face a winter tomato, never quite the red they get in summer, with white blonde hair, like dandelion fluff and cobwebs, stuck to it.

Something between a moan and a hum came from Shinny.

"Sorry about that, ma'am." He had to drop the *ma'am*. "I know you are not all right, but we're going to get you comfortable real quick. My housekeeper Nita will help you into a bath, and don't worry if it stings at first because the longer you soak, the better it will be for your skin." He pulled on gloves. "Just grab my hand and I'll help you up. That's it." He let go long enough to unlatch the tailgate. "Okay, now just slide on down."

The screen door slammed and Nita came out, rubbing wet hands on her jeans. "Mary and Joseph! What is this?"

"Poison oak, Nita. Put on something that will protect you because I need you to get her into a bath. You'll get the whole story eventually, when we get this lady comfortable. Short form is she came out of a rafting group on the river."

"Poor thing."

Shinny nodded. The medicine seemed to be wearing off, unless it was just that she was forcing herself to be more alert here, to be on guard as if she had the power to decide whether to trust these two. Glen held the door open with his heel and guided her in. At the bottom of the stairs he turned her over to Nita, who had protectively clothed herself in one of her husband Rafael's flannel shirts buttoned to her chin and a pair of work gloves.

"Not hot water, Nita, but not ice cold either. We should start with soda to take out the sting until I can I get some chickweed. I'll boil up some Oregon grape root and we can apply that, or you can if you don't mind, with cotton to dry up those blisters."

Then she was in Nita's care, the whole scene like a hospital where absolute strangers handle the body casually as if it were a head of lettuce to prepare for salad, pulling off her clothes, washing her. She tried to maintain a sense of self independent of the swollen red knees and blistered thighs, stretchmarked stomach, small breasts drooping like collapsed tears, but this kind young woman only knew what she saw. Shinny felt the need to apologize.

"Not a problem," Nita clucked.

"Maybe not a problem for you."

"Okay, I know what you mean. Here, you sit. You're gonna feel lots better when you get in this bath."

Downstairs in the big kitchen, Glen heated water in his enameled-steel kettle and found a tray. Filled a blue teapot with a handful of dried flowers, added extra valerian to help her relax. Fiddled through his stores for a fresh jar of the plantain salve he had mixed himself from leaves of the fresh plant infused in oil and left for weeks, then blended with beeswax. He believed it would relieve the sting somewhat. Set all this on the counter.

Voices came from outside the window where Rafael was organizing a crew to weed and thin the purpurea fields. Glen hollered to him. "Show them the chickweed and have them put it in separate bags, will you, Rafael?"

When the water stopped running upstairs, Glen carried the tray into the room that used to be Evan's, a guest room now. Before she became too sick to work, his wife Louise had made it her business to get the house in order. So matter of fact. If you don't sell, it will be nice for you, Glen. We haven't put any money into the house since we shut down the dairy. Three years after he last heard it in weakened form, her voice still spoke clearly as the day she married him. I do, she said out loud to the minister. Oh do I, she whispered in Glen's ear. It'll be a project for me, I won't spend much.

Out of dairy into herbs, one of the first in the valley to commit. Seven years later Louise did not have to worry so much about what she spent. Glen would have happily gone into debt, in any case, to grant her wish. She stripped the shellac off the fir planks on the floor of this room and the upstairs hallway, though he protested: it wasn't the floor he cared about but the corrosive stripping substance. Nothing can hurt me now, she reminded him. She gave up before he did. Resigned herself. Took as one of her last pleasures in life the re-creation of the rooms in the old Schroeder house. The guest room a trumpeting yellow this time of day with the sun beaming in as it would for another twenty minutes or so, until it moved up above the window. Yellow walls, furniture painted blue. Sunflower pattern on the bedspread, the curtains. He set the tray down on Evan's old desk. Placed the jar of salve on the nightstand.

"You gotta close the curtains in here, Glen, it's way too bright." Nita stood at the door, squinting.

"I know it, but it won't be in a minute." Reconsidered. "You're right, Juanita, as always. I guess she might want to sleep. I'll close them."

Out of the soothing bath into a pretty, shadowy room where she found tea, toast on a plate. Thing is, it hurt to hold anything. Nita saw the problem and offered to feed her.

"I'm not really hungry. Do you have a straw? I could drink the tea like that."

"A straw! Good idea. I don't know if Glen has any here but I got some at home for the kids. I'll be right back."

Sedated by the tea, the comfort, the lingering histamine fighters, Shinny slept until late afternoon when the collected heat of the day elevated her skin temperature, burning her awake. She groaned, fought the light sheet, then, panicky at the intensity of the throbbing itch, cried out, bit the cry back. Help, Mom. Help me!

It was sunset before she saw Glen again. He carried a tray with more tea on it and soup lukewarm enough to pass through a straw.

"It won't help to starve yourself," he chided her, his gaze on the reproduction of van Gogh's sunflowers framed above the bed where Shinny lay.

"Thank you. You are very nice. Nita, too."

He didn't answer with the not a problem phrase that rolled so automatically off Nita's tongue, and not only hers: no problem or not a problem. No problemo. Shinny sucked up the soup and slept again.

Glen returned in the morning, knocking first, then opening the door a crack. "Good morning, did I wake you?"

He had not. She had been drifting in and out of sleep for hours. When she tried to consider her situation she only despaired. It was easier to cross over into unconsciousness.

"Do you mind if I come in?" He rolled his lips together. "I want to determine whether there's been any change at all. There might not be any change for the better that we can see because it will take a while, but we don't want it getting worse."

"How long is a while?" she asked as she extended her arm.

"This acute stage can last for days and even weeks. It all depends on how good you are at fighting off the poisons, and by the way, you ought to imagine that, if you can, fighting the poison. We're doing the right thing for you. Tea will help quite a bit by flushing out the toxins, so you should drink every bit as much as you can stand to drink. When you're ready for another bath you tell Nita and she'll fill it up with some stewed chickweed, which ought to reduce the itching considerably. Then she can paint you with this." He held up a brown glass jar. "The juice of Oregon grape root, and it'll turn your skin yellow but dry it, too. Fact is you need something stronger. Chinese medicine if you can get it when you're back in your own territory. I've heard it can clear a bad case up to fifty percent in less than a day."

Mattie liked to play a game called Jenga, in which a tower of uniform wooden rectangles were balanced so intricately that only the most thoughtful, careful player succeeded in removing a piece without collapsing the tower. Shinny could move, but sudden moves irritated her already wildly irritated skin and upset the relative comfort Glen and Nita had created with the baths, the salve, the cool clean sheets, the endless tea. All the tea had already forced her up and into the bathroom down the hall several times in the morning and early afternoon. Now she had to go again.

The astronauts had walked like this, wide-legged on the moon, she remembered, and worked with hands as apparently clumsy. But they couldn't have been as fuzzy headed or they would not have remembered how to get back to their spaceship.

"Damn!" she said as loud as she dared, because it was bad form to complain in front of these kind people.

"I know it's a bitch," Glen had said that morning. "But you just hang on and we'll do all we can. Your friends will be back for you tomorrow and you'll be on your way home."

She watched him from behind the mask of her swollen red face, the platinum hair that sprouted out from her scalp. Would she ever be able to hold a hairbrush again? She couldn't even bring her thumb and her index finger together as the rash was especially virulent in the delta between them. Glen's shower-damp hair bore the marks of his comb, thinning hair that crossed his scalp in long shallow swells. He'd pushed his glasses up on top of his head to examine her hand and was frowning at it seriously. She smelled soap. She noticed the bumpy red skin of his throat; unusually large earlobes tanned like the rest of his skin. He didn't seem like the kind of man who would use the word *bitch* except to describe a mother dog.

Later, she watched from the window as he strode the gravel path from the house to the barn. She was going to have to find some way of thanking Glen and Nita and she had to start thinking now: Heather was coming for her tomorrow.

Having more money was giving her a kind of freedom, making a different person of her, too: Carter Biggs had been right about that. She could pay her own way now instead of hobbling through life on favours she could never wholly reciprocate. It was good, clean. She could write cheques for Glen and Nita and hand out Canadian coins to Nita's kids. I'll make it right with you, she had promised, convincingly, she hoped. No problem, Nita repeated. Pretty, capable. Nothing would be a problem for Nita, Shinny suspected. Glen only shrugged. Gentle Glen.

It was actually more comfortable here in the bathroom, which was shady, than in that sunny bedroom. She turned on the bath taps and spilled the rest of the box of baking soda in, wrestled out of the big T-shirt Glen had given her to wear. When calculating how much she owed them she was going to have to remember items like this—the T-shirts she had used, the baking soda, the food. She would ignore her usual thrifty impulses and be generous, enjoy it, as she had when the money from the sale of her mother's house came through and she wrote out cheques for each of the girls. Lawreen applied the money to her townhouse mortgage. Annette bought a second-hand truck and some new goats, and though she sounded delighted with her purchases, Shinny wondered if it would have been fairer to give Annette more, since $10,000 Canadian wouldn't go as far in California. Then Lawreen reminded her that trucks were cheaper there, and goats couldn't cost too much, and though Lawreen was biased because she envied Annette's bond with Smokey, Shinny would wait until she visited Annette to make up her mind. Then there was Elfie, who—despite her bursary—needed the money most. How far $10,000 would go in Italy, Shinny didn't know.

When the tub was three-quarters full, the perfect, soothing lukewarm temperature, she turned off the tap and heard tractor engines. The rash had not spread to her torso so far and if she was careful not to touch herself it would stop at her hands and arms, her thighs, her face, all of which still blazed. The bath relieved everything but her face, which she had to mortar with Glen's salve to leash her manic urge to scratch it.

Suppertime. Glen sliced some just-picked beans into a pot of soup and made another tray for Shinnny. He had heard the toilet flush, she must be awake, and Nita had gone home to feed Rafael and the children. He covered the bowl with a plate, as the hospital kitchen staff used to do, and the memory of the hospital returned him to the days when he sat beside Louise's bed trying to persuade her to eat. He brought the gourmet brands of ice cream she used to love, but it got so that she would turn away when he showed up with a new flavour, frown as if disappointed that he could not accept her imminent departure. Preferring to abandon herself to the inevitable rather than fight it, as Glen believed he would, she resented his attempts to cheer up her final days. She breathed shallowly until her heart finally stopped, freeing her from the "prison of the flesh." The way the minister spoke at the funeral, death must have been a relief. Heaven at last, no earth-bound husband to tend to any longer, no more worries about her only son, her grandkids down there in Oregon. Glen's sadness mingled with deep anger at the church for having convinced Louise that the real life lay beyond this one. This one temporary but that one eternal. So they said. Rounds of anger gunned through his stomach at the recollection. He wasn't the only person in the valley who did not attend one of the five churches in town, but he was one of the few.

So, a napkin, a spoon. A glass of cold tea.

"Are you awake in there?"

"I'm awake."

"Nita's out and I've got some supper here."

She made no attempt to sit up to receive the tray, and so he shoved aside some of the clutter that had accumulated on the bedside stand and set it there.

"Feeling any better?"

"I don't itch quite as much, at least I don't think I do."

She had slid down in the bed so that the blue sheet covered a good part of her face and she spoke through the cloth. He saw that she was embarrassed about her appearance. "Can you handle this soup? My specialty vegetable. I'm a plain cook but not a bad one."

The sheet lifted with her long breath out.

"I could leave you to it if you'd rather. Or I could call Nita."

"There was a straw . . ."

"This won't work with a straw but I could feed it to you. I used to feed my wife."

She scooted over to give him room to sit on the bed. Sighed the sheet off her welted face. "I don't feel like me."

"I know you don't." He settled the tray on his lap and dipped a small spoonful out of the bowl. "Try not to worry yourself, just open when you're ready. I'll be real careful not to spill."

"So you let him feed you?"

"Well . . ." How could she explain? Someone at a control panel might have been pushing buttons that determined what would happen next. The poison oak had launched her towards a planet where pain made the rules. Now she had re-entered an atmosphere more familiar where Tina, with Homey, and Lawreen, with Mariah, listened to her report on the experience. Both mothers held fast to their children to keep them from wandering over to Shinny, who, though still blotchy with poison oak rash, felt considerably better just being home. "What else could I do? But it was weird."

She had kept her eyes down while he filled the spoon and raised it carefully. Opened her mouth as widely as possible so that the soup could pass between blistered lips without irritating them. When the spoon reached her mouth, she had to raise her eyes and then she saw his, above the little window in his bifocal lenses, focussed hard on the spoon. They did not speak until she finished the bowl. She concentrated on his ear lobes, which were the size of a dollar coin and soft as horse lips.

"Enough? I could get more."

"No, thanks. It was good." Woman, mother, hardware clerk relinquished their customary dominance to the obedient child. At the same time, those quiet five minutes or so, him dipping into the bowl, carefully bringing the spoon to her mouth, her stretching her jaw to receive, was embarrassingly intimate. She moved her eyes down from his ears to the hairs between the joints of his crooked forefinger, his flat, scarred nail. Regretted the view he must be getting of the many fillings in her teeth. When he turned away from her to set the empty bowl on the tray she slid back under the blue bed sheet and stayed there until he left the room. If she didn't look at him, he wouldn't see her.

Tina understood exactly what she meant. "Sounds kind of sexy to me."

"Oh well you. And remember little pitchers." Lawreen pointed to the top of Mariah's head. "Then what happened, Mom? Did Heather call or anything, or just show up?"

"They just showed up, and they were pretty nice. I think they felt guilty. They squeezed together to give me a seat to myself."

"Typical you, Shinny, to see self-preservation as niceness. Nobody wanted to sit with you."

"I know that."

"Is your face always going to be red, Grandma?"

"No, honey. It's getting better."

Lawreen rose then, without releasing Mariah. "We have to pick up Mattie, Mom. I'll stop in with him tomorrow. He can't wait to see you and he wants to hear all about the rafting. Say goodbye to Grandma, Mar."

" 'Bye, Grandma. I hope you get better quick. One, two, three!" She flashed the smile that had won her roles in two commercials and one movie of the week.

" 'Bye, sweetheart. Say hi to your brother. Next time you see me, I'll be back to my real self."

They let themselves out and Tina sighed. "I guess we should go, too. Do you need anything?"

Shinny shook her head. "Guess not. You could get Homey a cookie for the road, if you want, and turn on the kettle while you're there. I have to make my own tea now."

"Sounds like such a nice guy. Was he cute?"

"Oh Tina. Who thinks 'cute' at this age? He was kind to me. That's more important."

"So he was fat? Ugly?" she called from the kitchen.

"He was just a man, about my age, glasses. Good build, not fat, I mean. I really didn't even think of how he looked. And I hope the same was true for him."

Tina returned to the living room where Shinny lay on a sheet spread over the couch. The sun had moved away from the balcony and a breeze nudged the white curtains as evening approached. Free of his mother's arms, Homey toddled towards the open glass door. "Homey!"

"He'll be okay. The rails are too close for him to fall through and there's nothing to climb on." Not since her flowers had all died of thirst and she had hauled the containers away.

"We're going anyway. Hey, I didn't mean anything. It must have been terrible. I'm glad he was nice." She reached up to tighten the tie on her ponytail. "Call me when you get your pictures back, okay? You know, despite what happened to you, I'm still sorry I couldn't go. The rafting sounds great."

Shinny did not have her chequebook with her and she had very little cash, all of it Canadian. "I'm going to make this right with you." Glen and Nita stood side by side on the porch. A couple of Nita's kids, a boy Mattie's age and one younger circled the driveway on their bikes. Over two days' worth of care and she could not give her caretakers a thing. "I'm going to mail you something, to thank you."

"It's not necessary. We were happy to help out, isn't that right, Nita?"

"Sure."

Glen had flipped dark lenses down over his bifocals. The red cap shaded his forehead.

"Come on, Shinny. They understand." Nice Lynette, gloves on, helped her into the van.

"Thank you, really," she called over her shoulder. The women in the van made a chorus of the words. "Thank you!" Everyone tired but happy, on their way home. They were careful to keep their enthusiasm under control, so as not to make her feel worse, but she knew from the satisfaction in Heather's voice that it had been another successful trip—except for Shinny, a footnote. They could afford to be generous now. "Can we get you anything, Shinny? On the way home?"

Nita had mixed her a yoghurt milkshake before the group arrived and Glen had packed a shopping bag full of tea and plantain salve. "I'm going to send you a cheque for this," she promised again, though he seemed not to care whether she did or didn't.

"You can do testimonials, when I develop my own brands and get into advertising. How about that?"

"Sure, I'll do that. I'd do whatever you want."

Nita laughed.

When she could hold a pen she was going to write that cheque, but for how much? Phoebe, the young, blackhaired lawyer who had led the singing every night, would do it with flair: a cool five hundred, leave it at that. Half a thousand dollars, to thank him. Some people spent that much on their children's birthday parties.

The pile of mail Tina had pried out of Shinny's box teetered on the coffee table next to her supply of ointment and Kleenex, her mug of herb tea. It still hurt to force her fingers together to do the simplest things, and she feared contaminating everything she touched, but she could see several rising suns in the upper left-hand corner of some cream-coloured envelopes, and one of the distinctive blue airmail envelopes Elfie used. There was a postcard—this was easy to manage—from Mattie, from camp. "Don't exactly wish you were here, Grandma, but it is fun."

She settled her head on the pillow, closed her eyes. Glen had advised her to give it a few days before seeing her doctor about cortisone. "That can be nasty medicine." Nice Glen, alone, but not plagued by it. He had a life. She liked that, and his long legs in jeans. The slight twang in his voice. The truth was she might have been attracted but what a waste of energy under the circumstances, and they would probably never see each another again.

The mail, what to do? Use her teeth? A person had to be inventive at times like this, as her father had demonstrated when the sheer physical effort of accomplishing ordinary tasks had not defeated him. He had used his crutch to measure distances, to point out curiosities. Other times he had leaned on it as if it were all that supported him.

She tackled Elfie's first, which was the most difficult to manage because the writing was actually on the opposite side of the envelope. If she tore the paper she might miss something important. "*Cara Mama.*" A letter written over a month ago, from the summer camp where Elfie and Brendan had gone to teach. Shinny instantly recognized the injured tone of the words from Elfie's adolescence, when the sheerest suggestion of criticism or rejection chased her inside herself where she would hide for hours, days, behind doors thick as a bomb shelter's. Brendan was the star there, and Elfie jealous? But what was this about Smokey? The fool!

She held the phone with a paper towel, punched buttons with her least afflicted finger.

"Yes?"

Oona. A dreamy, distracted woman. Oonie-loony Annette called her. But you couldn't dislike Oona, unless for her abstractedness. Smokey, whose proceeds from marijuana farming allowed him to retire early, had been forced to become a more active father to Aidan to give Oona the time she needed to dream the shapes she wove into fabric and sold for big money in San Francisco.

"Oona, it's Shinny. Are you feeling okay? How's the little one?"

"Oh Shinny. I'm fine and so is the baby. Smokey is just putting him to bed. Do you want to talk to him?"

Shinny had to stop herself from replying sarcastically. Oona couldn't help it: her imagination was far more compelling to her than the real world. The challenge of dragging her into reality kept Smokey interested: he had not succeeded yet. She would bear the children but they would then be his to raise.

"I'll get him."

Losing track of children. What was he thinking? Several minutes passed and Oona returned to the phone. "Oh Shinny, he must have gone out." Probably hours ago. If Shinny hadn't called, Oona might not have noticed he was gone until he returned.

"Just have him call me, okay?"

It was coming like a train, the light a distant spark, the far sound rattling the track these many miles away. Unless the train was travelling on a parallel track and while the draft of its speeding passage would chill her, the locomotive would not run her down. Some secrets lasted a lifetime. That opera, for example, in which the troubadour went to his death without knowing for certain that it was his natural brother who ordered his execution.

She twisted herself off the couch and moon-walked into Elfie's room, pushed the play button on the tape Elfie had sent, *Il Trovatore*: if she listened to it more often, she might like it better. The big bass voice of Ferrando told the story of the Count di Luna's brother who had been bewitched by a gypsy later burned at the stake. *Ha, ha, ha, ha, ha-ha.* She remembered swinging on tree swings with her sister Carol, chortling in voices

they thought operatic. They had heard opera at their grandparents' house, not listened to it but heard it in the background
when Grandpa was resting in his room. Oh Elfie, honey. I had
to wait until you were old enough to understand. Was she old
enough now? Should I just fly right over and tell her?

It might be days before Smokey called. Shinny couldn't plan
on him doing what she wanted him to do when she wanted him
to do it. It was his characteristic undependability that had sent
her out that night in the first place.

The anxiety started her itching again and the itching height-
ened her anxiety, and the opera didn't help, all that excited
music. She didn't want television, either, but she wanted diver-
sion. Before she returned to her resting place she fished a table
knife out of the drawer in the kitchen and awkwardly slashed at
one of the envelopes that bore the rising sun logo of
Vistagrande. The monthly report from Carter Biggs with a picture of Carter wearing a checkered lumberman's shirt, jeans,
resting against a boulder by the side of a lake.

Friends,
Something different this month. In the course of examining the
properties of some of the mineral exploration companies we're
involved with, I took a side trip to a town that was little more
than a camp when I lived there for a time as a child. My father
was on the team of geologists that had made the discovery which
gave birth to the new mine and the little town. Curiosity drove
me to return and the fact that I had no appointment until the
next afternoon made it possible for me to indulge my curiosity. I
found a thriving community, dependent mostly on the mine, but
also on tourism which developed because the area had opened up.
Night does not fall in northern Canada until well after ten o'clock
and the mosquitoes were out in force well before total darkness,
but still I could not resist trying out one of the Lodge's canoes and
paddling out to the centre of the lake to watch the stars.
Mosquitoes and stars—opportunities too—all in abundance.

Flashing Yellow

*You will see from your statement this month that my
Vistagrande growth fund is outperforming expectations. Our
pattern of diversification has served us admirably, with big
gains in commodities, metals and some of our high tech
companies.*

*My job is to pick stocks and I can do a better job travelling
than when I'm in the office because I'm getting a broader view of
the world. By the world people in our business usually mean
emerging markets in Asia and South America. But there are
certain things you learn in terms of investment philosophy that are
accumulated from the mistakes you make. Canada has long been
seen as the premier mineral exploration country in the world. The
hours I spent on that lake reminded me that it would be a mistake
to overlook the potential of our native land and waters. Next
month I intend to continue this theme with information about
some very innovative mineral exploration companies that have
come to my attention.*

It helped. She imagined Carter out in the middle of the lake,
his ideas powerful as pesticides, holding off all the mosquitoes.
She had followed his advice and taken charge and the trip had
turned out to be a minor disaster but she could learn from her
mistakes. "There are certain things you learn in terms of investment philosophy that are accumulated from the mistakes you
make." More of that cryptic talk. Her mistake might have been
to think of giving up before experiencing the essence of that
surging river. Yet there was room to consider that she might have
changed her mind: the poison oak had put the kibosh on her
opportunity, but who knows what she would have done if she
had been able to do it?

The mutual fund statement showed that she had earned
almost a thousand dollars last month for doing nothing but
turning her money over to Carter Biggs. At least that had been
a good decision. Not only was she wealthier than she had ever
been, despite leaking money like a cracked hydrant this last

month, but she was going to be wealthier still. And she did not feel uncomfortably bloated as she had when she deposited her inheritance but satisfyingly padded. Soon her money would be earning more than she was.

The phone rang and she picked it up clumsily, without remembering that she had intended to touch the receiver only with a paper towel.

"Shin? Are you back? Did you have a good trip?"

"It was good and bad, but there was a letter from Elfie when I got home, Smokey. She said you said the new baby would be number three! How could you do that?"

"I said that? Well, hell, Shin. A guy potent as me does lose track. Just kidding. You know I didn't mean anything. She's always been mine. You worry too much."

Bearish since she had met him, Smokey had developed a basketball-sized gut and strands of white iced his thick hair and his beard. When Shinny drove Elfie down to California last summer to say goodbye to him Smokey had joked about aging, but it didn't bother him, she knew, not with a wife barely thirty, a fifteen-month-old, a baby on the way. He didn't hug Shinny the way he always used to, spontaneously, with feeling, and she missed it while understanding that Oona, vague though she always seemed to be, might take exception to their closeness.

Crying in the background, then sniffling, as Smokey lifted Aidan onto his lap.

"I'll write again, or call. Make some kind of joke about going senile. Hey, Babe, I keep my promises. You know that."

"Just be careful. I live in terror."

"I will, but it's crazy to live in terror. The Elf is old enough to take the truth."

"The truth is one thing, but how would she take the fact that we've lied to her all these years? That's the part that bothers me. I don't ever want her to know."

"Hey, it's safe with me. You know that. Twenty-three years."

"Twenty-four, if you want to be exact. Twenty-four yesterday, in fact. Anyway, do what you can to set her straight. How's Aidan?"

"Teeth. Or an earache or something. I'm wonderin' if I'm too old for this."

"Fatherhood or Oona?"

The wind through the opened glass door had turned chilly. She would slide the door closed and turn on the TV, drink some of the tea Glen had given her.

Smokey chuffed. "Just leave it, Shin. It was a slip of the tongue. Want to say hi, Aidan?"

Shinny heard the little one whimper. No, he said. Well why would he want to say hi? What was she to him? His father's ex-common-law wife? Big whoop, as Mattie would say.

Joe, the former Portuguese bull-fighter who owned Joe's Café across the street from A and C, had ordered a pair of lesbians off his premises earlier in the week because they had French-kissed at one of his tables. In protest, gay people from all over the city had gathered on the Drive to pace the sidewalk and chant, "We're here, we're queer, get used to it!" Shinny studied the group from the window where Carlo had arranged a modest back-to-school display—lunch kits, stacks of lined notebook-filler paper, umbrellas—next to clear-ance fans and picnic ware, plastic bird baths and statuary that had not sold earlier in the season. Diane and Lynette might be demonstrating and she had not seen them since the trip. She could run across, say hi, thank Lynette, as she had meant to do. Anthony made jokes about what he could put on sale, to take advantage of the specialty crowd.

"How 'bout hand tools, eh Carlo? A power drill! That would do it for them."

Carlo emerged from the office with a catalogue in his hand

and motioned Anthony over to the counter. The ethnic make-up of the neighbourhood had changed and Carlo wanted to acknowledge it and at the same time attract new customers with tortilla warmers and corn grinders.

"Their own stores stock that stuff, Carlie. We don't have enough shelf space as it is."

"I'm not talking big quantities. Try a few of these for Christmas. I'm thinking we get in the spirit, say we know you're out there."

The demonstrators had blocked the street and affected not only Joe's but the stores around them. With no customers to serve, Shinny remained at the window. Not just gay women were marching. There were men, too, and the quartet of older women who showed up at political rallies, the Raging Grannies they called themselves, who stood directly in front of Joe's door singing verse after verse about the importance of tolerance, to the tune of "John Brown's Body." The crowd listened to a few verses before bursting out with cheers and songs of their own.

"I say we stay Canadian. Let them think of A and C as their Canadian goods store, Carlie. Keep it pure."

"So cappuccino machines are Canadian now?"

"Sure they're Canadian. Everybody drinks cappuccino."

After trying to turn left through four light changes, Ken let Matthew out of the car at the intersection and instructed him to walk the block to A and C: traffic was that thick. "Just go straight to the hardware store, okay, Matt?"

"Okay, Dad." Matthew could see the A and C sign clearly enough, half a block distant, but if he went straight there he would have to pass a camera crew and he didn't want to be on TV. Something else: he remembered the second-hand shop in the block of stores between the corner and the store where Grandma worked. He and Shinny had stopped there once before and the reek of grease from old frying pans, dust, shoes that had gotten soaked and forever after stunk like wet cardboard had revolted him. Grandma liked a table lamp with a wire base shaped like a sleeping cat, but she thought it was priced too high. Matthew wanted nothing from here, no matter the price, though he spent some time examining the pocket knives in the glass case by the counter.

School started in ten days and he needed artifacts. Pictures at least. What else? What might they have?

He held his breath and walked in. The proprietor, whose face was folded and jowly as pig parts, leaned against the doorframe watching the street action, which made it easier for Matthew to browse. A shoebox full of old postcards, some of them brown and white, some in watery uneven colour. Paperback books crammed together, spine up, in shallow cardboard boxes. Dishes that didn't match. Jewelry. Anything good? He couldn't tell. Shoes. Oh yeah. Bring in a pair of shoes for the box. My great-grandfather's shoes. Big deal. Further in the back, old clothes. Shoes would be stupid, but a tie, maybe. An old-fashioned tie made of silk, not from the gangster, but another relative. The '20s. Stock market crash, flappers. He had the teacher's list memorized and kept his eye out for objects that fit the decades he was missing, that he could pass off as heirlooms. Okay, so his great-great grandfather on his mother's father's side was maybe one of those big bankers, investors who lost everything in the crash.

He fingered a drape of individual ties; which was the oldest? He could ask the storekeeper, but he had only five dollars and if he emphasized *old*, the man might think he had something special, a real antique. Matthew had already investigated the antique stores close to his neighbourhood. Out of his league. The things in this store were not antiques, only old. How old things came to be antiques he wasn't sure, but the antique stores definitely smelled different: dust, sure, but mingled with the stronger odour of furniture polish and deep head-clearing whiffs of camphorous mothballs.

He selected a wide striped tie with a shiny, pebbly surface. The white between the deep red stripes had yellowed, the dark blue label on the back was stitched right into the fabric and the name of the manufacturer—De Witt—was sewn in a script that appeared old-fashioned to Matthew. He looked hard but did not see a date. Well, who would put a date on a tie? Duh! Still, he worried. Maybe it wasn't old enough, or good enough to have belonged to this stockbroker ancestor. And here was a stain—grape juice or chocolate milk, something brown. Maybe blood?

He would get a lot of points for a relative who killed himself when the stock market crashed. His teacher had told them about men jumping off buildings on Wall Street, but they must have killed themselves in other ways too. He couldn't have slit his own throat or there would have been more blood. Maybe shot himself?

"Are you looking for something, sonny?" the shopkeeper called from the front.

"Just looking." He put the tie back on the rack with the others. More neckties dripped out of a round cardboard hatbox on the table next to the clothes rack. Ties, yellowish handkerchiefs folded up. Woolen scarves in dark colours, toques. And here, at the bottom, an incomplete manicure kit and a wallet. A leather wallet that might originally have been brown, might have been black, worn to the colour of old asphalt. Soft, curved rather than flat. And something in it. Cool! He had to be careful or the shopkeeper would know he really wanted this. A business card in it, advertising a delivery service, Bernard's Parcel Delivery. A four-digit phone number! And on the back a note, written by someone with a shaky hand, in black ink: Preston—100. Oh boy! There was no price tag on it. He could only hope.

"Uh, sir?"

"Yeah?

Matthew stared at the pouches beneath the man's eyes. Great swags of skin, a wart on one. It was impolite to stare, he knew, so he moved his eyes to the pocket of the man's pink shirt, concentrated on the lint in the seams.

"How much is this?"

"That wallet? I'll give it to ya for $2.50."

Holee! I'm gonna get change!

Shinny never did spot Lynette and Diane, but before the demonstration was over and business returned to normal for Saturday, a television news crew set up in front of A and C and the reporter interviewed Carlo. Watching him on TV that night, Shinny was relieved that Anthony had left for lunch by that time. He would have been sure to bluster about the loss of sales. Carlo came across as more open-minded. "We generally say live and let live," he began, "but I can understand Joe's position, too." His bald head shone as it tilted from side to side and his voice was soft and even more squeezed-sounding than usual, as if someone were sitting on his chest.

"You should have plugged us," Anthony complained to his brother the following day. He was thinking of outright advertising, the special coming up in the next flyer: electrical accessories, toggle plates, dimmer switches, electrical tape, box connectors. "Live and let live. No matter who you are, you need light, and A and C has switches on special this week. Carlie, you know what advertising like that is worth?"

The scarlet reflection of the canning shed undulated in the oily harbour water, seagulls screamed for something, anything, then gave up as they realized Shinny had nothing to give. Wiping the bench with her rag before sitting, she bent to collect an empty chip wrapper, a straw with pink goo in it. She had picked up worse, a used but luckily empty condom one time. Her rubber gloves went into the garbage with that bag full of crud and she brought a new pair the next time. Had they done it right here on her bench, who-ever they were? A prostitute probably, because this was the east side waterfront, where the "girls," as they called them, "worked," as they said.

Sorry, Mom, she said, and heard her mother, in Elfriede's characteristically weary tone, remind her that she had not thought of this possibility when she chose the location for the bench, but had gone ahead and followed her first impulse. Sure the scenery was pretty, but think of what you could pick up. Yet Shinny had found only the one condom in all these weeks. So maybe prostitutes did not do it on park benches. Maybe the condom belonged to a teenager. Thank God he'd used it. Thank God they had not got so carried away that they pulled down their pants, pressed their hips together, ravenous, aching to join. Like she and Larry, in Larry's parents' car. "We better be careful," she had whispered. There were trees so determined to grow they sprouted out of cracks in sidewalks.

Who's to say, her mother said, resigned.

That's right, Mom. Who *is* to say? Shinny stretched her legs out towards the path. Barely a trace of the poison oak rash left. Too bad her debt to Glen and Nita had not faded like the blotches on her skin, but stained her mind as something unfinished. Glen had returned the cheque she sent and she had rejected the idea of mailing chocolates or smoked salmon that would spoil in the sun before someone collected them from that humped metal box at the end of the long driveway. She would drive down. Take Matthew on a camping trip. Knock, knock. Nita would come to the kitchen door. "Yes?" It would take her a minute to register that this perfectly ordinary-looking woman was the same pathetic creature who took refuge here six weeks earlier.

"Sheeny?" she would ask, a trace of Spanish altering her pronunciation.

In his last letter, Carter Biggs had suggested that his clients present units in mutual funds or individual stocks as gifts to children, who would benefit educationally as well as financially. Shinny intended to look into this possibility for Matthew, but it didn't seem a proper thank you for Glen and Nita. Glen turned down a cheque for $350; I doubt he'd be impressed with mutual funds, she tried to explain to Carter, who had joined the circle of people she talked to in her mind. She spoke and he answered in his monthly reports and the occasional article on the business page in the newspaper, which she scanned every day. Glen doesn't care about money too much, not mine, anyway.

Unattached, kind, attractive in his country way, a widower.

She had reached the age where available men were not those whose relationships had ended because their partners found someone else: death had become the principal competition. Did Glen talk to Louise the way as she talked to Larry, to Mom?

A couple wearing athletic shorts, T-shirts and ball caps jogged past. Joggers used the park less often than bag people and single men from the residential hotels up on Hastings and Powell. Cyclists occasionally wheeled by on their circuit around the waterfront. If they glanced at her she would nod a greeting, secure, proprietary on the bench she had paid to have placed here.

The sun had dipped behind the promontory that excluded witnesses to its final drop over the watery horizon. At Canada Place, the windows of a white cruise ship glowed as twilight advanced. Shinny collected her gloves and her garbage bag, the rag, her plant sprayer, and started back down the cinder path to the parking lot just as a cyclist sped towards her, head down, so intent on motion she worried he would slam straight into her.

"Hey!"

Her sudden shout caused him to squeeze the brakes on his handlebars instinctively and he lost control. The wheel skidded, he flew off his bicycle and landed on the grass. "Fuck!"

"Are you okay?" He raised his arm to release the strap of his helmet and she saw an abrasion that stretched from his elbow to his wrist: blood bubbled and dripped. "You're not okay. Sorry, but I thought you were going to ride right into me. Maybe I can help."

"Why did you yell?"

"Because you were coming right at me. I didn't want you to run me down."

"If you hadn't yelled, it would have been fine. I'm not blind."

"It wasn't my fault. I was on the right side of the path."

"You shouldn't have yelled."

Shinny thought him a jerk for blaming her, but she could hardly stand here and argue when he was bleeding.

"Can you walk okay? Does your arm hurt? I've got a spray bottle here and some paper towels. We could clean the wound. Don't worry, I'll be careful. I raised three kids."

He stood, sniffed. "I'll be all right." His nose bulbed out slightly at the tip, as hers did. Ginger brows, matching wisps of longish hair over his balding head. Hey wait a minute. I know this man.

"We should try to stop the bleeding. Here, let me look at it."

She took his hand and stretched the forearm gently. He started to pull away. "It'll just take a minute. I should clean it, in case of infection."

The sweat he had worked up evaporated quickly in the evening sea air. It smelled of tobacco, though he didn't have the breath of a smoker.

"What are you doing with a plant sprayer?"

Long arms, reddish hair on them. "I used it for cleaning that bench over there. I donated that bench, actually, in memory of my mother. That's her name on the bench, mine, too. People call me Shinny."

"I've sat on that bench."

"Well, good. That's what it's for." More like the bowl of an old pipe—a grandfather memory—and some spicy soap. She blotted the wound with her last clean paper towel. He grunted. "Stings, I guess." Should she mention that day at the park, canoeing? He probably wouldn't remember her. "Too bad I don't have any disinfectant. But it should be okay until you get home. Can you still ride? Because I could give you a lift. What's your name?"

"Andrew. I'll check out my bike. Let's hope it's all right."

He was going to squeeze every ounce of advantage out of this. She picked up his helmet and saw that it was damp inside. Sweat-damp plastic, the plastic smell and the spicy scent—ginger, maybe. Or maybe it was his hair, what there was of it, that made her think of ginger. Shampoo or aftershave.

"Here's your helmet. Do you have far to go?"

"I'll be all right," he scowled.

"Did you ever try canoeing again?" That got him. "Weren't you part of the canoeing group at Deer Lake this spring, with your son?"

"My nephew."

"I thought I recognized you. I was there with my grandson, Mattie. Well I'm sorry about the accident. Take care of that arm."

"Yeah, thanks. I will." More polite now that he realized they shared history.

Shinny continued on to her car. It would be something to tell Mattie, how she had seen the man from canoeing, the one with the boy who had followed Mattie around. Not his son but his nephew, so he was not a single dad as Shinny had assumed, or a dad taking his son out, but an uncle. Maybe not married at all. A nice big hand, too, bigger than hers, and that smell. Her skin lifted with the rising of the wavy down that covered it, and she felt herself open like the sea anemones she sometimes found with the kids in tide pools at the beach. Crazy. The cyclist had to be ten years younger and he had blamed her for his reckless biking.

"Stupid," she shouted into the windshield of her Pony. But hadn't it always been like that, her body yearning in a direction opposite from where good sense should lead?

Wasn't it ever like that for you?

Elfriede lifted her eyebrows, blinked. Even now she would not reveal those secrets, if there were any. Certainly no recent ones, for Shinny's father Joseph had died when Shinny was thirteen and he had been crippled for half her life. She tried to think back to her young childhood, when he had been a normal, healthy young man with a head of thick, wavy hair, smiling in photographs with Shinny or Carol on his knee. Neither photographs nor mind pictures showed him embracing her mother, not even on their weddding day: blonde Elfriede in a light-coloured suit, a hat with a veil, a corsage, Joseph also suited conservatively, that smile, that hair. The two stood side by side, touching just barely. His arm was not flung around her; she was not snuggled in. Had they just argued about something? She would have had to love him to endure the man he became. And there was that note Shinny had found, a birthday card from her to him that referred to a rendezvous under the covers.

It never became easier for him to move with his crutches. Elfriede would stroll, small steps, beside him, as if this were the pace she preferred, while he thunked along, eyes down, breathing heavily. Often he preferred to move by himself. "Go ahead," he would shout at them. Released, Shinny would hurtle off to wherever she did not have to apologize for being whole.

She struggled to picture her father alongside her mother in heaven, but the image that developed showed Elfriede alone, in a chair much like the one in which she had inhaled her last earthly breath. If he were in heaven—and he was never a bad man, only increasingly short-tempered and he had reason enough for that, having been forced to quit his good paying job at the mill and sell insurance for a living. If he were in heaven, he would be happier and they might get along as well as they must have when they first met. If there was any kind of privacy up there he might even kiss her; they might embrace. And then would her mother swell as Shinny had tonight, in the presence of the cyclist? Her breasts strain against the fabric of her brassiere, her genitals tauten? Would she long to continue touching, embracing until he moved into her tightly as a plug in a socket? Or was that even possible up there?

Damn! She had missed her turn and was now approaching the inert ship at the bottom of Burrard. She would have to drive back east to Oak Street to reach Ken and Lawreen's townhouse. It was later than she had planned to arrive, too, which meant she and Ken would have to mount the canoe on the roof of her Pony by streetlight. Well, it wasn't her fault.

[three]

An electric blue shark, a lime-coloured whale, sea horses in vivid pink—fluorescent shapes Aunt Elfie had glued to the ceiling above her bed. When Mattie slept in Elfie's room, he liked to imagine himself a transparent jellyfish floating among those exotic shapes on the ceiling. They were supposed to glow for up to thirty minutes after the light went out, but already they were drowning in the black ocean of ceiling. Matthew switched on the bedside lamp to fuel them. He wasn't sleepy anyway.

"You okay, Matt?" Shinny called from the hallway.

"I'm gonna read a while before I go to sleep, Grandma."

"Not too late, though."

The clutter against the wall under the window included a net bag containing envelopes of hot chocolate and dried soup and ichi-ban noodles that Shinny had bought for her rafting trip. Mattie tore open the hot chocolate mix, licked his finger and dipped it into the chocolate powder, sucked it off. The camping gear rested on the two cardboard cartons of Great-Grandma's things that Grandma had brought up from her storage locker in the basement.

"I combed those boxes, Matt. I just couldn't find anything I thought you'd find interesting for school." Mattie pictured a giant comb with teeth widely separated enough for thick envelopes and cardboard file folders to pass through.

In lamplight the vivid colours of the sea creatures were disappointingly dull, almost dusty. He would nuke them with light for ten whole minutes before he switched off the lamp. But what to do? The shelves underneath the window supported books Elfie had left behind: *The Young Violinist*; *Grove's Dictionary of Music and Musicians*; *Milton Cross's Stories of the Opera*; *Techniques of Bowing*; *Mozart*; *Fiddler's Almanac*; *Watership Down*. Nothing to read here, and he had left his own book in Grandma's car, for the trip tomorrow.

The pulpy smell of the boxes drew him, dampened cardboard that had dried like the old shoes in the second-hand shops, both having been drenched in previous lives. The flaps of the top box, though folded closed, were not otherwise sealed. Hmm. The best thing he had for the millennium project so far was the wallet he had bought from the thrift shop. A real note in there, in real, if faded, ink: Preston—100. He doubted that Preston had owned the wallet. Preston probably owed the wallet's owner 100 of something, or maybe the wallet owner owed Preston. Unless Preston was not a person at all but the name of a store or a business. Mattie glanced at his watch, which was the type that could be set to beep at a certain time, like an alarm clock. Three minutes had passed since he set it. Seven to go before he could turn off the lamp. He was going to have to get his story straight before next week, when school started, and he had been thinking about it a lot. The story wouldn't come, not like the one about his gangster uncle, and the grandfather who died saving his pet dog. He could rocket off from stories that had the slimmest link to fact, but without any kind of explanation at all for the wallet he was stuck. He needed just the right amount of information: too little left him in outer space, too much buried him under the object's reality.

None of his fabrications about the wallet or the business card had settled comfortably in his mind, and he had to convince himself first: when he could make himself believe a story, he felt it had to be true. The wallet had never belonged to anyone in his family—at least it probably hadn't belonged to anyone in his family. But what if Great-Grandma used to have a big clear-out, like his mom liked to have once a year? What if she had put a bunch of old stuff of her husband's, or her uncle's or brother's, in sacks and given it away or sold it? What if, by coincidence, it had ended up in the second-hand store down the street from A and C? Grandma Shinny had passed along fragments of his great-grandparents' lives, but what about all the things even she didn't know?

Mattie's fingers twitched with the need to rub the worn-soft leather of the wallet again, but he had concealed it behind his Goosebumps collection at home. He pictured the faded part where the wallet had folded all these years. The compartment where he had found the business card with Preston—100 written in ink on the back. Bernard's Parcel Delivery, and that four-digit phone number: 9730. So maybe it was Bernard's wallet and he delivered parcels and Preston had 100 parcels to pick up?

Truth and fantasy confronted one another as if across a trench on an ancient battlefield located in his stomach. He opened the top carton without even thinking of what he was doing, pulled back the flaps and released more of the smell of time: the process of decomposition temporarily arrested.

He shook the rest of the hot chocolate powder directly into his mouth and dove into the box.

Birth certificates, marriage license, a death certificate with the same official border and seal as the birth certificates. School reports: Carol Ann Shinnan, Sharon Marie Shinnan. Instruction manuals. Warranties. Bank statements. The program from Elfie's first recital. A dried-up bouquet of flowers wrapped in cellophane. A batch of Irish Sweepstakes tickets rubber banded together. A child's book in Dutch. Birthday cards, also banded togther, many of them featuring tulips. Matthew curled his toes into the rose nap of the carpet. He took out the pile of birthday cards and placed them on the floor, then the sweepstakes tickets, the brown envelope containing all the records of births and deaths and marriages. Hospital bills.

Water pelted the wall behind the bed: Grandma was taking a shower. Mattie didn't know what he was looking for; Grandma had already said there wasn't much and from what he had seen so far she was right. Property tax notices, a batch of newspaper and magazine clippings that reported on the polio epidemic. But he lifted things out all the same and arranged them on the carpet in order, so that when he put them back it would look as if they had never been touched. Matthew had discovered a place in himself shadowy as the fold where he had found the delivery service card and, relishing the cool isolation, he dwelled in there for longer and longer periods of time.

A picture of a sailor, Great-Grandpa probably, geeky-looking in a sailor's white cap, the dark suit with the stripes around the square collar, the knotted tie. Below that more paper. If Grandma Shinny had not brought this box in from the old garage out in Meadowvale, the mildew that spotted them grey here and there would have continued to process all these papers into powder: there would be no proof that her family had existed at all. Mattie fumbled through a crumbling-edged stack and found a letter in an envelope that had never been mailed. Addressed to Otto Vanderclag. He broke the seal easily, as all the glue had dried. *Dear Papa*—it was hard for Mattie to read the old-fashioned writing, but here was another 100. This time he knew the hundred referred to dollars because there was a dollar sign alongside the number. He tried harder to read the letter. *Dear Papa, I need to borrow again. $100 please. The Veterans Affairs promise to help . . .*

The water stopped, shower curtain rings clacked against each other as Shinny stepped out of the tub. Mattie tucked the letter into its envelope and piled the contents of the box carefully back in their original order, pressed the flaps into their former position and jumbled the camping gear on top. A quick assessment assured him that the pile under the window looked as if it had never been touched, except for that one packet of hot chocolate powder. He switched off the lamp and stared at the glowing sea above. Tangerine swordfish. Squid with lavender tentacles curly as Mariah's hair. Brilliant fuchsia sea horses rocking through the inky deep.

August 15, 1999

Cara Mama,

I hope you are not still thinking of coming over here this fall because I won't be here. I'm coming home. This place has been awful. Beautiful torture. First of all, they treat us as peons. We thought it was something special, to be invited to teach here, but all we've been is policemen for some spoiled rich kids. Some are talented, but most wouldn't make the string section of the poorest orchestra. It's not like the Suzuki camps I used to go to—nothing like that kind of discipline here. If a kid doesn't want to practise he doesn't have to. They don't even have to read music every day. The cook calls it camp feel good because the kids' parents feel good about sending them here! In the end there's supposed to be a recital and group performances, but I don't know how they're ever going to be ready. On top of that, this bright hot light is killing me! I wish it would rain—a big summer downpour, just one day! Worst of all, Brendan and I broke up. I'll explain when I see you but it had a lot to do with him becoming an egotistical jerk. I'd leave

124

right now except that if I do I won't get paid. As soon as I do get paid I'm going to hop the next train to Milan where I have to clear up some things and say arrivederci to the one teacher I'm really going to miss, and to Carlo's nephew and his wife and their kids, who were so nice to us. I always meant to write Carlo and Joan.

Shinny woke to a sky the colour of ruby red grapefruit flesh. Red sky in the morning, sailor take warning, her father, the stricken old sailor used to say, yet no clouds threatened the climbing sun as she and Mattie left the city and drove southeast towards the border.

"This is going to be cool, Grandma." Mattie leaned forward as if to speed them on.

"You bet, but we're not going to try the river in this canoe, okay Mattie? I don't want you to think we're going to because I don't want to disappoint you. That river's too much for us. The lake will be good enough."

"I know, Gran." He smiled with his whole face, too happy to worry about displaying the slightly protruding front teeth he usually tried to conceal beneath his lips.

They crossed the border with no difficulty: a non-threatening, middle aged woman, dressed in unremarkable summer clothes, shorts, shirt, sandals, accompanied by a young boy. Her present age conferred a satisfying invisibility, still too young to be easy prey, yet old enough to be credible. The border guard did not doubt for an instant that Matthew was her grandson, as she claimed, instead of some strange boy she had stolen away for nefarious purposes. And yet, as if simply having been scrutinized implied wrongdoing, her shoulders fell with relief as the Pony rolled over the speed bumps on the U.S. side and she escaped to the village of Blaine, where she filled her tank with cheap gas.

Matthew fiddled with the radio trying to find a station that played something he recognized.

"Why don't you get out the map and see if that exit we want has a number?"

He did, and predicted it would take them well over an hour to reach it. "Do you want me to do anything else, Gran?"

"We're okay for now, Matt, but thanks. It's great to have a navigator along." She loved Mattie as dearly as any of her girls. She loved him for his slightly chubby, serious self and also for the way he dragged her out of her customary rut. Canoeing had led to rafting, and while that had turned into an adventure different from the one she had expected, here she was, making a return trip. Children forced people out of their houses and apartments, out of their neighbourhoods and into the world. With her money growing each month and Elfie in Europe, she would just go ahead and book an airline ticket. Why not?

Mattie unrolled the Spiderman comic he had tucked into the side pocket of his backpack and lost himself in it as mile after mile sped by. Although she had lived with the metric system for most of her adult life, Shinny's sense of a kilometre continued to be foggier than her sense of a mile. Not so for Matthew, who had never learned to think of distances in miles. Big hairless knees. Parts of him grew faster than others. Shinny reached across the small space between them and tweaked his elbow.

"What?"

"I was just thinking of what a great kid you are, Matthew."

He shielded his grin with the comic.

"We should talk about your project while we're together. Are you ready for school? Did you find everything you needed?"

"Maybe not everything."

"So what do you want? I said I'd help."

"Thanks, Grandma. It's okay." He went back to fiddling with the radio dial so she let it drop and slipped into the highway daze familiar from school holidays, when she and Elfie used to drive down the Interstate to visit Smokey and Annette.

It was just as well Brendan and Elfie had not returned for the summer, for considering the snags she had almost caught herself on in Europe, Elfie might have unravelled the fabric that Shinny, with Smokey's big-hearted assistance, had woven so carefully twenty-four years earlier. Life went on. Elfie and Brendan would have their own children, and then—so far out on the limb of the family tree—roots could be forgotten. Elfie's life might have been different if she had known the truth, but better? Shinny didn't think so. Elfie would have thought herself a bastard. Love Child—that song, by the Supremes. "Love child, love child, never meant to be. Alone, afraid, misunderstooo-ood . . ." Elfie, conscientious, sensitive Elfie, would have grown up embarrassed about her promiscuous mother: considered Shinny whorish to have gone out looking for casual sex, worse to then advertise her abandon with a pregnancy, a fatherless child. Elfie would have seen herself as the poor sister, Smokey's charity case, and she always had seemed needier than the other two, as if she had known all along that she would never obtain what she most desired. But Elfie did not know, and if Shinny could manage it, Elfie would never know. What could that tall, carroty-haired man have done for her, anyway? If Shinny had been able to find him and convince him that Elfie was his, he might have helped her with music, but Elfie had found her way without his help. Those music genes in her had demanded expression, and now look at her. Discovering the true story at this point in her life would only jolt her, like a train car banged onto another locomotive, one heading in a direction wholly different from where she thought she'd been going. Jolt and no doubt sadden her. She would question her entire existence, feel herself a fraud, perhaps; wonder who she would be if Shinny had married her father. No, despite what Smokey said, no.

"Gran?"

"Yes, Mattie?" He had finished his comic and she had not noticed, but he didn't seem unhappy.

"Maybe you should get in the right lane now. The exit is coming up, I think. See? There's the sign."

Shinny had rented the lightest canoe available and it slid easily off the roof rack onto her and Mattie's shoulders. Wouldn't Andrew be impressed, she thought, to see how competently she handled a canoe now. "Funny I ran into that man from canoeing, wasn't it Matt? Such a small world."

Matthew did not know whom she was talking about: he barely recalled the kid that had followed him around the Deer Lake Nature House, but Grandma seemed excited to have seen the man again. "Yeah, Gran. Funny." He led the way to the lakeshore where they gentled the craft down into launch position.

"Cool. That water's so clean, isn't it, Gran?"

"I think so. It sure looks clean. Our leader . . ." An image of Heather's face framed by elaborate head gear, like a character from a science fiction movie, momentarily distracted Shinny. "The woman who guided our group said that the river comes off a glacier."

"Really cool!" She moved to his side and put her arm around him. He didn't mind it when they were alone, in fact he liked the comfortable weight of her arm and the lingering baby powder smell of the deodorant she used. The lake lapped the shore placidly as a cat but out towards the middle a gleaming ribbed band warned of the force of the river moving through. If they stayed out of that current they should be fine; Shinny wasn't taking any chances with Matthew.

They zipped on their yolk-coloured PFDs and after the anxious moment of transition from land to water, they were off.

"Hey Matt, we're doing it! Now let me see if I remember what I learned at Deer Lake." She had to concentrate the first few tries, but Matthew's firm strokes propelled them into deeper water quickly and she picked up his rhythm in minutes.

"I wish we'd see a moose or something."

"I don't think there are moose here. We saw raccoons. One of the ladies saw a deer. I didn't see it. Lots of birds. Even a big owl, a screech owl. A couple of those ladies really knew their birds. Look, there are some little ones." She pointed to a shady spot where dippers skimmed the water surface for insects. "And look up there!"

"Those aren't birds, Gran, they're bats."

"Really? Well, they sure look like birds. And there's fish in here. See? We should have got a licence. Of course, we'd need a fishing pole.

"Yeah."

"What's wrong? Wouldn't you want to fish?"

"We wouldn't do much good. I've hardly been fishing and you haven't been, have you, Gran?"

"Once or twice maybe." A boy from Meadowvale wanted to date her and didn't care that she still loved Larry. He had not been especially close to Larry but had played on the same football team at Meadowvale High. Not a starter as Larry had been, but second string. The irony of it made her cry—as if she needed any reason back then: with Larry gone she was going to have to settle for second best for the rest of her life. Elfriede urged her to date.

"Go on, Sharon. Let me take care of the baby. Have some fun."

So she went. He drove a Chevy that belonged to his dad and brought a picnic he had got his mother to pack for them. Roast beef sandwiches, lemonade, chocolate cupcakes. She could remember the food but she could not remember his name.

"I know a great spot. You'll love it," he promised. It was a pretty spot, except he didn't understand that every time he reeled in she expected to see her baby daughter's dead father emerge from the brown water. The Fraser. Hadn't he considered it might bother her to spend an afternoon within shouting distance of the place where Larry's body had washed up? Stupid. Thirty-five years later the memory still angered her.

"Fishing's not hard, Matt. We'll ask my friends at the farm about a good spot. We'll pick up some gear. What do you say?"

She glanced over her shoulder to see him squinting beneath the suede bill of his new ball cap. With his shirt off it was obvious that he had not lost any weight this summer. A nicely tanned rim of flesh bulged above the waistband of his sateen shorts. Still a baby, really, despite the serious eyes.

"Hot?"

"Yeah. I'm gonna swim when we get back. How 'bout you?"

"Sure. We'll do everything."

In their absence the campground had filled with vehicles and a few more tents. Children sculpted mud castles on the shore of the lake while their parents prepared supper on charcoal and propane barbeques. The rhythms of pop and country music clashed from portable tape decks.

"It's like a party," Shinny said, unsure if Matthew, with his wilderness experience, would think it tacky. They propped the canoe against the Pony and pulled the cooler and a carton of groceries out of the hatchback. "Maybe you can find some kids your age."

"Is it okay if I open this, Gran?" he asked, holding up a bag of chips.

"Sure." It was not Mattie who cared about wilderness purity, she reminded herself, but Heather and the rafting group. Camping in campgrounds with other families was a perfectly normal, even pleasant way to spend a weekend. Little clearings divided by trees and bushes. Everyone playing woodsman. Not the wilderness, maybe, but not the city either. "When I was with those women we ate wild plants for dinner."

"What kind of wild plants, could we get some?"

"One night we had stinging nettles. You and I might be able to find some of those." She dumped coals into the barbeque, squirted starter fluid over them, lit a match and dropped it and flames sprung up along the irregular trails of blacker black.

"Whoa!" said Matt.

"Thing is, Mattie, I don't know wild plants too well. I might pick something that's poison."

"I wouldn't want to eat stinking nettles anyway, Gran. We can pretend our hot dogs are something."

"What, Mattie?" She hefted the cooler onto the picnic bench and took out a beer for herself, a rootbeer for Mattie.

"I don't know. Moose dogs?"

The cold beer was just what she needed. After the drive down the Interstate and the exertion of canoeing, the alcohol produced an immediate haze through which she watched Matthew's loveable face shift expression as he struggled to imagine himself in a scene from the century before. Lawreen planned on braces this year, which would be good for Matthew, Shinny knew, but she would miss the sweet way his two white front teeth rested on his lower lip when he forgot to move his top lip down over them. He had zero interest in looking for playmates among the other campers.

"Or maybe deer. Say maybe I shot it with a bow and arrow, okay Gran?" She nodded. "Pretend I'm the man of the family since my dad got killed by a bear, and you have lots of other kids to watch so it's up to me to hunt for food. I bring this deer in on my horse." He grabbed another handful of chips.

"Okay."

"So then what?"

"Hey Mattie, you're the one with the imagination."

"Okay, so then we'd skin it, I guess, and cut it up and roast it over the fire."

Shinny smiled into her beer bottle. They used to do this when Mattie was younger. He would choose the subject and start the action, and though she would have to take a turn eventually, think of what happened next, he often put the stories together himself.

"And the Indians nearby would smell the meat and come to our fire."

"Friendly Indians?"

"Yeah, friendly but starving."

"You mean you shot a deer when they couldn't?"

"That's what I mean, Gran. I'd be like this cool hunter. All the Indians would be sick, starving, and I'd save them."

"Well okay, but the truth is that Indians are probably better hunters, Matt. The Indians that live in the bush are different from the ones you see downtown. It was usually the other way around: the Indians saved white settlers from starving."

"I know." He scouted the fringe of bushes around their campsite until he found a stick he wanted. Returning to the table, he pulled out his pocket knife and began shaving the end to a sharp point. "It was just a story, Gran."

Later, full of marshmallows, lathered with mosquito repellant and content, she knew, from the duration of his goodnight hug, Matthew fell asleep on one of the air mattresses Shinny had bought for the trip. A woman she had chatted with as they waited their turn for the outhouse, who had camped here once or twice a summer for years, assured her there was no poison oak in the park; news that confirmed that group camping had its benefits. Yet she wished that the person in one of the campers nearby would shut off his radio, or tape player, whatever it was, broadcasting rock music through the fibreglass shell of his camper into the crickety night. She wanted to listen to the crickets without the accompaniment of anything other than the beat of the lake on the shore.

Mattie's breaths came so faintly she switched on her flashlight to check him. Of course he was fine, sleeping on his back, his mouth open. She hoped he was having good dreams. Maybe they could make a habit of this, camping, just the two of them. She could afford to take time off now, if Anthony and Carlo would let her. She could buy a fishing rod and all the gear; they could learn the names of all the stars. But they would have to become braver. Tonight, as soon as it was completely dark and most of the other campers had gone to sleep or at least quieted, Mattie had snuggled closer.

"Aren't you cold, Gran? Shouldn't we go to sleep?"

"Sure, we can do that."

He perked up enough for one last fantasy. "Let's pretend your story, that the Indians saved us. They sling us over the backs of their horses and ride us to their camp. They give us our own tepees and cover us with wolf skins. In exchange I show them how to . . ."

"Not deer skins? What happened to the skin of the deer you shot?"

His sleeping bag zipper whizzed. She heard rustling nylon. "It's hanging up. The women are going to make clothes with it. Anyway, in this story they shot it."

"Okay. So they cover us with wolf skins. Then what? Then what, Mattie?" she repeated softly, because talking too loud in the dark seemed rude. But he was gone, fallen into sleep that fast.

With Mattie it would be okay. She would not feel awkward about dropping in at the farm tomorrow. Mattie could pass out the chocolate maple leaves that she had bought for Nita's kids. But yes, they had better go early. A day as warm as today would finish her ice, and God only knew what happened to smoked salmon in this kind of heat.

Annette once told Shinny that she could never be disappointed if she did not expect anything. Advice that came from some religion Nettie had taken up down there, as Shinny recalled, and logical enough, yet who could live without expectations of some kind, no matter how modest? She had only looked forward to happily surprising Glen and Nita. As for disappointment, Nita had been pleased enough to see her at the door, and if she had plans for the day, Shinny could hardly suppose she would cancel them on a minute's notice. And Glen—where else would a farmer be at harvest time but in his fields? Shinny had let the purple cone flowers she saw dropped at intervals along the road entice her into imagining that Glen had purposely scattered a flowery path for her to follow to his door. Ridiculous. He didn't even know she was coming.

"So Matthew is your oldest daughter's boy?"

"That's right, Lawreen's. She has two. The other's a girl, Mariah. Mariah's a little actress." She reached into her bag for her wallet. "Here's Mariah."

"Cute."

While Nita studied the picture, Shinny resignedly catalogued the sunflower print curtains, matching toaster cover, a cookie jar dominated by a huge sunflower top, salt and pepper shakers to match on the shelf above the stove. An unlikely decorating scheme for a single man, unless Nita had chosen the fabric and the knick-knacks to soften the clinical appearance of the brown eye-dropper bottles and separate jars of dried grey leaves, the bunches of weeds tied together at the stems and hanging in front of the window above the sink. Aside from the bedroom upstairs, with its own bright sunflower motif, and the bathroom, Shinny knew the house and its occupants no better than Nita and Glen knew her. Of course they had exchanged words, but the conversations were limited to necessities. In pain, mortified about her appearance, she had barely looked Nita, and certainly not Glen, in the eye.

Nita's son David had taken Mattie down to the river, and when they returned, David was going to have to go with his mother to town, for school supplies. Shinny regretted that she would not see Glen. She had endured the cold campground shower to wash her hair and borrowed a gas-powered hair dryer from the woman who had reassured her about the poison oak. She was dressed in the white pants she brought for this visit, and the peach crocheted top that complemented her hair colour. Sitting at the picnic table with polish, remover and cotton, she had carefully stroked copper lacquer onto each short, broad fingernail.

"Why are you dressing up, Gran?"

"It's not really dressing up, Matt. I'm just cleaning up to go visit those people I brought the presents for. I was such a wreck when they saw me the first time, you know what I mean?"

She told herself that she was not trying to impress anybody, certainly not Glen, not as a man. For though he was a man and a single man, and, as Tina had reminded her, widowers naturally missed a woman in their lives, and though she had dreamt of him or not him but some man, maybe even the cyclist feeding her, not soup as Glen had, but iridescent ice cream that melted into separate colours as her lips touched it and ran down her chin, and that he craned over and licked it off, it was just an embarrassing dream. Sure she wanted a man—at least sometimes—but Tina talked as if to hook a man Shinny literally had to find one that stood separate from the herd, rope him or net him or drag him in. No, despite that dream, she was not here for Glen the man, but for Glen the generous person who had helped her when she was in need. Annette had also told her that dreams were unfulfilled desires: thank God they had their place and wouldn't hang out like a panting dog's tongue. Shinny only wanted Glen and Nita to see her as whole, a healthy, not bad-looking woman for her age, if you ignored the bursts of red veins alongside her nose and the spots on her hands and her permanently pleated throat. But by the time she and Mattie had organized their things and hoisted the canoe on top of the car and driven the windier than she remembered road along the river north to the farm, it was after eleven. People had lives. What had she been thinking?

She sipped her iced tea. "Funny, isn't it? I was here over two days and you knew nothing about me. I could have been a psycho, an axe murderer."

Nita shrugged. "No way you were going to hurt anyone else, Sheeny. You were in a bad way." Pretty, with her tan skin, dark lips. About Annette's age, or even younger—the ponytail gave her a bouncy, teenage look—and three kids already.

"Anyway." Shinny scooped up the picture and replaced it in its plastic window. "Lawreen has got Mariah into acting. It leaves Mattie on his own a lot, and so I thought I'd kill two birds, you know. Treat my grandson and stop in and visit you folks. I tried to pay Glen."

"Oh, Glen. He was mad about that."

"Maybe I should have brought him something with sunflowers on it. He sure seems to like them."

"That was Louise. Glen's wife. She loved sunflowers. The last year, when she was sick? Rafael and me, we just came the year before and then, boom . . .," She flipped her hands palm side up. "Poor Louise got cancer." Sniffed. "I started in the house then, more as she got sicker. She worried a lot about Glen. You know, her cakes always won the prize at the fair, she liked to sew a lot. She wanted to leave the house nice and bright for him so he would not be sad. She knew she was going to die, right from day one. Glen did not believe her, but she turned out to be right. So that last year—and I was pregnant, too, with Tracy—we shopped by the catalogue. I finished the sewing when she got too weak. She started with the kitchen—she did all this." Nita waved her arms behind her. "The last thing she did was that room where you stayed. Glen had to finish painting the furniture because the chemotherapy made her sick. He didn't want to do it. But she made him. Then . . ." she swallowed and looked down into her glass of tea. "He got a sunflower carved on her tombstone."

"Oh, how sad."

"I know."

They sat in respectful silence that lengthened awkwardly. Shinny rattled the cubes in her glass with her spoon. "That was good, Nita. Thanks. I guess I have to wait until Mattie gets back, but then we'll go. We don't want to hold you up."

"No problem. You make yourself at home. I got to give that little one a bath. You want to come over?"

"You go ahead. I'll just wait on the porch in case Mattie's looking for me."

Disregarding her white pants, Shinny sat on a gable-shaded step which gave her a good view of the gravelled area around the big ogee-roofed barn. Glen would be coming back for lunch, Nita had said. Shinny and Mattie could stay, but Shinny did not want to accept another meal. The whole point was to give, in thanks, not take more. Farm machinery clattered way off in the fields and a grassy scent, not as clean as grass but more complicated, blew back her way. When she squinted she thought she could see actual bits of things that might be petals from the purple coneflowers Glen trucked to a nearby farm to be milled into powder for echinacea medicine. She closed her eyes and took a deep breath, and imagined her lungs as colanders that would strain into her only the healthy material in the air.

Then the low-gear whine of a car up the long driveway, a truck rather. The same bruised-looking dark blue pick-up truck that had carried her back here from the river camp, parking next to her dusty white Pony with the red canoe overturned on the roof rack. She stood and, remembering her white pants, she brushed at her bum.

"Hi!"

"Well, howdy. You are lookin' much healthier."

His slightly jutting chin gave his face the forward thrust she remembered, and deep smile gulleys accounted for his naturally pleasant appearance. He wore his red cap, jeans, a dark blue T-shirt.

"So you recognized me after all," she said, extending her hand. "It's okay. I don't have anything contagious any more."

"Well, I do and it is called dirt. Come on in." He started up the stairs, then stopped, turned. "Did you say hello to Nita?"

"I sure did. In fact we've been drinking iced tea. I've got my grandson with me. David took him down to show him the river. I was just about to leave."

"Already?"

"Matthew and I came down to canoe on the lake. Since we were in the neighbourhood I wanted to give you something you can't send back, though you can feed it to your dog if you don't like it. Nita put it away to keep cold."

Glen opened the fridge and lifted out the package of smoked salmon, a full side of it packaged in gold foil and clear plastic.

Haida designs on the label. Seventy-fish dollars' worth of fish. "Hoo-ee. No dog's going to get his teeth into this. It's nice of you to think of us. Now can you sit a minute while I sluice the field off myself?"

He ran himself a glass of water first and drank it down, removed his hat and his glasses and set them on the counter and washed right there at the kitchen sink. Poured liquid soap onto his hands, splashed water onto his face, the thinning waves of his light brown hair. This was better, she had done the right thing.

"Where has Nita got to?"

"She's getting her kids ready to go to town for school supplies."

"That's right. She told me so this morning. School starts next week already." He towelled his face and arms dry, and his hair, which stood up like a joke wig until he smoothed it down with his hand. Grey brown waves like ripples the outgoing tide leaves on sand.

"She left your lunch on a plate; she wasn't sure if you were coming back. And I know it's a busy day, so don't let me interrupt your routine."

"A very pleasant interruption." He smiled at her with his lips closed and the surface of his eyes watery as if melting like the ice cream she had dreamed, and it occurred to Shinny that the expectations that had humiliated her less than an hour before might not be out of line after all.

Dixie, the lab-collie cross, loped ahead of David. Mattie followed black and white shorts, a green T-shirt, brown legs down a footpath bordered by high, dried-out grass. David was just his age, just his height, but rangier. He wore his thick-soled black and white runners without socks and he spoke without his mother's accent. She called him Dabid. Dabid, you show Mattie around. Don't be gone too long, Dabid.

Though he did not talk, David twisted his head around every so often to see that Mattie was still behind him. As they neared the river, David broke the silence between them by hollering the obvious: "Here it is."

"Cool." It wasn't as wild as his Grandma described, not here in its wider bed between sides that stretched to less than Mattie's height above the water level. Here the river curled swiftly along, like a snake surprised in the sun. Clear, green, white where it splashed against the rounded umber rocks. Not too deep, at least it didn't look too deep from where Matthew stood.

David caught Matthew studying the opposite bank, which was slightly steeper, a slope of pale grass and ochre dirt and green-black pine needles. Some straggly blue asters. "Wanna go across?"

"Over there?"

David had picked up some pebbles, not many pebbles where they stood, more below, brown, black, some light ones beneath the water, and threw them. He couldn't mean anywhere else.

Mattie shrugged. "How?"

Turned out David had a knotted rope he could sling across from this side. He hung onto the rope and half-ran, half-paddled with his feet and he touched the other side in seconds, shouting his excitement, his black hair wet, face streaming, his green T-shirt pasted like a rain-soaked leaf to his brown chest. Matthew shaded his eyes with both hands to frame David beneath the arch of his fingers.

"This way," David shouted. He looped the end of the rope around the big tree and it made a line Mattie could hand himself across above the water.

"Come on!"

Mattie weighed more than David, he was sure of that. Still it looked a strong rope, thick nylon, bright as a lemon. Nothing could break ropes like this. It was hard even to cut through them. He'd seen his dad resort to fire to divide one by burning right through it. The rope was smooth, so it wouldn't kill his hands, not that he feared so much for his hands, and even if he couldn't hang on it wouldn't be much of a drop, the river was not so deep he would drown or anything. Glacier water, his grandma had told him. So cold as thawed ice, which might even feel good because it was so hot here.

He stepped into position, about halfway down the bank where he could reach up and grab the rope, test his weight on it. The sun blinded him; he would have to feel his way. Okay. It was easy to hand himself along at first, when his toes were still touching ground. David wasn't saying a thing and Mattie didn't look across to see what he was doing. Okay, okay.

Ah! Breath squeezed from every cell so that he was momentarily light-headed as his body hung from the rope. Stomach suddenly sick He swallowed. Do it! He had to get going or his arms might break off at the pits. Concentration. He moved his right hand over, felt water breeze just under his feet. Moved his left. Then froze as a screech pierced the river rustle.

"Jesus, Mary, Joseph! Dabid, if you don't die I'm gonna strangle you! You get back here! And help this boy!"

Shinny grabbed Glen's arm with both hands and the tendons in her throat stretched as she clenched her teeth.

"Don't let go, Matthew. Don't be scared!"

"He's okay, Ma!"

Dressed for town in clean jean shorts, a black tank top, earrings, lipstick, nail polish, her ponytail coiled into a bun, Nita continued to screech. "You're gonna be in big trouble, Mister! Wait 'til I tell your old man!"

Matthew's armpits sizzled and dripped as he hung there rotating his nose to deal with an itch.

Shinny covered her mouth with her hand as Glen strode to the river's edge.

"Come on, son, you just have to slide your hand a little this way," he coached.

"Dabid, I could kill you. I'm so sorry, Sheeny."

Matthew had not moved more than half a metre away from

the bank, so it was easy to heft himself back. He did it with a single lunge and touched the dripping toes of his Adidas back to the gold-brown dirt where Glen stood, hand extended.

Only then did Shinny permit herself to breathe. "Oh, Matthew, you scared the life out of me."

David untied the rope from the tree and half-swung, half-splashed back across the river.

"Your new shoes for school! You idiot! I been telling you a hundred times! *Madre de Dios, tú eres loco?*" Nita berated David, mostly in Spanish, all the way back to the house.

"Since Evan grew up I've forgotten how much natural trouble a boy can get himself into, but it looks to me as if you survived this one. Are you okay, son?"

Glen continued comforting Shinny with tales about the things boys do, particularly the troubles his son Evan had gotten into, but he was speaking from another planet as far as Shinny was concerned. She held Mattie's hand, shook her head, sniffed back tears, tried to control her quivering mouth. "Oh, Mattie."

"It wasn't any big deal, Grandma. Really. I could have done it. It wasn't like you said."

"Not here it isn't, but it gets that way. Gee, Mattie!" Shinny pictured the river as it narrowed and roared, foaming excitedly not far downstream. Despite his bravado, Matthew would never have been able to swim it.

Glen stopped at the back steps. "Come on in now and let's have some of that salad Nita made up this mornin'. I will bet you it's tuna fish, which I like, but if you prefer somethin' else we can slice some of your fine salmon and Matthew, I keep peanut butter for my grandkids if you don't like fish, and I have Coca-Cola. Would you like a Coke?"

He pushed up the bill of his cap, which exposed his forehead to the sun, the jutting chin, the smile-incised furrows in his cheeks. Regret welled in Shinny's heart, but the image of those white river lips nibbling at Mattie's feet, trying to pull him in, had shattered the mood entirely.

September's child on the A and C calendar was a boy with blue jeans bunched around his waist, a ball cap pushed sideways on his head. He held a satiny red ribbon in one hand and the collar of his prize-winning calf in the other. This was the month that seemed to Shinny the real start of the year, as if the entire city, the country, possibly even the world were collectively turning the same page, beginning the next chapter. Kids in school, winter chasteningly close. The September flyer advertised furnace filters, floor diffusers, air deflectors, digital thermostats and more of the houseware items Carlo believed would make or break the business. The neighbourhood had changed from one of owners to one of renters and most potential customers left furnace problems to their west-side landlords, who bought supplies at one of the hardware superstores.

"But everybody needs a toaster, a nice set of mixing bowls, muffin tins."

"Carlie, you forget. We got a hardware store."

Shinny left them to argue: it was still light outside and she would have to walk home in the dark soon enough. She set her bag of Portuguese buns and a litre of milk on the lobby floor and checked her mailbox, which was, amazingly, empty. Up the concrete steps to the second floor, down the carpeted hallway, where she set the bag down again in order to unlock the door. Inside and through the kitchen to the living room where she found Elfie asleep on the couch. Elfie? Shinny had to clap her hand over her mouth to stop herself from cying out. No letter since that disturbing one about Smokey's gaffe and now home? Was she so angry that she could not bring herself to call for a lift from the airport? Then angrier still when she found no place to put her violin cases and her bags because Shinny had been using her room for storage?

Shinny loaded up everything that did not belong in her daughter's room and dragged it into her own, then tiptoed back into the living room where the last light of day fell through the sliding glass doors in a slanting gold parallelogram that illuminated Elfie's fair hair. She did not appear to be angry so much as vulnerable, her tanned knees scrunched up towards her chest, her hands curled in a single bud beneath her chin. Shinny moved closer, to breathe in the aroma Elfie had brought with her from Europe, anticipating sun, garlic, tomatoes, and got some of that along with stale sweat and the generic, rather papery ambiance of airliners.

Sensing Shinny's closeness, Elfie opened her eyes. "Mama?" she whined sleepily, spreading her arms for a hug as she stretched. She had woken this same way when she was a child, a swan embarking on morning.

"Elfie, honey. Such a surprise! What happened?"

"Didn't you get my letter?"

"I haven't got a letter from you in weeks."

"Then you don't know. Brendan and I broke up. I had to leave. I'm sorry, Mama. I know you wanted to come over."

Relief on one hand, concern on the other. "Don't worry about that, honey, I was only coming because of you. To tell you the truth I was worried about going somewhere I couldn't speak the language." She was hugging her now and Elfie was digging her chin into Shinny's shoulder, another childhood habit, the playfulness a tactic meant to camouflage her need. "Tell me."

Elfie pulled away, stood on her tiptoes and reached to the sprayed plaster ceiling. Although children supposedly achieved their full growth by eighteen, Elfie appeared taller and sturdier. Despite how she must be feeling inside, she looked healthy—a beautiful girl: Brendan had to be a fool to let her go.

"I really need a shower, Mama. Can we talk after?"

"Whenever you want, honey. Gee, it's good to see you again. I'll make us some dinner. Or we could order in. I can afford that now and you always used to want to."

"Yeah, I used to, but I couldn't eat a thing tonight, Mama. Thanks anyway."

While undisputedly affectionate, the "Mama" sounded to Shinny like a big woman in a black dress, with greying hair coiled in a bun on top of her head—the image from the label of a jar of spaghetti sauce. "Just something light, honey. I have some of those buns you like."

When the bathroom door closed Shinny instinctively clicked on the television—it was "Home Improvement" time—then clicked it off. She had to make something for dinner and what did she have? In the scant year the Elf had been away, she had gradually abandoned the habit of shopping regularly for groceries. There were eggs in the fridge, cheese. Frozen pizza shells in the freezer but no mozzarella. Tuna fish, tomato sauce, peanut butter, single portions of dried soup mix in colourful cartons and envelopes.

"Did you call your sister?" she shouted. "Should we invite them for dinner?"

"What?" The water streamed down hard and Elfie liked it hot, which meant there might not be enough for Shinny's customary soak before bed. Well, if not, who cared? Elfie was home!

"Never mind."

Steam and the scent of strawberry shampoo billowed out from

the bathroom. Elfie emerged with her wet hair combed smooth, a big white T-shirt skimming the middle of her thighs. So tan, white-blonde hairs shone on her legs like fish scales. Shinny had set their oval pine table as if for a celebration, using the dark green cotton placemats the kids had given her for Christmas, the thick red candle she had not put in storage but saved for rainy days, to brighten the apartment with an open flame.

Elfie wanted only coffee and dug through her suitcase to find a package she had brought from Italy. The strongest espresso, which she brewed herself while Shinny finished her own omelette, then Elfie's, who continued to maintain she was not hungry.

"I'll just nibble on a bun with the coffee. Want a cup, Mama? It's great coffee."

"Sure, I'll have some."

"I brought you another present, too. Just a minute." She vanished into her room again and reappeared with a larger package, wrapped in dark tissue paper.

"A purse! Wow! It's beautiful, Elf. Looks like it cost a lot, though, and you shouldn't have spent your money on me." She hugged it, unzipped it to examine the little compartments, three of them, all lined in black satin.

Elfie saw lines she did not remember mapping her mother's skin; the brown eyes seemed to have sunk more deeply, too, and shadowed the skin beneath them. The new shorter hair style suited her age, an attractive woman still, especially with the blush she brushed onto her cheeks, the bronze lipstick. Her big hands were somehow bonier, though, the skin on them looser and patterned with deep cut skeins. She was obviously delighted with the purse, which temporarily improved Elfie's mood. Then tears massed in her eyes.

"What?"

"Nothing. I'm just glad I'm home."

Shinny knew that espresso was meant to be sipped from little cups, sets of which A and C displayed in the window of the hardware store alongside small chrome pots and the bulkier cappuccino machines. Elfie was drinking it out of a mug.

"I am too, honey. And thank you for this," she said, patting the purse. "How did you ever have time to think of presents? Tell me what happened." Whatever it was had nothing to do with all Shinny feared; not when Elfie had brought her this beautiful gift and hugged her with such sincere need.

Elfie leaned back in her chair, propped her feet on the chair opposite, lifted her hair with the back of her hand to dry it.

"Carlo's nephew's wife, remember? Marietta? I called her when I got to Milan and she took me around. She listened, she was glad I decided to dump him, but she said she was sorry it meant I had to leave Milan. They were great, Mama. I have to tell Carlo."

"But why, Elfie? You never told me what happened."

"It's like I said in the letter." Then she remembered. "But you didn't get the letter. That was one thing, Mama. The mail. Most people use e-mail now. You've got to get a computer. Anyway, we broke up. He got to be a real jerk at camp. Too much attention from the girls, and then another counsellor came. Our age. A real Roman vamp. Heels this high on her shoes. Of course she had to be a cellist too." Elfie shivered.

"Are you cold, Elf? It's getting cool at nights now. First day of fall next week."

But it wasn't the temperature of the room that caused Elfie to shiver so much as the memory of Brendan on the tiny stage of the recital tent at camp, and Mimi, both with their cellos, improvising, flirting. He had not seen Elfie standing at the back, in the shadow of the support poles. She suspected nothing at first but glided into the spirit of the improvisation, each of them borrowing riffs from the standard cello repertoire, and twisting familiar phrases in play, like jazz musicians. It was great, Elfie thought. Then they moved into a call and answer style that began with liturgical formality and moved into seductive dialogue, low, even bowing accelerating to a climax she was not about to let them reach while she was there to witness it. She tried the Suzuki method of staying still, concentrating on the soles of her feet, but she couldn't help herself from shouting: "Brendan!" He snapped to and anger quickly replaced alarm as he saw that it was not the camp leader who was calling his name.

Shinny reached for another bun. If she didn't soak up the coffee she would lie awake all night. "And you two together for so long. I always liked Brendan, too. But they get it in their heads that they're God's gifts." The attractive ones attracted, that was the problem. "To tell you the truth, Elfie, Lawreen's father was a little like that. It's the big shots you have to watch for, the handsome ones or the football stars, like he was. Or in Brendan's case, the talented ones."

Handsome, too. Too handsome, although before Italy he had always underplayed his looks, worn the baggiest T-shirts and cotton pants, scuffed running shoes, let his black hair shag out. He dressed up only for recitals in soft, dark clothes that accentuated his caramel skin, his perfect white teeth and nails that would have been perfect too except that he chewed them. Elfie loved the contrast of her winter pale legs entwined with his dusky ones, but the image hurt now.

"So you just put up with it?" Her voice dropped as thoughts of the recent past dragged her down.

"Well, you know what happened there, Elfie. He died."

"I know that, but was he fooling around on you before?"

"No; I don't think so, anyway. We were out on a date together when it happened. I guess he had gone out with another girl not long before, though, because his parents always claimed he was finished with me." Like walking on a bruised foot, the memory managed to throb through the emotions that had piled atop it during the thirty-five years that had passed. "It's why they never accepted Lawry. But we'd been going together for two years. He did want to get married. I even had it on a Valentine's card— from that very year. But you know all this."

"You never told me the details, Lawry did. She made it sound more dramatic, though." The story Elfie knew from her sister was that Larry's parents were horse snobs who looked down on

Shinny because her mother was the widow of a barely employed cripple. Elfie hated the thought of her grandmother being snubbed, and none of them had ever known their grandfather. Long before Elfie was born, Shinny had regularly threatened to march Lawreen up to the Blakes' front door and somehow force them to acknowledge their granddaughter. But she never had, and Lawreen had not approached the Blakes herself, despite her fantasies of claiming what she always said was her rightful inheritance. Now Meadowvale Stables was shut down, the Blakes dead.

The room had darkened and the candlelight wavered over Elfie's narrow face, the smooth skin, freckled in a saddle over her nose, the thin lips that worked the notes when she played her violin. Shinny wished she had more wisdom in these matters, but her life stood as an example of what not to do when it came to men. How could she advise her daughters? Strong-minded Lawreen didn't need or want advice anymore, and Annette, gone for over ten years now, had found her own way, with Smokey to back her up when she needed him. But here was the Elf, the most fragile, whose life this last year in Europe with the young composer she loved seemed to have vindicated every poor choice Shinny had ever made. Now what?

"Did he apologize or anything, try to make it up, or was that, that?"

"There was a cove we used to go to, did I tell you about that?"

Shinny nodded.

"I didn't even want to go there any more, but it was the only place where a person could get away from the campers. I swear!"

She had written Shinny about the treacherous cliff path they had to step down to get there, and how they had invented backpack slings for the instruments they sometimes brought with them. Brendan could never bring his cello, of course, so would borrow a viola and Elfie would fetch bread and olives or cold polenta and sometimes the sour wine that was so plentiful in the kitchen. They would lie on their backs and watch as the sea mist fashioned the most transparent veil between the ocean and the glitter-strewn black velvet above it, and one night before all this happened they saw meteor showers. The sounds inspired Brendan, the water rustling in as it did on every sea coast, but there, because of the pitch of the shore, echoes of splash, gurgling. Rocks knocking against each other like maracas. He would listen, distracted, sometimes forgetting she was there. She didn't care that he forgot her in his listening. Her teachers used to tell her that she had a direct line from her ear to her fingers: she could play whatever she heard. Brendan had the greater gift of being able to draw from the world a path that led inside himself to his musical imagination. She would lie back and watch the shape of his head as he turned to catch a nuance of water on rock, here a spray, there a trickle. Eventually, before they climbed the rock steps that led to the trail back to the camp, he would lie next to her and kiss her freckles first, which is how he always started, and then her neck, and when they were finished making love, if the surf was not too rough and the moon bright enough, they would swim or at least refresh themselves with seawater.

She opened her violin case one tiresome morning when her main job was going to be trying to coax her charges to practise, and found a note from Brendan asking her to meet him at the cove that night. She would not be a wimp about this. If he wasn't prepared to leave camp with her immediately, they were finished. Finished. As she related the story, parts of it, to her mother, the word rang in her head with the despairing finality of Azucena's cry: "*Figlio mio!*"

"So that was that, then?"

Elfie stood at the glass door hugging herself. The sounds of cars cruising, the bus stopping and starting made it hard for Shinny to hear.

"What did you say, honey?"

"I said, what do you think, Mama?"

Shinny thought it probably had been, which was too bad, because Brendan had become one of the family, more or less, and it was hard to think of anything soothing to say that wasn't a lie.

Although Elfie insisted she never wanted to hear from Brendan again, she collected the mail as soon as the postman exited the co-op each day. Shinny missed the ritual of stopping to check her box on her way through the lobby, leafing through bills and junk mail for one of the familiar envelopes from Vistagrande and, lately, Glen. He had written to thank her for the smoked salmon and hinted that he might see her again before long, as he was contemplating a trip north to attend a meeting of organic growers. Contemplate was the word all right. He would sit on the porch, or stand gazing at his fields, considering the work he would miss by leaving for a few days. Contemplate her, too, a single woman about his age, not afraid of adventure, if sadly prone to adventures ending in near disaster.

The sight of Matthew dangling above the river had whipped Shinny right back to the railway bridge and the loss of her first love in the wider, muddier Fraser. She and Matthew sped north and were idling in the line-up of cars at the Canadian border before she recovered from the scare that drilled down to the well of dread she thought time had finally capped, and then she regretted leaving so quickly.

Up the stairs, down the hallway to the door of her apartment. The opening aria from *Il Trovatore* thrilled her entrance just as if she were sweeping onto a stage. *"All'erta! All'erta!"* Shinny would normally have cautioned Elfie against having the volume so high, but the music seemed to revive the sad girl a little and after more than a decade of hearing Elfie practise, from the rasps and squeaks of "Twinkle, Twinkle, Little Star" to complex Bach partitas, Shinny had learned to tune her daughter's music in or out, depending on her mood. The neighbours were not as flexible but it was only just after six.

She shook some saltine crackers into a bowl and set the bowl on the pine table next to the mail. No Riverbend Farm stamp in green ink today, but two envelopes in the pile bore the rising sun logo of Vistagrande. Reviewing her statement first, she saw that her money continued to grow, a satisfying feel. Carter Biggs had warned his clients not to view their dollars as ducks putting on a little fat each year until they were big enough to paddle over to where the big ducks played. All the same, Shinny couldn't help thinking of the earnings as thick white down, which would keep her warm if the climate changed and instead of getting warmer, as scientists were predicting, the world was suddenly locked into a new ice age. The second envelope contained a letter from him.

Dear Mrs. Shinnan,

I hope you are satisfied with your decision to buy into Canada's premier no-load mutual fund family. The statements you have been receiving should assure you that it was a wise choice. As an investor in Vistagrande's Growth Fund, you hold shares in companies poised to earn solid profits in the near term.

While growth-oriented, these are still good bets for the cautious investor and relatively new market player such as yourself.

I'm writing today to give you the opportunity to join us in a *riskier venture, with the potential for dramatically higher returns. Our new Futures Fund invests in junior resource-based companies, such as Esperanza Explorations, which has reported impressive results from an exciting find of manganese nodules on the ocean floor just off Vancouver Island. You have undoubtedly read reports of Esperanza in the news media. My own background in geology, as well as the Biggs "hunch" factor tells me the Esperanza property surpasses the potential of the highest grade land-based ore body in western Canada. The company has a simply designed retrieval system and a newly developed underwater exploration vehicle which promises to aid company geologists in further examining the extent of the nodule accumulation. Esperanza shares are now conservatively valued at $12.00, but as news about the company's technological developments spreads, share value is bound to skyrocket. This is a Canadian company mining Canadian territorial waters using Canadian developed technology, a golden opportunity for Candians to invest in the country's development.*

You will no doubt have been warned away from funds such as this by market commentators who emphasize their riskiness, and there's no doubt that more risk is involved. All of us who manage money are reading the same music, it's just that some of us conduct the orchestra differently. I'm as familiar with the signs of failure as with the signs of success, and one sign of success in the case of Esperanza is the company's reliance on a combination of earth and marine scientists. That's why I bought Esperanza for Vistagrande's new Futures Fund.

If you have any questions, call my office and we'll send out a prospectus immediately.

Odd that he should compare his decisions about money to music, with that opera alternately cresting and pooling around her.

Aside from the raft trip, which was really her fault for having too literally interpreted the message she received over television that Saturday night, she would have to say that Carter Biggs had given her only good advice. If he were the leader of her tribe, as she had imagined him during the meeting at the trade and convention centre, she would be obliged to prostrate herself in thanks. Now he had word from neighbouring tribes of great riches that could be scooped up from the ocean floor. Amazing! And patriotic. She kept her bank statements in a metal file box, in a haphazard pile she intended to organize some rainy day. The most recent showed that little more than half of what she had received from the sale of her mother's property remained in her account. But there was still enough cash to buy the van she thought she wanted and take a vacation, and contribute more to the Parks Board, for that tree she had been thinking of and had not yet done anything about. Should it be a blossoming tree, a conifer? One of those willows whose branches gracefully brush the ground?

But you don't want to spend it all, Sharon. Her mother's words sounded in her mind as clearly as if Elfriede were standing in the room, her voice every bit as sonorous as the Count di Luna's guard. You want to be careful, keep some aside. Government bonds are always a safe choice. Forbearing, cautious Elfriede. The considered approach to life had skipped a generation, like twins, and shown up in Lawreen, even Elfie, who, despite her mother's encouragement, planned to take her time before making her next move.

Da, dah, dah, dah dah, dah, dah duh. The opera music swelled enchantingly, and Shinny could now whistle many arias as she unconsciously whistled Bach and Vivaldi. Elfie had been nicely on her way, sailing on music and love, until that sexy cellist got her hands on Brendan. Now the poor thing had no job, no money, no dreams. Shinny's challenge was to get her to dream again; then, if Esperanza shares shot up, she could cash in her Futures Fund to make Elfie's dreams come true.

But first they had to eat. She dragged her old enamel soup pot out of the bottom cupboard, filled it with water and set it on the stove. Elfie collected the mail but she had not cooked a meal for them since she had returned. So meek, though,

Shinny's slightest criticism lacerated her: she retreated to her bedroom and turned on the opera, or that lugubrious cello music.

"Why don't you play your new violin for me, Elf?"

"I will," she promised, yet she had done no more than lift the white satin cover to display it and run her finger around the f holes. "Isn't it beautiful? From Cremona, just like the violin of the little girl in the Vivaldi story."

"But better. That was just a story. This is real and look at the wood! Wouldn't your grandma be impressed? Play something for me, even just a scale so I can hear it."

Elfie hesitated, looking to the instrument itself for direction, then carefully replaced the satin cover and closed the case. "In a bit, Mom."

It surprised Shinny that she missed the softer "Mama."

Frozen pasta sauce, salad from a plastic bag with already cut vegetables and shredded lettuce. Cheating, but who cared. When Elfie felt better she could plan the meals.

"Elfie! Supper!"

No answer, only Leonora warbling to her maid the story of how she met the troubadour she loved. "*Tacea la notte placida.*" So like a waltz Shinny could not resist lilting around her tiny living room, dipping and turning between the couch and the basket chair, skirting the console that held the TV, imagining herself in a violet ball gown and satin shoes instead of the loose cotton pants and pullover she had worn to work; secure, no—adored—in the arms of her lover. She pictured Glen without his ball cap, his wavy hair neatly combed. Glen in a swallowtail coat and a high-collared white shirt set off by a black silk tie. The two of them gazing into each other's eyes as if there were no furniture to dodge but a ballroom of space in which they could swirl and swirl until another suitor appeared at her elbow, taller, fairer—the ginger-haired cyclist Andrew, who, being younger, cut a trimmer figure and steered her into a shadowy niche of the ballroom where moonlight blessed cascading blossoms—wisteria, perhaps—which perfumed the air and made her swoon against his shoulder until he circled her back into the light of the crystal chandeliers where yet another suitor, not as tall, but confident, a little king or emperor whose step owned the floor, commanded her into his arms. Carter Biggs. She offered her face to the ceiling, eyes closed, and the accumulated stress of the day drained away. Da, dah, dah, dah, dah, dah—dah, dah, dah.

The same melody, each note of which Elfie anticipated because she knew the piece so well, dragged through her with the sluggishness of a recording played at a speed lower than intended. She and Brendan had squeezed each other's hands, enraptured by the heights of the soparano's fabulous range. Now Leonora's maid would warn her of the foolishness of her love for Manrico. Scolding, preaching. Now the Count would appear; Leonora would mistake him for Manrico. The Count would proclaim his love in the soaring *"Il balen del suo sorriso,"* which Brendan had haltingly sung to Elfie one night on their beach. Only a few phrases, until Elfie's laughter discouraged him. "Sorry, babe," she had whispered, her lips against the salty skin beneath the collar of his shirt.

Romance had not worked out any better for the lovers of Verdi's time than it was working out for her. She had been staring at the sprayed ceiling for so long she could discern cobweb tents between its miniature plaster peaks. If only she could shrink and somehow encase herself like a caterpillar inside a paper cocoon.

When Shinny caught her breath she called for her daughter again. "Elfie?" She wouldn't kill herself, would she? Plenty of jilted lovers tried it. There was a window in her bedroom, she could jump, or she could have found pills somewhere. With passion inspired equally by the music and motherly concern, Shinny rushed to Elfie's door and beat on it.

"Elfie? Are you okay?"

"What? I'm fine. Just not hungry. I ate snacks before you got home," she shouted.

Why did she bother to cook? Elfie was never hungry.

"Turn down your music then, will you, Elf? It's really loud."

Mattie drew the same teacher in the same five/six split, but it would be better for him this year because in addition to knowing Mr. Fong's likes and dislikes and the excuses he would probably accept, Mattie was one of the older kids now. In the second week of school Mr. Fong announced that the grade six kids were to write a family history as their major language arts assignment of the term.

"Use the things you have collected for the millennium box and ask your grandparents for help if you need it."

"How long does it have to be?" one of the kids asked.

"I guess it depends on how big your family is," Mr. Fong joked, still in an upbeat mood after the summer break.

That fall in schools across the district teachers incorporated into every subject the history of the century about to pass. Lawreen thought they were making a mountain out of a mole-hill: it was just a change in numbers. But Matthew expected something momentous to happen. For one thing, it would be the best New Year's eve of most of their lives. Then, on

January 1, the entire school would gather at the excavation site in the courtyard to bury the millennium box. The students speculated about who would find the box and open it and examine the artifacts they had collected. Would those who made the discovery be able to read the English language? Would there even be such a thing as language in one hundred years or would people communicate telepathically, and would they be human or alien? Matthew listened to these conversations without participating. He could spare no fantasies for the future, not with the past yet incomplete.

In math, Mr. Fong discussed the controversy regarding the year the new millennium would actually begin.

"So when is it really?" a student more extroverted than Matthew asked.

"It depends on whom you believe," the teacher admitted. "Both sides argue a pretty good case. I tend to agree with the historians and the Royal Greenwich Observatory that because there was no year zero, the millennium will begin in 2001." Despite his personal beliefs, however, Mr. Fong had decided his class should celebrate with the rest of the school and most of the rest of the world.

The science theme for the month concerned the major inventions of the last hundred years. In social studies, Mr. Fong listed all the wars Canadians had been involved in, the First World War, the Spanish civil war, the Second World War, the Korean War, the Vietnam War, plus the wars where Canadian soldiers had acted as peacekeepers, in Cyprus, Somalia, Yugoslavia. He asked kids who had relatives who had served in any of those wars to raise their hands. Matt raised his, because there was that picture of his great-grandfather in the sailor's cap, and he could find more stuff, in second-hand stores and used-book shops. He thought of submarines. His great-grandfather started on a regular navy ship but moved into submarines. Submarine intelligence. He spied on the enemy from under the water, using a periscope, an eye sticking up out of the water to spot potential threats, like a spy-hopping killer whale. What enemy, though? Japan? Germany?

Sometimes Lawreen seemed nuts to Matthew, like for instance the way she was going on about the tooth Mariah lost today, that Mattie helped her pull out. He heard his mom tell Grandma, on the phone, that big teeth weren't as cute as baby teeth and that this might be the beginning of the end of Mariah's career. Matthew wondered how that would be: with time on their hands his parents would notice him more and that could be both good and bad. Anxious for morning to come so that she could see what the tooth fairy had left for her, Mariah went to bed earlier than usual and Matt would not have heard the conversation himself except that he had thumped downstairs to retrieve a volume from the set of encyclopedias in the living room bookcase and got sidetracked by the sitcom his dad was watching. He heard his mother's voice from the kitchen, during a pause in the dishwasher cycle. The O word came up, orthodontist, and he curled his tongue up over his two front teeth. He regularly tried pushing them back, thinking that if he kept at it he might not have to suffer braces.

Although Mattie was supposed to be in his room by nine, Ken let him perch on the edge of the leather couch, to maintain the illusion that he was just passing by. Through the fifteen minutes Lawreen talked, until the end of the show, Mattie scooted gradually closer, until he was within reach of his dad's hand. Ken grabbed Mattie's shoulder and hauled him back. They rarely cuddled any more and Mattie liked the give of his dad's arms and stomach. He kept the S volume under his right arm, though not to hide it, for he was gaining confidence in himself as a storyteller: his parents believed anything he told them. The encyclopedia? Oh, just some research for school.

When the show was finished, Ken watched Mattie trundle up the stairs to his room. A pleasing boy, low-key by choice, it seemed, often in his own world, doing fine in school, no behaviour problems. *Trundle* was a word Ken's mother used, "Trundle off to bed now, honey," and it had once perfectly described the rolling motion of his little feet; but Matthew lumbered heavily now, trudged rather than trundled.

"Is your project coming along okay, son? Do you need any help?" Ken called after him. Mattie was fast getting away on them, Ken felt, yet he also believed that his son knew where he wanted to go.

He situated himself in front of his computer and opened a new file.

My Family
by Matthew Webster

Part of my family came to Canada from Holand and the other half started way back in England but Im not sure when they got over here. My great-great grandfather was a soldier in Holand who fought in the resistance. HE became a spy and worked on submarines during the first world war. If it wasn't for him the German army would have won the war because he was the guy who spotted a big ammunition dump hiden on the coast. It was such a big defeat for the GErmans that no one even says his name. Some angry GErmans might still want revenge on his descendants, including me, that's why I'm not saying his name.

To escape from the Germans who were hunting the whole family one of my uncles moved to south america where he got involved in a crime ring. This was before cocaine. They were smuggling other illegal things I can't say what. Meantime, my great-great-grandfather the war hero moved to the Fraser Valley and started a peaceful farm so no one would suspect. My great-grandmother was born on the farm. She met a salor who also worked on submarines, like her father, and after WW2 they got married and had my grandmother Shinnan.

Across the valley there was a famous horse farm where people raised race horses. The people had one son, Larry, who was too big to be a jockey so he was going to be a animal doctor instead. He met my grandmother and they got married. They were having a picnic one night when his dog Sky got away and started walking on the trestle across the river. My grandfather went after him to save him and they both fell into the river and drwoned.

On my dad's side his grandfather was a bnaker who lost a lot of money in the stock market crash. Until then the family was very rich then came the crash. They lost everything even the airplane his brother was working on that was going to fly around the world faster than the first guy who did it whose baby got kidnapped.

After that my great grandfather and my great uncle started a delivery business. The card shows it as Bernard's delivery service. That was my great-grandfather's first name.

Okay, so somebody named Bernard had a delivery service. But who was Preston? He reached into the secret compartment under his desk for the candy he had stashed there and tore open a bag of Skittles.

"Matthew? Are you finished with your homework?" Lawreen called as she pushed through the door.

Meaning to hit close, Mattie instead mistakenly deleted what he had just typed, so he would have to start over, and that sucked, but it was better than having his mom read what he wrote.

"Just about, Mom."

Lawreen's short hair dripped with water from her shower. She was dressed in her track outfit, the soft grey pants, the grey sweatshirt. Taller than Shinny, just as slim, a pretty, angular face, her father's straight perfect nose and blue eyes, a kind of miracle, Shinny believed, considering that blue eyes travelled in recessive genes.

"Elfie's going to pick you up from after-school care tomorrow because Dad is taking Mari downtown for that shoot. Okay?"

She snapped his bedspread to straighten it, picked up the socks he had left on the floor, ran her finger across the edge of his dresser, to check for dust. Mattie had his super hero figures lined up there, he hated it when she did that. She was coming closer, to kiss him goodnight. "You weren't into some game, were you, Mattie? You know the deal about keeping the computer in your room."

"I wasn't. I just finished working on my family history. Honest." Then he remembered the Skittles.

"Oh, Matthew, where did you get these? Did Dad buy them for you? You were going to cut out candy, remember?"

She snatched them up, only half a bag gone, and leaned down to hug him. Instead of saying he was too fat, she encouraged Mattie to exercise and eat fewer snacks.

"I remember." She smelled like shampoo and soap and the apple she had eaten while she talked to Grandma on the phone.

"Maybe you could try going to the gym with me."

"Maybe."

"Better turn that off now, honey. Get some sleep."

She closed the door behind her. At least she hadn't seen the family history file. He didn't have to finish it tonight, it wasn't due until Monday, but he'd thought of something to add.

He clicked open his school file, hoping he had not lost all he typed tonight, but he had; the screen was blank. So he repeated the title and underneath it he added the bit he had just thought of: *During the 2nd world war, the submarine was attacked and my grandfather was taken prisoner of war. The Japs kept him in a little room, so little that his legs went bad and he had to walk on crutches for the rest of his life.* This sounded less pathetic than the polio story. He imagined that shrunken great-grandmother of his writing her war hero father to ask for one hundred dollars. Mattie had five hundred dollars in his own bank account and even if money amounted to more back then it was still sick, he thought. *Papa, can you let us have $100.* Except he wasn't really a war hero, Matthew had made that story up. At least he didn't think his great-great-grandfather was a war hero. Nobody had ever said so, not as far as he could remember.

In his hiding place beneath the desk, Mattie found a full package of Jolly Ranchers. He unwrapped a grape-flavoured square and sucked it hard while he shut the computer down. Lime came next, more sour than the grape, the insides of his cheeks contracted right down to his jawbone. He chewed it finished and went out to the bathroom. Except for the light that seeped through the window from the street and the stripe beneath his parents' bedroom door, he walked down a hallway whispery dark. Then laughter burst into the near-silence of the house from whatever TV show they were watching in bed. When he was little he used to open their door and run in and shake his mom's arm, or his dad's, until one of them pulled him into their warm nest. The memory slowed him, though he knew it was no use, that even if he wanted to lie there with them they would send him back to bed. Even if he wanted to, which he didn't.

He scrubbed his teeth with the electric brush and scanned the mirror for signs of facial hair. Some guys had the beginnings of moustaches at eleven. He pulled his upper lip down to cover his front teeth. Nothing.

Back in bed he unwrapped a cherry, which clashed with the taste of the toothpaste until it was almost gone, when the cherry flavour dominated. The next little square of candy would be lemon, he knew from experience. Still, somebody in the factory might have felt rebellious one day—put two cherries, his favourite, in a row.

Having noticed how much Mattie enjoyed the glow in the dark shapes on Elfie's ceiling, Shinny presented him with a similar set, but of the heavens, for his own room. When he turned out his light he saw stars, several glowing moons, meant to be arranged around Jupiter, Saturn with its ring. Ken had promised to help Matthew place the stars in their proper constellations, but he had not yet got around to doing it. Tonight, Mattie put his desk chair on his bed and stood on it to rearrange the stars in clusters, bursts of stars. In the dark, when he narrowed his eyes, they resembled explosions. His great-grandfather, the submarine spy, had picked out the target, then watched through the periscope as blast after blast destroyed the enemy's ammunition dump. While the sky blazed red he sat cool, undetected. In fact, he refused even to admit it was he who identified the targets because he feared revenge. So he didn't accept the medal the Allied Forces offered him, declined to have his name included in the roll of heroes. That's why no record of his achievements existed, only the legend that had been passed down by the men who were with him on that submarine, all of them, unfortunately, dead by now.

Invention had proved to be as delicious as candy, and as ultimately unsatisfying. One story demanded another, yet people believed what he told them and it seemed to be true, that old saying: what you don't know won't hurt you.

Three weeks after Shinny and Mattie waved goodbye to him at his farm, Glen Schroeder phoned Shinny with the news that he would indeed be attending a meeting of organic growers at the end of the month, in a suburb of Vancouver. Was she free to have dinner with him after the meeting?

"Free? Let me think." Fool, she told herself. Don't play this game. "Yes, I believe I am, Glen. That would be nice."

She mailed him directions to her co-op then worried, the day he was due, that her letter had not arrived before he left. He had her phone number, he could call when he got into town, except that in her fluster—they had not made any plans to meet again when they said goodbye in the summer; there was only that hint in his letter; had he been thinking of her? did he miss her?—she had neglected to ask him what time his meeting would finish. She might still be at work when he called and what then?

"Carlo," she said, when they were alone in the store, "I've got to leave early today, okay?"

"Is it Elfie? Maybe we could help out. Joanie and me, we could take her to dinner. Maybe a concert." Carlo had been worried about the young musician for whom he felt such affection. From the heights she had reached in Italy, she had fallen like an ambushed bird.

"She still doesn't want to go anywhere, but she can't stay home forever. You remember what it was like, don't you, Carlo?"

His eyes closed and his thin-lipped smile broadened to expose his teeth. "Too well," he said. "But it's hard when you're young, eh, Shinny?"

Not only when you are young, she thought, though she refrained from speaking the thought because she didn't want to reveal too much. "Anyway, it's not Elfie this time, it's a date, but you have to promise not to tell Anthony."

"Somebody we know, eh?"

"No, it's just that he teases, you've heard him. Please, Carlo?"

"Go! But tell Elfie we want to see her."

"It's only been a few weeks, give her time. She's not only sad, she's embarrassed; she thinks it's her fault that it didn't work out."

Rap music blatted through the cracks around the sheets of plywood covering the broken windows of the house across from the co-op. Squatters, she suspected, but how did they get electricity? The house had finally been condemned and would soon be demolished to make room for the townhouses pictured on the development permit affixed to a post in the weedy front yard.

Shinny had time to change clothes, maybe shower first. She had asked Elfie to tidy the apartment, and Elfie generally did as she was asked. What Shinny told Carlo was half true: Elfie went out, but only to see those people who had nothing to do with her life pre-Europe. Instead of renewing contacts at the university music department, she had registered with JOBWORKS, an agency that supplied temporary office workers. She wanted money to travel, but not back to Europe; eastern Canada, perhaps, or even south, to the States.

"It would be a bad time for that, with the new baby coming."

"Not so bad. Annette said they could probably use the help."

Shinny didn't want to encourage her, but if she protested too much Elfie might surface long enough to wonder why. So far, so good—those bells that had rung from Europe seemed to have been false alarms and the ancient guilt they awakened had slunk back into a crevasse in Shinny's mind.

"Are you sure you don't want those students? You used to love to teach."

Elfie said she would think about it.

Shinny set her bag of wine on the floor to press the elevator button, then transferred the plastic sack containing the focaccia bread and sausage to that hand, adjusted the shoulder strap of the big handbag she carried to work every day, and picked up the wine bag with her free hand. The elevator took so long descending she just about gave up and took the stairs, despite her load. Then she heard the whirr of the mechanism, the click as the elevator reached the main floor. The doors slid open to reveal Mrs. Ferishenko inside, leaning on her walker as if on display. Startled at first, Shinny recovered quickly enough to edge her foot against the door.

"Senk you." Distant, aristocratic Mrs. Ferishenko kept her hair dyed brown and her lipstick fresh all day.

"I can wait."

"Senk you all da same, but I von't be going back up just yet."

"Okay then. See you." Mrs. Ferishenko had taken the suite of Archie Gillespie, the old man Shinny befriended soon after she and Elfie moved into the co-op. So far she had not been able to strike the same accord with the Russian woman. When they passed in the lobby or hallway, as now, or found themselves sitting next to each other at the monthly co-op meeting, Mrs. Ferishenko received all overtures politely but gave nothing back.

"Elf?"

No answer, and she had tidied the apartment as promised. Shinny had time to shower, dress in her calf-length black skirt and the high necked black sweater that concealed her fluted throat—nothing too fancy, as if she expected high dining—low heels, the same outfit she wore to the Vistagrande meeting and to her mother's funeral. She had coloured her hair and visited her hairdresser for a trim early in the week, not wanting it to appear "done" just for tonight, and painted her nails with white polish this morning. The trick with hands like hers, she had read, was to blend nail colour with skin colour so as not to draw attention to their size. She didn't think about her hands until she dressed up, when they looked ungainly to her as lawn rakes at the ends of her arms.

When the knock sounded on the door at five to six, she licked her lips and swung the door open with a big smile, and found Elfie there, frowning.

"Sorry, Mom. I forgot my key. You look nice."

"Do you think so?"

"I do. Really nice. And you don't have to worry about me. I'm kind of tired. I'm going to take a nap."

"Carlo was asking about you, Elf. He and Joan want to take you out. Will you call him?"

"Sure, Mom. I will. Just not tonight, okay?"

So Elfie would be home; of course she would, she lived here again, but the fantasies that had been keeping Shinny awake all week could never play out in her bedroom with her daughter on the other side of the wall, asleep or not. Just as well, for the better a person got to know another person before they had sex, the greater the chance the relationship would last. All the advice amounted to what her mother had told her for years—look before you leap. Still, at nearly fifty-five, she worried about her ability to leap at all: if she looked too closely she might be afraid to leap, and how many opportunities could a woman her age expect?

When the second knock rapped on the door, she was calmer. She took a deep breath and twisted the knob and there in the hallway stood Glen, looking handsome in a corduroy sport coat, dark twill pants, his thin wavy hair neatly brushed to the side. No red ball cap tonight, no swallow-tailed coat either.

"Hello!" She wanted to hug him, but held back lest he misinterpret her pleasure in seeing him again. People in Vancouver fell into each other's arms on any excuse, but Glen came from the country where a hug from a woman he barely knew might put him off.

"Hello." A tissue-wrapped clutch of peach gladiolas in one hand and a bottle of wine in the other. He thrust them both towards her.

"Flowers! And what a beautiful colour! Thank you. Come in and sit down and I'll pour us some of this. I have some too. Do you like white or red? I wasn't even sure if you drank."

"I drink some."

"Well, good; I do, too." She waved towards the living room: "Anywhere you're comfortable." But he followed her into her kitchen-galley instead and leaned against the fridge while she hunted through the clutter beneath the sink for a vase tall enough to support the gladiolas. The tallest vessel she could find was a gallon jar Annette had filled with sun-dried tomatoes and sent to her last Christmas. Orange flecks of oil still clung to the sides. She shrugged. "This will have to do."

Amid the scents of the food she had set out for snacks, Shinny breathed Glen's particular essence, murmurs of grass and flowers and damp earth, the cloth of his coat, the heat of his skin. He carried in the plate and set it on the square pine table. Shinny followed with the wine and glasses and a corkscrew in the shape of a fish.

"Cheers!"

"About time, too," he said, unable to fully conceal the question Shinny saw in his eyes before she glanced away and settled on the basket chair that faced the couch. Would this be it, then? Was she reading him right? Elfie coughed.

"That's my daughter, Elfie. She's not feeling well. I didn't have a chance on the phone to tell you she came back from

Italy." In fact, she had hardly had the chance to tell him Elfie
lived in Italy. The litany of the past new acquaintances custom-
arily recite, barely begun during her poison oak episode, had
been interrupted by Mattie's near accident at the farm. Now she
couldn't remember what she had actually told Glen and what
she had imagined telling him. "I told you she was studying
music there, didn't I?"

"You mentioned a daughter in California." He took off his
glasses and set them on the coffee table. Without them he
looked younger, and so more desirable, in his view, though
Shinny saw him as unfinished without them, as if she had
surprised him in his pajamas. She shifted on her cushion and her
wine rocked up to but not over the rim. Glen rubbed the bridge
of his nose then put his glasses back on. The fact was he could
barely see without them.

"That would be Annette. Elfie is the youngest. She and her
boyfriend went over to Italy to study music in Milan." Shinny
wanted to explain, yet she felt defensive for Elfie: she would
have to tell the story in such a way that her daughter emerged as
the victor, not victim. It was simpler to leave him with general-
ities and change the subject. "It didn't work out the way she
wanted and so she came back a few weeks ago." There, she'd
summed it up in a sentence, leaving the whole complicated mess
for the time being as she would leave an unpleasant job that
would nevertheless have to be accomplished at some point, and
speeding onto her lunch break. "But what a coincidence that
your meeting should be up here. I didn't know there were so
many organic herb growers."

Outside, darkness had claimed as much of the city as was
possible with traffic lights and street lamps, distant squares of
white from downtown office buildings and vehicle headlights
competing with night. Shinny had left the sliding door open a
crack for air that, while not exactly fresh, textured the atmosphere with the fetor of damp dead leaves, car exhaust, deterio-
rating vegetables from the stand at the corner. The colder days

and nights to come would lock the odours out and Shinny would notice their absence like a hay fever sufferer notices when she can breathe again. Same with the sounds. Though Glen heard traffic slowing to a stop at the intersection a block east and start up again, motorcycle engines, the occasional horn, wheels of skateboards rolling down the sloping street Shinny's window faced, the apartment felt quiet to her and she wished for once that Elfie would play her opera or even that sad cello music to alleviate the uncertainty of the silence.

"You'd be surprised," Glen replied, uncomfortable as Shinny and disconcerted that this should be the case at his age.

"And it went okay? What do organic growers talk about?"

Glen had kept his shoes on, which people in Vancouver generally didn't, while Shinny curled her toes in her stockings because the innards were spilling from the embroidered cotton house-slippers she had bought from a Chinese shoe repair shop. Shoes on, knees together, resting the base of his wineglass on his thighs. Compressed, as though he might knock something over if he moved too quickly.

"We generally talk about ways of improving our crops without chemicals, although this one had more to do with how to get the message out to consumers, to improve the market for our produce and the products that come from them, like the medicines I gave you."

"Oh."

She attempted to see the room as he would see it, small, minute compared to his house, space enough for a three-seater couch, which she had covered with a woven, forest-green throw, the basket chair, the console that held the TV with the VCR on a shelf directly beneath and below that her books: the *Illustrated Medical Encyclopedia*, the big dictionary Mattie and Mariah used to sit on to reach the table, an oversized illustrated book on the redwoods of California that Annette had sent, the Canadian encyclopedia, the music books that didn't fit on the shelves in Elfie's room. She didn't need to live in such a small place, she could afford something grander. If Elfie stayed she would look for a larger apartment, maybe one of those new townhouses that would be built across the street.

"I bet it would be hard for you to live in a place like this. You'd feel cramped, right?"

"I imagine," he smiled. Then, as if to test himself, he stood up and edged around the coffee table and made the sliding glass door in two strides. "But you have the advantages of the city where there must be a lot of interesting things going on all the time."

"I made a reservation at a place we can walk to. An Italian place. This used to be a real Italian neighbourhood. Now we have a little bit of everything."

She saw from the stripe of worn leather that he used to notch his belt tighter. The cotton plaid shirt, a triangle of white T-shirt underneath, showing at his throat, which had rings like the rings of trees. The deep smile lines.

"El Salvadorans and Guatemalans, and of course Chinese, and Vietnamese and Koreans. East Indians. You can tell by the restaurants. Do you like Italian?"

"I am actually glad you made the choice because I would never know what to choose from that impressive variety. As you must have noticed, where I live our choice is limited to Bonnie's Café and McDonald's, on the Interstate."

His sentences would wind around her silkily, making a pod in which they would stretch out along the length of one another. It was happening, the anemone sensation, petals opening, tentacles waving. She looked beyond him to the sliding glass, where a darting light grabbed her attention.

"What's that?"

Glen turned back to the window. "Looks like a flashlight to me. Odd. That house is boarded up."

"Nobody's supposed to be living there, but squatters have been. It's going to be torn down any day now and then we'll have to live with construction all year. What's he doing? Is that a ladder?"

"It's a ladder, all right, and it looks like whatever's going on is not good. I believe someone is trying to break into that house, Shinny."

"Do you think? Oh but it could be one of the squatters. That's probably how they get in and out."

"You ought to report this, in any case. I'll go over and see what I can do."

"I don't think you should do that, Glen." But he was on his way to the door.

"Just call the police."

"Okay, except that they probably are squatters and I don't think . . ."

He didn't wait for the elevator but took the stairs and jogged out the entry doors, surprising Mrs. Ferishenko, who, in her effort to simply make it home, had not noticed any ladder, any flashlight. Glen excused himself, and sprinted across the street as the 911 attendant came onto the phone.

"Fire? Ambulance? Police?"

"Police!"

"Go ahead."

"There's a break-in. Robertson and Bennett. It's going on right now, a friend of mine ran over to try and stop it."

"All right, there's a unit on the way. This isn't your residence, Ma'am?"

"No, I'm calling from across the street. I can see it all from my window. I don't think he should have gone over there. The place is boarded up. But I think squatters . . . Nobody would break in a squatters' place, would they? What would there be to steal?"

"Just stay on the line, Ma'am. You say a citizen is attempting to intervene?"

"A friend of mine from the country. He's not used to city ways. Here's the siren!"

"Mom? What's going on?" Hair mussed from her pillow, eyes swollen as they always were these days, Elfie hugged herself and coughed. "I thought you were going out."

Shinny held her hand up, for silence. She couldn't take in both voices at once. "The police got there. Should I hang up now?"

"What's going on?"

Shinny put the phone down and hurried to the balcony to better see the action across the street. "It's Glen, the friend I was telling you about. He went over there to make a citizen's arrest or something. I wish he would have stayed out of it. Oh my God, is that him?"

In the revolving red beams thrown on the house by the police cars that had sirened up, three figures scrambled down the ladder, knocking Glen to the ground in their hurry to escape the uniformed police who blocked their paths. One officer intercepted a person and wrestled him to the weeds in front of the house. Two other officers trapped the second. The third escaped. Glen struggled to his knees.

"Look, he's hurt! I should get down there!" Shinny slipped her feet into her duck shoes and grabbed her jacket.

Elfie returned to her room for her quilt, which she wrapped around herself like a cloak, and returned to the balcony to watch.

[four]

Their latest encounter ended with Shinny watching Glen drive away maimed. She had steered his pick-up out of the cramped space on the block, because his bruised shoulder prohibited such complex maneuvers. He would not stay the day and he would not take the painkillers the emergency room physician prescribed because he feared falling asleep at the wheel.

"Maybe I should just drive you home. I bet I could get the day off." The odds were long, though: Anthony had plans for an insulation blow-out sale this weekend.

"No, I'll be all right now that you've got me pointed in the right direction. Thank you all the same, Shinny."

Grey beard fuzz and the odd dirty eggshell colour of the sky accentuated his exhausted complexion. Shinny checked the rearview mirror: any minute a car would putt up the street or roar around the corner, wanting to drive the narrow strip between cars parked on both sides, the passage Glen's truck blocked.

"You better get in." She set the emergency brake, slid out and hugged him lightly so not to hurt or confuse him. Stale sweat smothered his hayfield country aura, but after having spent what was left of the night on the couch, so that Glen could rest in her room, she smelled like no rose herself. "I'm really sorry about all this. You are a kind of hero, though. You did break up a ring of drug peddlers."

"A small ring." He kept his good hand just above her waist. "We'll try it again," he promised and he bent a little to kiss her forehead before climbing into the truck. She raised her hand to wave and saw disappointment complicating his understandably strained features. Impossible at their ages to pretend they were not both thinking the same thing.

She got to work late and found Anthony and Carlo unrolling a broad paper scroll Anthony had commissioned a neighbourhood artist to letter with the words *Fall madness! We're going batty with batting!*

"Sorry," she called, picking up Anthony's end of the banner so that he could tape it to the window. Neither of them remarked on her tardiness, though Carlo smiled, thinking he knew the reason for it, thinking it a happy reason. How could she explain? Such independent movers as Glen who instinctually took matters into their own hands hardly existed in the city.

When the sign was in place and the door open, Anthony put on a beanie with a propeller on top, which he had bought in 1960 on the midway at the Pacific National Exhibition. He planned to station himself in front of the garden shop and talk people into the store. Fat pink plastic-wrapped bolts of insulation material were crammed into the narrow yard where racks of flowers, herbs and vegetables lingered until just last week. By bringing in a whole truckload, A and C could offer a lower price than the hardware superstores. A table just inside the door displayed weather-stripping alternatives, space heaters, also paint,

for last-chance painting during the Indian Summer that was
bound to bless the city sometime in October.

"We've got ladders for people who've got bats in their
belfries," Anthony hollered. "We've got ladders for people who
need batting in their belfries."

"Hey, have you lost a little on top?"

When Carlo was within hearing distance, he quipped back:
"It's obvious he has, and I'm not talking about insulation."
While not the natural showman his brother was, he enjoyed the
hoopla as much as Anthony did.

But Carlo seldom had time to duck outside. He helped customers find what they wanted inside and assisted Shinny in
ringing through orders, so that no one had to wait too long.
Shinny liked working with Carlo. They could man both regis-
ters during a rush, and when business was slower but steady, one
could handle transactions and the other bag. It had to do with
size: Anthony, the heavier brother, spilled into her space but
Carlo's slimmer, shorter body fit alongside hers easily.
Sometimes they reached for bags beneath the counter at the
same time, too preoccupied to acknowledge that they were moving in concert: synchronized hardware handlers.

"So you had a good time?" he asked during a lull. His eyes
gleamed the rich brown of horse chestnuts kids in the city called
conkers, but he tactfully refrained from winking.

The weekend after the sale, Shinny tucked in her handbag a box
of expensive chocolates and the invitation she had received to a
reunion of the 1999 Take Charge! rafters—a celebration of their
accomplishments, the end of the season. For Shinny, an excuse to
discharge a months-old debt of gratitude to Lynette. Then she
could not bring herself to join the hearty women at the False
Creek community centre but drove instead to the railway overpass
flanked by the grey marble lions. It would just be too awkward.

Seagulls. A couple strolling east. Late afternoon on a dull

October day. The canning shed displayed the sombre shade of dried blood instead of its usual radiant crimson. Shinny could not see the mountains and the clammy air chilled her and she had no cleaning supplies because she had not intended to come here. The best she could do was to pick up the garbage strewn around, not much garbage this time. Polish the plate. With a tissue wrapped around her forefinger, she dug her nail into the cut of each letter, quietly uttering the name they spelled, almost as if waking her mother, a kind of incantation. Grey sky lapsed into plummy twilight, though it was only just four, and dots of light outlined the shapes of docks, silos, the tugboat landing across the Inlet. Shinny had heard of people who saw visions of deceased loved ones, figures materializing like images on Polaroid photographs. A gift; you either had it or you didn't, and she must not have it, for if she was ever going to see her mother, this would be the perfect place. The foreground appeared starker than usual against the smokey blue rumour of a background. Shinny had little to say to her mother today except to request another chance with Glen. I'm taking it slowly this time, Mom, just as you always wanted me to. An improvement, see? And the usual wish that her mother guide Elfie through this next change. Did Mom know the truth about her youngest grandchild? If she could read Shinny's mind, hear her thoughts, she must know it but Shinny skipped over that file for the time being, as if ignoring it would delete it and there would be nothing for Elfriede to read.

It was almost a year now. Barely a month after Elfie left for Europe Mom was gone, having expired without a fuss. Heart arrhythmia. Elfriede's neighbour Margaret found her stiff in her chair the next morning, Sally Jesse Raphael on the TV in front of her, the TV so hot Margaret just about burned herself on it, she said, but Shinny doubted it. TVs didn't get that hot anymore. Hot TVs would be a safety hazard and manufacturers could be sued. Margaret, Elfriede's long-time neighbour, had walked over to shoot the breeze, as she did most mornings—to check on Elfriede who was the older by fifteen years; entered through a wide open door, she said, though it would not have been wide open, only unlocked, which made it seem wide open to Margaret, and found her friend sitting peacefully in front of her television. Nothing odd about the scene at all at first glance except for Sally Jesse, a show Elfriede never watched, preferring Oprah, and not even too much of Oprah lately because they went so far, those guests of hers. Sally, Elfriede's silence—which Margaret took as slumber at first—then a closer look at the dry staring eyes, the stiffness of the fingers, the hotness of the TV. But it had not been literally hot, Shinny knew, just as the door had not been literally wide open. The heat had come from Margaret herself as she ignited with the sudden terrible realization of death.

Shinny took the box out of her handbag and pulled at the shiny gold ribbon, tore off the marbled paper. Lifted the lid. A warm smell, chocolate, even in this weather. She chose a vanilla cream, her favourite. Soft-thick on her tongue, a lingering pinch of sweetness in her throat. Then a milk chocolate haystack. Mom was gone but Elfie had returned. Instead of sitting here mooning over her departed mother, she should be working harder to help Elfie make a new life. The white peaks of the trade and convention centre's sails off to the left reminded Shinny that she had the money to actually set Elfie up: in fact, if her fifteen thousand doubled in a year, as Carter had hinted it well might, she could help Elfie do whatever she wanted to do.

Shinny chose a third chocolate, a caramel so sticky she had a hard time pulling her teeth apart to chew it. Her mouth was full when a silver bike rolled to a stop beside her and Andrew set his foot down.

"Hi!"

Hand over her mouth, she held up the box to explain. "Andrew!" The lump of caramel fisted down her throat. "I was going to give these to somebody, and then it didn't work out. Want one?"

He wore black spandex cycling shorts and a green nylon windbreaker. Black and white athletic shoes, white socks that stretched halfway up his calves. The weather and the exertion had reddened his face to the shade of a raw clay pot and his ginger eyebrows glistened with moisture.

"That's a big box."

"It was going to be a thank-you present."

"But now you're not thankful?"

"I'm thankful, I just waited too long. I don't even really know the person I was going to give it to, and the nice thing she did happened months ago. It just got to seem embarrassing. Here, have one. They're good."

"I can't eat chocolate. I break out in hives. The bench is looking good. Your mother would be pleased."

"I think she would. She's buried way out in Meadowvale, so I don't visit her grave much."

Andrew swung his leg over the crossbar and wheeled his bike to the side of the bench. Shinny moved from the centre to the edge. Andrew took a bottle from the holder attached to the bike's frame and drank from it. The chocolate had made Shinny thirsty but she did not know him well enough to ask for a drink.

"Do people visit graves any more? I take that back. My parents still visit my brother's grave. I visit Ty, it seems more relevant."

"I used to visit my first husband's grave." Shinny referred to Larry as her husband because their actual relationship and all that stemmed from it was, like so many of the details of her life, too complicated to explain in a sentence or so. "That's out in Meadowvale, too. And we're going out there next week to put flowers on my mother's grave. It will be the first anniversary of her death." She hesitated to say she felt close to her mother, heard her voice more distinctly here at the bench, because she had not told anyone about the voice, not even Elfie. Do you feel her here, Elf? she had asked. Elfie's chin had drooped to her chest and she had turned to Shinny with swimming eyes.

Shinny had taken her hand and squeezed. Elfie had wanted to comfort her mother but had not known what to say. The bench was just another place in the world Brendan was not.

"So it was your brother who was Ty's dad?"

"Mmm."

"Must have been young when he died."

"Forty-five."

"That's young. Do you mind my . . ."

"Asking how he died? No, it was freaky. One of those galloping viruses. You wake up with the flu, next day you're in the hospital. If you're lucky they can save you. Seems hard to believe it can still happen, but it did. Lucky for Eric it was over before he could really appreciate what hit him."

The damson sky had acquired a velvety nap, air dense with suspended rain. Shinny shivered and folded her arms across her chest so she could shove each big hand into the opposite sleeve of her jacket. Andrew should have a bench for his brother, or something, somewhere to go. There was no reason to ghettoize the dead in cemeteries. Whole neighbourhoods could be embroidered with flower-adorned altars, such as the ones spontaneously created by neighbours and friends for victims of crime. Candles could burn at the bottom of skyscrapers from which construction workers had fallen to their deaths.

"Were you close?"

"As kids we were. My big brother, eh? I looked up to him, but he got to be quite a loner. He took an apartment in the West End, which is where he met Jeanette actually. But we didn't see much of each other for a few years and then, when we did get together . . ."

The roar of a seaplane lifting off eclipsed his words. Unaware that Shinny could not hear him, Andrew continued speaking. She leaned over, frowning, folds gathering at her throat as she cocked her head in concentration. She had not expected him to sit down in the first place, never these confidences. Bone-smooth skin, as if he shaved hourly. She imagined her cheek against his, cool and sleek, like the back of a spoon, then chastised herself on Glen's account, although infidelity hardly applied at this point. Go for it, Tina would say. She advised the same when Shinny reported Glen's visit.

"He wants you, Shinny. Don't let him get away from you."

"I can't just go there, Tina."

"Oh, Shinny. You're going to end up alone forever. Do you want that?"

". . . and it's hellishly busy out there. Teaching, private students, recitals. I was just getting started at City Hall." Andrew paused, watching the plane career over the harbour, then gain altitude, heading west. "Jeanette—that's Ty's Mom—may be getting remarried. Ty may have a live-in dad again."

"You sound sad about that. Did you want to marry her?"

"Jeanette? No way, she's not my type. I'm not sad. I'm happy for her, happy for Ty that he'll have someone around whenever he wants him. A guy Eric used to work with, in the music department of UBC. Two kids from another marriage. Ty'll have stepsisters. It will be one of those blended arrangements. A family."

"I suppose you could be sad about your brother being replaced. Unconsciously, I mean." She hated herself as soon as she said it. Lawreen talked this way, and Annette, basing their analysis of people on family relations, as if family were a big net that kept everyone trapped beneath mesh they could see through but never escape.

"I suppose." He capped his water bottle and replaced it in its holder.

"God, that chocolate made me thirsty! You know, my youngest daughter is a musician. She went to UBC."

"She probably knows Keith then. What does she play?

"She plays the violin, and she's good. It's not only because I'm her mother that I think that, she really is. She got accepted at a famous school in Italy. In Milan."

"Hmm. My brother spent some time in Italy. I think it was near Milan."

"He played the violin too?"

"No, the piano. Keyboards generally, but especially the piano. Jeanette still has the baby grand my parents bought for him when he was a teenager. He moved it everywhere he went. Cost a fortune."

"How do you feel about sharing your water bottle? The chocolate made me so thirsty."

"Look, the cap can be used as a cup. Don't worry about it. Finish it, if you want."

She did finish it, hardly thinking of what she was doing, distracted now. It was not just the chocolate that made her crave water, but the dry mouth of fear. A baby grand. That wing silhouetted in the white grey dawn that sprayed through sheer curtains. Although colours were fading in the shrinking light, there was no mistaking the red of Andrew's hair. And his nephew Ty had Elfie's green eyes; Shinny had noticed the similarity way back at Deer Lake.

"Uh-oh, she said, "here it comes".

Rain. Inevitable, yet also sudden, as if someone had punched the air: soft fine drops exploded in a shower that might last minutes or days. Shinny stood.

"Thanks for the drink. I better get going. You too. You'll be drenched."

The chocolate she had eaten was working through her like a laxative. She hauled the hood of her jacket over her hair, but she might have hauled it right over her eyes, for all she could see through the darkness. "See you another time, then."

"Yeah. See you."

His tires chewed the cinder path east as she ran in the other direction, to the parking lot, thinking that if she beat the rain and the night she might escape nauseating possibilities as well.

The next day Shinny's family gathered at Ken and Lawreen's condo. A white linen cloth covered the dining room table, which was laid with Lawreen's best china, also white, with a delicate wreath of blue flowers circling the edge. An arrangement of dried wild grasses and golden chrysanthemums decorated the centre of the table, and crystal wineglasses were set at each place. Mattie's and Mariah's contained apple juice that resembled the sparkling golden wine the adults were drinking. Turkey, candied yams, mashed potatoes, wild rice stuffing, Lawreen's special pickled red onions, whole cranberry sauce, crusty rolls, Brussels sprouts, green salad, the pumpkin pies Shinny baked for dessert. Lawreen had followed the recipes printed in *Canadian Woman*, in an article entitled "How Working Moms Prepare a Great Thanksgiving Feast." Mattie wore his best, dark brown cords and a white shirt, Mariah a new sapphire velvet dress. Ken clipped on a bowtie for the occasion. When the food was on the table and everyone was seated, Lawreen stood in the doorway between the kitchen and the dining room attempting to freeze the scene while it still had the gloss of the picture beside the recipes in *Canadian Woman*. She aimed her camera, "Smile everyone!" Then she thought of a new angle and climbed on the kitchen stool.

"Be careful, Lawry."

"Okay, now." This was better. The uncarved turkey gleamed a perfect golden brown and everyone's upward-turned faces appeared hopeful. With his new mustache grown out, Ken finally looked his age. Shinny was smiling so broadly that her wrinkles deepened to luge-depth, but Lawreeen didn't register the changes in her mother's appearance except to note that she was wearing her black skirt and sweater again despite being able to afford to buy decent clothes for the first time in her life. Mom was Mom. Elfie's smile looked forced and was forced. Mariah was perfect, even with the missing tooth. Mattie kept his lips pressed together.

"Just smile a minute, Matthew. Then we'll eat." Click, flash: Canadian Thanksgiving, 1999.

Shinny lifted her glass for a toast. "Thanks," she said, and they reached to clink with each other. "Thanks!"

"For what, Grandma, thanks for what?"

Shinny saw that Mariah was serious. "For all this food, Mari, for all of you, for our good luck compared to a lot of other people in the world. What do you have to be thankful for?"

"I got the part in the series." She tilted her head prettily, her actions self-conscious now, her beauty irresistible. Elfie leaned over and impulsively kissed her as if congratulating her niece for being so sure of love.

"And what about you, Mattie, honey, what do you have to be thankful for?"

Mouth full of roll, he popped his eyes and raised the drumstick Ken had just dropped on his plate. The chewing noise created a moat inside which he enjoyed a castle of silence.

"All right!" Shinny felt she should stop right here because it had been hard to persuade Elfie to join them in the first place;

no point pressing the thankful bit, not with Elfie slipping lower by the day. The nutmeg skin she returned with had faded after a month in Vancouver. Against the black of her dress, she was peeled almond, her smile a fan fallen open, no more emotion than that. How long did it take to recover from a spoiled love affair? Shinny tried to remember but it had not been the same for her, with children. Children allowed their mothers no time to languish. Languish, a love-affair word. She thought of Glen, the pressed flowers he had sent to thank her. Did she have the energy? She might, but she had to take care of Elfie first, do something to help Elfie make a new life away from Vancouver and all its reminders of the past. Toronto? New York? Canadian money would stretch further in Toronto.

Shinny needn't have worried, for Elfie, a pro, understood when it was necessary to rise to the occasion.

"I'm thankful to have two such great kids as my niece and nephew, my perfect big sister."

As the tone of her voice climbed, Shinny's stomach twisted like good intentions in destiny's breeze. She started to speak, to save her, but Elfie was not finished.

"A fabulous brother-in-law, and most of all, Mom."

"Oh Elfie, stop."

"Really! This is supposed to be a happy occasion. What about you, Mom?" Lawreen took her place at the end of the table opposite her husband, noticed cranberry sauce dribbling onto the tablecloth already.

They couldn't know how precarious their existence sometimes seemed to Shinny, surprising they existed at all, amazing they had survived childhood, these two, and Annette, and now there were Matthew and Mariah.

"So much. Sometimes I can't believe it, all of you."

"Don't forget Annette."

"Never."

"Or Dad," Elfie added.

"How could I forget him?"

Lawreen addressed the mashed potatoes she was spooning onto Mariah's plate. "Or the people who have already gone."

"Of course." A procession of them lit up in Shinny's mind: Mom, Larry, Mr. Gillespie. Dad, so long ago. Grandma, Grandpa. Had that tall carroty-haired man joined them? Was the dad Elfie referred to really Andrew's brother?

"White meat, anyone?" Ken asked. Matthew held up his plate. He wanted a little of everything.

During the week a letter postmarked Italy arrived at the co-op, addressed to Shinny in Elfie's small backslanting script. A letter nine months lost.

January 30, 1999

Dear Mom,

Thanks for the cheque. I didn't think it would be so much. Do you know what I'm going to do with it? I bet you can guess. I found a violin from the Cremonese school, not a Stradivarius, but close. All I have to do is touch the bow to the string and it sings. Thrilling! Brendan says so too. But it won't all go for the violin. We're going to treat ourselves to a trip to Venice. That's the plan, anyway. But Brendan is madly working on the string quartet he wants to submit in order to be accepted to the composition master class. We're working with two of the other students on a performance of it, and if we can win a slot at the festival in Siena, we're going to introduce it to the music world of Italy! Then, in the fall, there's the Internazionale, back in Cremona. A stringed instrument exposition they hold only every three years.

I hope you feel better now, Mom. We all miss Grandma, but you most, I know. I think of her just about every day and I have that Thanksgiving card taped to the wall above our bed just next to the picture Lawreen sent me of Mattie and Mar. I never got a Thanksgiving card from anybody before. I just imagined her going into downtown Meadowvale with Margaret, buying it, making

191

another trip to mail it. *Of course it got here after she died, which made it even sadder. It must have been hard to sort through all her things. I wish Aunt Carol would have stayed to help.*

We visited Carlo and Joan's relatives. Really nice. They invited us back, too, for a musical evening. Give Carlo a hug for me and thank him, again, will you, Mama? Tell Mattie he promised to write and I haven't heard from him since Christmas. You've got to come visit us, Mom. This country is so old. You should see the Duomo. It took centuries to build! It's more musical here than in Canada, too, Mom. More exciting. Course it could be all the coffee everyone drinks. Including me!

> *Con amore,*
> *sua figlia*
> *Elfita (You like?)*

Heartbreaking that such hope should have come to this. The evening news was about to begin when Elfie came in late from her shift at the data-processing office.

"Hi Mom. I'm really beat," and went to her room without supper again.

"Aren't you hungry, Elfie?"

She called through the bathroom door. "I had a big lunch."

"There's soup."

"Maybe after my shower."

Elfie had a willow-switch body similar to the one that had thrilled Shinny so that night, freckles on his shoulders, his arms. In the light of the candle burning on the windowsill, his shadowed skin had the cast of solid marble with all its subtle shadings, its mysterious veins. Slender was one thing, but how far away was anorexia? The trick was to get Elfie interested in playing music again. Shinny wondered if she should call Elfie's old teacher to ask about connections in Toronto.

The commercial finished and the news began with the grainy

image of a window, an underwater window, two hands silhouetted against it. The announcer began: "Tragedy struck the founder and chief geologist of Esperanza Resources, Eberhard Stuibel, when the company's newly developed and highly touted personal submersible lost power at 3000 metres. A warning: the following footage contains images that some viewers may find disturbing."

Hand over her mouth, Shinny watched as the light shone from eyes terrified but also enraged. A big man in a high-tech diving suit punched at a control panel, trying to force to life the connection between his craft and the mother ship; then the silhouette of those hands against the grainy window.

The news anchor returned, looking grim. "The tragedy follows news last week of disappointing assay results from the company's initial nodule harvest at the Esperanza underwater mine." Distracted by romance, Shinny had not been following the business news as she used to. "Trading is expected to be halted in shares of Esperanza when the Toronto and Vancouver stock exchanges open in the morning.

"Carter Jack Biggs, one of the Bay Street insiders whose Futures Fund invested heavily in the company, says he isn't running scared yet, but those who have depended on Biggs's famous sixth sense may be."

And then Carter himself, dressed neatly as usual in a suit, caught coming out of his office, frowning. The camera revealed a smattering of city lights beyond his generous office window.

"Eberhard Stuibel was a pioneer. Like the prospectors who trekked over the Canadian Shield and the northern territories, he broke new ground in mineral exploration and development. His death is a tragic . . ."

There was no ring around him this time, only white flashes from cameras and the artificial brightness of TV lights, gone now as the image of the anchorman returned. But he had looked at her directly, maybe not only at her but also the hundreds of other people he had convinced to invest in his new high risk mutual fund.

"Esperanza had gone into production only last month. Exploration reults were positive. We're sure that the nodule deposition is simply uneven. That's what Eberhard was down there trying to prove. To investors my advice is—hang on. Out of respect for Mr. Stuibel, give his dream a chance."

Was it possible to lose the whole $15,000 barely a month after she wrote the cheque? Could it go that fast, all that money? Enough to pay the rent on her co-op apartment for over a year? More? Enough for rent and food just gone? Would this be it? How could she set up Elfie? And why was she even thinking of money when that poor man had just died in the most horrible way? Trapped, helpless!

She clicked the TV off and heard the Bach cello music Elfie played more frequently now than the opera; melodies heavy as motor oil that oozed out from beneath her door and stained the entire apartment with sadness.

The third week of October, a Saturday. Weather warm with a crisp underlayer during the day, near-freezing at night. Sidewalks glazed slick in the morning. Elfie stood in the small reception area of the office where she had been working since late September. Grey carpet, a room divider in complementary grey tones. White walls. A sophisticated phone, also grey, that rang discreetly—didn't ring so much as hummed notice of incoming calls. The one picture on the wall a Robert Bateman print of a fat sheep. Behind the room divider, keyboarders entered amorphous words and numbers off documents the clients wanted processed. Data processing. The big contract had necessitated an extra processor, Elfie, but now the work was finished and Elfie was needed no longer. Joy, the office manager, thanked her for her good work.

"I'd like you back if we get that contract we bid on."

"What day would that be?" Elfie asked.

"I'm not sure. It's not definite."

Joy was a big, pretty woman who wore short skirts, though

her legs were thick as railroad ties, and had beautiful thick dark hair; a crescent of tiny silver rings and studs pierced her right ear. Her people skills had catapulted her to the position of manager quickly. She did not want even temporary employees, such as Elfie, quiet and diligent Elfie, to feel they were being fired when they left. But Joy's kindness was unnecessary in Elfie's case as she had never expected this to be more than a temporary job.

"Gayle and I always go for sushi on Saturdays. Want to join us?"

Elfie declined. She was not hungry but she had nothing else to do until Monday, when she would call JOBWORKS to report that she was available. She started walking east—towards home—and saw opportunities to kill herself everywhere she looked. She could step out onto any intersection on Hastings Street, into the path of delivery trucks and commuters storming through. Perhaps wait for a moving van. She could blow her paycheque on drinks in the stinking Hastings Street bars outside which men and women loitered, their faces and in some cases bodies deformed by alcohol their mothers had drunk, or they had drunk, by punches or bites or acne or makeup too pasty or runny. She could hang around Cordova Street until dark, her presence alone alerting the druggies who always needed something that everything she had was theirs to take. She could jump off one of the bridges—the Lion's Gate to the west or the Second Narrows further east. Remembering the quandary Shinny always fell into when she had to drive to the north side of Burrard Inlet—which bridge should we take? Which would be fastest?— Elfie snickered at the thought of having to decide which to choose to jump off and laughter's close relation opened her heart and her view for several blocks. Mom would die if she killed herself. But now, in Gastown, she could see through the spaces between buildings the railway tracks and the waterfront park where Grandma Shinnan's memorial bench sat. I could lie on the train tracks, she thought. Walk into the oily harbourfront tide.

Earlier this month, on the anniversary of Elfriede Shinnan's death, Shinny had brought Elfie here after returning from the cemetery at Meadowvale. "I think she would have been happy with this, don't you, Elf?"

The sandbag that was her heart prevented Elfie from speaking. It was hard, even, to swallow. She nodded agreement, though the bench made her mother happier than it would have made her grandmother, she suspected. Grandma liked it out in quieter Meadowvale. The people around here, the junkies and schizos, would have frightened her. Shinny had become so accustomed to the city she didn't notice and Elfie hadn't the energy to confront what would surely be Shinny's denial of that fact. Sadness being harmonic, thinking of Grandma, whom she missed, meant also thinking of Brendan. Brendan was out of her life for good, yet, instead of closing over, the space he left continued to expand, as if the tide receding from the shore of the inlet would never rush back but ebb and ebb until all the muck on the harbour floor lay exposed.

She stopped at a brackish pond fringed by cattails and rushes where a great blue heron stood in stillness absolute. Brittle maroon claws from the Japanese maple mingled with yellow willow spears on the ground. If she could achieve the heron's perseverance, might change come of itself?

"But I could be with you, Grandma," she whispered, moving on to the Elfriede (nee Vanderclag) Shinnan bench. Elfriede Shinnan did not speak to her namesake grandchild as she did to her daughter. That is to say, she spoke, but her words did not penetrate Elfie's consciousness. Had Elfie been receptive she would have heard her grandmother's gasp: No! No! But the Bach suite in D-minor for unaccompanied cello dominated Elfie's mind and distributed her emotions on its melancholy scale. Da, da, da—da, da da, da, da, da, da, da . . .

She bent to unbuckle her high Italian shoes—no sense wasting them—and rested her forehead on her knee. Almost three months of this. Enough. Unfolding her body to stand and shake off first one shoe and then the other, she saw a cyclist wheeling towards her and impulsively stepped into his path. He squeezed his brakes barely a metre from her.

"Jesus, not again!"

She fainted.

Because Elfie's voracious anxiety consumed the few calories she ingested each day, her weight had fallen to just over a hundred pounds. She was nothing to lift, though Andrew was careful in case she had bumped her head when she hit the ground. He felt for her pulse, which beat weakly, splashed her face with water from the bottle he kept attached to his bike frame, then proceeded to administer the CPR he had learned as a teenage lifeguard. Pinching the nostrils of Elfie's narrow freckled nose, he fingered her thin parted lips further apart and moved his fuller, redder lips over them.

Elfie fought to consciousness through the gale-force of his breath in her throat. She was being smothered by a bicycle-helmeted man who was too old to be Brendan, and she started sobbing.

"Thank God!" Andrew helped her up and onto the bench. This side of emaciated, with long-fingered hands, long legs, green eyes streaming. She jabbed at her running nose with her wrist. His spandex cycling tights had no pockets which might contain Kleenex or a handkerchief, though he felt for one just the same. "Are you okay? Look, your shoes are unbuckled. That's probably why you fell. Didn't you see me?"

Sobs quaked up from her chest, preventing her from speaking. The sharp briny wind off Burrard Inlet pierced through her light jacket and she curled into herself to resist the external chill. Andrew didn't know what to do. There were social service agencies on the town side of the overpass, on Main and Cordova Streets. She could have drifted down here from a woman's shelter but he didn't think so. Her neat black pants, the stylish impractical shoes, the expensive jacket did not look like the clothes of a homeless schizophrenic, and a purse hung bandolier-style over her chest and her shoulder. A panic attack?

"I'll help you get where you need to go if you'll tell me where that is. I can lock up my bike. Or I'll put you in a cab."

Still no words but longer intervals between the sniffing. He said, "You know it's funny, well maybe not funny to you, but this is the second accident I've had here. Except I guess this wasn't my accident."

Pretty hair, the creamy yellow of fresh split alder, obscured her face. Not wanting to alarm her on top of everything else, he consciously restrained himself from moving an arm around her shoulders, as was his instinct.

"Last time a woman who was sitting here yelled at me and I lost my balance. Fell off. This is that woman's bench, a memorial to her mother."

The light head lifted a little, the eyes pounced at him. A marbled red and white face, green eyes greener in their net of pink veins. The saddle of freckles.

"I mean it's a public bench. People can donate them in memory. That's what she did. See? The plaque?" He felt successful for having distracted her until the olive orbs in the red net sank beneath rising water.

"It's my name," she confessed. "My grandmother. My mother donated this bench."

"So you're the daughter? The musician?"

She nodded, sniffed.

"Have you been sick?"

Elfie had barely the strength to hold herself upright, but it would be okay. The music inside her head had stopped. This man would let her lean against him, and he was trustworthy. He knew her mother. She wiped her face with her hands then held them together as if praying. "Yes," she admitted. "I have been."

When Shinny got home from work that evening she found Andrew at the door preparing to leave. Elfie had made coffee and eaten a banana and a slice of toast at Andrew's insistence. She had washed her face and lathered it with aloe vera lotion and combed her hair and now, except for redder than normal eyes, she looked herself again.

"I was feeling sick," she explained. "I fainted. He found me."

"So this time it was your side that went down," Andrew joked, as if he and Shinny were engaged in a contest. "She's okay now but I'd try to get some more food into her."

"Well, thank you. Are you really okay now, Elf?"

She nodded but her eyes were on Andrew, who was holding up the piece of paper on which she had copied Shinny's phone number.

"I'll call later," he said. "To check. Take care of yourself, will you?"

His gaze excluded Shinny and the unmistakable affection of it tripped a warning signal that flashed yellow in Shinny's mind. That reddish hair in a thick fringe around his balding pate, and he looked taller than she remembered as he rolled his bike out the door into the hallway and stood at the elevator. The elevator. The green arrow pointing up. Green eyes.

"You know it's really weird," she said. "I know he cycles the sea wall a lot, but in all the time I've been there I've seen him only twice, that I know of. The chances of him meeting you must have been about as good as winning the lottery."

Elfie stretched out on the couch while Shinny heated the Alfredo sauce she had picked up at Oliveri's on the way home; easy and a favourite of Elfie's, before she stopped eating, that is. Feed her, he'd said, as if Shinny had not been! Who was he to advise her?

"I was really lucky he came along. Down there I could have been rolled before I came to." Elfie had forgotten her intention to walk into the sea. In her mind the story was set as told; weak, fainted, rescued. "He's nice. His brother was a musician."

"Yes," said Shinny, "I know."

"And he knows Keith, from UBC. Do you remember me talking about Keith?"

Shinny filled the sink with water, squirted in detergent. Dipped lettuce leaves, saw her error and pulled the plug, held the leaves under cool running water. Would the salad taste like soap?

"So my job ended today. I guess I was just feeling weak. I walked all the way there in those stupid shoes! Anyway, Andrew says he thinks he can find me something at City Hall, but he says I ought to talk to Keith first, because there might be something at UBC."

Andrew says, Andrew thinks.

"I thought you didn't want to teach. Yukio had students for you." Shinny poured herself the last of a bottle of wine.

"I know, but it wouldn't necessarily be teaching. Anyway, I'm going over there for dinner tomorrow night, with Andrew. I can ask about it then. Got any more of that, Mom?"

"No!"

She had her bath and watched figure skating with Elfie, and then she went to bed, though not to sleep. If Elfie and Andrew were going to date, she would have to tell Elfie the truth because Andrew could be Elfie's uncle and if that was the case, sex between them would be incest. But if she told the truth, Elfie would hate her. She would lose her chance with Andrew on top of having lost Brendan, and not only them but the person she thought she was. Her sense of self, her trust in her mother, Smokey, the man she had been calling father. So much loss! Could a sensitive girl like Elfie stand it? The traffic light at the corner sent ghostly reds and greens and yellows through Shinny's window, colours that changed at regular intervals, playing on the ceiling like the changing coloured lights of jukeboxes she remembered from her youth. Sometimes the beat of the lights and the music matched, but the lights alternated hue rapidly whether the rhythm of the music was fast or slow and watching them during slow numbers—"Love Me Tender"—could be disorienting. To think she had been attracted to Andrew. Embarrassing! She turned on her side, thrust her hands between her thighs. Her scalp felt as if it were literally bulging with worried thought. Elfie, before you get too involved with Andrew, there's something I have to tell you. And the $15,000 she had hoped would grow quickly enough to provide Elfie with an extravagant new start

virtually gone, though Shinny's anger about the money continued to be complicated by the sickening image of those black
hands against the window. Eberhard Stuibel. A terrible death and
one recorded like the explosion of the space shuttle years ago, the
spaceship with the teacher on it. How strange to watch someone
you love die accidentally: the moment when life met death more
dramatic, as when Larry fell into the river; the splash every bit as
loud in her mind now as it was the actual night. It was bad
enough that the image of those hands haunted her; what about
Eberhard's family? Then Carter Biggs on TV twirling his forefingers as he spoke, trying to put a good face on it all. Eberhard's
legacy. What? Nodules? A fascinating enough idea, little lumps
on the sea floor: Shinny thought of the plastic eggs that contained surprises for kids. The nodules were supposed to contain
valuable minerals. *Did* contain valuable minerals, except in
quantities lower than early results had indicated. A failure for
poor Eberhard, for Carter, for herself. But in my case it's only
money, she told herself, waiting for the comfort she hoped the
thought would drop softly as a cashmere cloak on her shoulders.

The next morning, although the store was closed on Sunday,
Shinny let herself in with her key and went directly to A and C's
office. First she called Carlo, who gave her a phone number consisting of many digits. Marietta, Carlo's cousin, would help;
Shinny only had to ask. Yet just thinking of Italy reminded her
of the opera, the havoc truth could wreak. Azucena got her
revenge but the Count had to live with his brother's blood on
his hands. In that case the sins of the father, who burned
Azucena's mother, were visited on the son. Father, son. Mother,
daughter. If Andrew and Elfie married and had children!
Shinny's eyes flitted from the piles of unsold insulation material
Anthony had stacked around the office to the picture she had
framed for Carlo, of him and Joan with Elfie between them, at
Elfie's going away party, as the phone in Milan rang and rang.

"You don't have to stay with him, Elf. You can live on your own and continue your studies if he really has turned into a jerk." The next words came out as programmed all those years ago by Shinny's mother: "Don't rush into anything."

"I don't think he's a jerk, I think it's just hard for him to resist flattery. He's going to have to learn because he's going to be famous." Fresh haircut, a big black sweater against which her skin appeared geisha white. The black shoulder bag, the violin case with its long strap. Still too thin but she had promised to eat a lot of pasta.

Marietta had learned from Brendan that he had been writing Elfie regularly but she had sent his letters back unopened. She was that hurt by his betrayal. "Call her. I think she really does want to hear from you," Marietta had urged. And it turned out as Shinny had hoped: Elfie dropped any notion she had about dating Andrew as soon as she heard Brendan's voice on the phone.

"*Figlio mio!*" Elfie sang, with the gypsy passion of Azucena, though of course Brendan was not her son.

"And you're sure you don't want to stay for Christmas, the new year? The new millennium?" She would not have asked if she thought Elfie would say yes but she missed her now, this awful weather, the apartment empty. One of the demolition crews that regularly worked the old neighbourhoods had finally smashed down the derelict house across the street. Shinny looked onto a lot vacant as the years she had left to fill.

"It's the Internazionale, Mom. The stringed instrument expo in Cremona. It happens only every third year. I really wanted to go and now, thanks to you, I can."

Because it was getting too cold to wear the expensive jacket she had bought for the rafting trip, Shinny hauled out the trench coat she had worn for years and inspected the lining, which hung beneath the hem. How to fix it? Mom had always done the mending she needed for herself and the girls. She should buy a new coat, but the thought of spending money now frightened her. Fifteen thousand! And then, not even a month later, a third of that to send Elfie back to Italy and give her a start, so that she did not have to depend on Brendan. Breathtaking, how money could fly away, except that in Elfie's, case it was money well spent; Elfie's happiness and her own reprieve. She poured another cup of coffee, weaker than the espresso Elfie brewed when she was home, and stared through the water that varnished the sliding glass door. Open space stretched between the co-op and the houses on the street beyond, a longer view.

She didn't have the right colour thread for this coat—she'd have to take it to a tailor. Instead she buttoned a heavy cardigan over her blouse and held the cuffs in her palms so that the sleeves wouldn't bunch up when she put on her jacket. Socks, duck shoes for walking up Robertson Street to A and C's. A bag to carry the Reeboks she wore behind the counter. She grabbed her umbrella last and paused at the door, as she used to do when the girls were little and she needed a moment to collect herself after they had wrestled out. Okay.

Though it was still four weeks before Christmas, Anthony liked to get a jump on the holiday and put shoppers in the mood to buy with festive reminders of the giving season. Over the weekend he and Carlo had strung coloured fairy lights around the display window and the main entrance. Shinny let herself in and called "Hi," but the store was empty. A flashing light led her to the message machine where Anthony's hurried voice informed her that Carlo had been rushed to hospital with a heart attack. Carlo? Her own heart drummed as she dialled Carlo's home number. Carlo's recorded voice had the squeezed sound of someone with laryngitis. Marlon Brando as Don Corleone. "Hello! You have reached the home of Carlo and Joan Emmanuele. Leave us a message and we'll call you back." Of course the whole family would be at the hospital. Should she open?

Nine fifteen. The nearest hospital was Vancouver General. By refusing to respond to the button-pushing instructions, Shinny made it past the automated information system to an actual person who agreed to page Anthony Emmanuele. An orchestral version of the old Beatles song "I Will" played in her ear while she waited, fooling with key matrices hanging from the revolving carousel on the counter by the register, wiping dust from the tin in which customers dropped coins to aid cystic fibrosis research.

"Anthony, it's Shinny. How is Carlo? Is he okay? I'm at the store."

A sob before he spoke. "So young, so fast. My little brother!"

"He's gone, Anthony? Already? No! I don't believe it!"

Shinny instantly visualized Carlo in the arms of the angel who was spiriting him away from earth. Her whole body yearned to reach up and tug him back. Not you! Not yet!

Anthony needed Shinny to take care of business, to post a

sign on the store and notify the casual employees. "Sure, sure. Anything," she agreed, sniffing and swallowing, trying to maintain some control of her emotions for Anthony's sake. Elfie was going to be devastated. Why did it have to be Carlo? Why did it have to be any of them? Mom, Larry, Princess Diana, Mr. Gillespie, John Lennon, the children of war, the man who had died that suffocating death underwater, Eberhard Stuibel? Each life seemed to be stamped with an invisible "best before" date that expired too soon.

She punched in the number of Ted, the warehouseman and part-time clerk.

"I have terrible news." With every repetition of that phrase, the reality of Carlo's death cut more deeply, as if the words were moving needles engraving permanent grooves on her heart. It wasn't just his Marlon Brando-like voice that inspired Shinny to think of godfathers in connection with Carlo. Because of him, Elfie had someone to turn to in Italy if anything went wrong again.

She pressed the security alarm switches to the "on" position and flipped the open sign to its opposite side. Most of the shopkeepers were just unlocking their doors. She couldn't pass without relating the shocking news, to Carmela, at the bakery, to the sisters who ran Oliveri's. Lou Lui who had bought the salad market next to Joe's Café. Joe himself.

"It's Carlo," she said at each stop, both corners of her lower lip dipping as if divining a new source of tears. "A heart attack. He was shaving and Joan heard a thump in the bathroom."

Jas, who ran the Commercial Drive branch of Patels, reminded Shinny that Carlo had only recently celebrated his fifty-fourth birthday. Anthony had bought an ad in *L'Eco d'Italia*. "*Buon compleanno!*" it had said over a picture of Carlo at four with his toy dog, a beautiful sable-eyed child whose hair was then dark and curly. Carlo had seemed older to her, but she supposed that was because he was one of her bosses.

After accepting the hugs and condolences of the shopkeepers,

Shinny had nowhere to go but home. She stopped at the super-
market first and bought a ham for the grieving family. But once
she had scored the fat in diamond patterns and studded it with
cloves and shoved it in the oven to bake, she still rustled with the
need to do something. There was a cake mix in the cupboard, or
she could try biscuits. Why not both? She had not cooked so
much since her mother was alive—just a year ago last summer,
when they threw the big send-off party for Elfie and Brendan.
Carlo and Joan, even Anthony and Adriana had come with *bon
voyage* gifts for the couple. So much had changed, Mom gone,
now Carlo. Carlo! His marble-bright eyes, his pleasant practi-
cality, his salt and pepper moustache, his white hair. No wonder
she thought him older. His white hair aged him, which was why
she preferred not to let hers grow in naturally but kept it dyed
the platinum shade she first tried out on Larry: platinum, the
colour of something more valuable than snow.

Though the oven racks were full, she set a stick of margarine
on top of the range to soften for cookie dough. Had she eaten
all the chocolate chips? She searched the food cupboard which
she had not seriously looked into since Elfie left. It needed re-
organizing, if not a thorough cleaning. She pulled out cans of
tomato paste and pitted black olives, half-used packages of mac-
aroni and rice. Before he left the office each night, Carlo liked
to straighten his desk. He had too much unfinished business to
manage a wholly clear desk, but he could and did gather up pencils and pens and drop them into the copper elbow joint he used
for a pen holder. Pencils all together, computer turned off, discs
in their protective sleeves, order books piled to the right,
invoices to the left. Those half glasses down his nose as he
studied the monitor screen, his enthusiastic broadcast of the
slightest percentage improvement in business, the slightest
losses. Used to drive Anthony crazy. "Who cares about an eighth
of a percent, Carlie? We gotta think big if we're gonna hold up
against those guys." Now what?

A few of the smaller old businesses on the Drive closed for the morning so that the various owners, long-time friends of the Emmanuele family, could attend the funeral mass at St. Jude's. Shinny wore her mother's good black coat, the coat she had last worn to the Vistagrande meeting, and made sure to stuff plenty of Kleenex into the pockets. The parishioners had decorated the sanctuary with fresh fir trees for Advent. Carlo's coffin, draped in a purple satin funeral cloth, rested in the centre as if in a forest clearing, same as Snow White, apparently dead of the poison apple the witch had given her, lay in her glass-domed casket in the forest, surrounded by grieving dwarves—an image Shinny remembered from the storybooks she used to read to the girls. In the story the Prince came along eventually and revived Snow White with a kiss, but Carlo's casket was closed, there would be no prince, and the trees in the sanctuary would be taken away between Christmas and New Year's.

Shinny had not been in a Catholic church, or any church for that matter, since childhood. The pews needed refinishing and tattered prayer books filled the compartments facing the kneelers. Organ music drowned the soft weeping of the Emmanuele women. Shinny did not recognize the hymn, which was appropriately sad but not as desolate as the cello suite Elfie had played and played. The night of the day Carlo was stricken, as Shinny lay wakeful in her bed, the Suite in D-minor purled darkly back into her mind.

The priest bustled into the sanctuary, knelt in front of the altar, then stood. The congregation stood, then knelt. Shinny copied the behaviour of the people around her, hardly thinking of what she was doing. A photograph of Carlo, framed in gold and propped on a music stand, faced the congregation. She concentrated on that because she did not know the prayers everyone was saying, she could not join in. The priest strode to the lectern, everyone sat.

"In the name of the Father and the Son and the Holy Ghost."

She crossed herself with the others, though she felt a sham.

She had put her faith in a man who managed money. Instead of believing that God made all things possible, she had convinced herself that the power lay in Carter Biggs.

"We have lost a good man," the priest started. "Carlo Benedicto Emmanuele. We have lost and Carlo has gained His Maker. Our tears are for our loss, the husband, the brother, the nephew . . ."

The boss, Shinny continued her own, more pertinent, list. Her friend and advisor, Elfie's patron. It was Carlo who had first suggested mutual funds as the place to invest her inheritance. "Study up," he told her. "There are good ones and bad ones."

But how was she to tell which was which? The business news media paid habitual respectful attention to Carter Biggs. Ken had approved. That halo: she had thought it might be a trick of the light while simultaneously wanting to believe she had been touched, that Mom or someone was pulling strings which would rain good fortune on her, like the contents of one of those gilt-edged clouds she occasionally saw at sunset, that billowed with promise. The sight of those beseeching hands on the grainy glass. She covered her eyes as if the picture were outside her mind. Esperanza was being investigated by the police, there had been rumours of fraud. An internal fight for control of the company. Contaminated by the bad news, Vistagrande's other funds had dropped in value.

Carter Biggs sent regular communiqués designed to comfort and encourage his clients. "Many of you have been scared away, but there was every chance you could have increased your investment tenfold in less than a year. Those of you who have not jumped ship still might. Technological difficulties can be worked out. Eberhard Stuibel took risks and up until that last tragic moment of his life his risks paid off. There is still every chance that the nodule deposit Eberhard discovered will yield the quality ore early results indicated. I caution you not to pull out now." He was not withdrawing his promise of riches, in fact he raised his estimate of potential earnings with each note, but any profits she made now would be tainted with the image of those hands. She should sign off, let other, more callused investors finance Esperanza's wild schemes. But Carter's optimism gave her pause. Carlo might well advise her to stay in long enough to recover her losses. Perhaps greed didn't really come into it when a person wanted only to recover her loss. Wouldn't anyone want to do that?

The priest continued the story of Carlo's life. "And after he served with the Candadian Forces keeping the peace in Cyprus, he came back to Vancouver and got himself educated. He earned his commerce degree from UBC. As you all know, Carlo never thought of a career outside the family business. It was enough for him to stay home, to make a life among his family and friends, his parish, his community."

Shinny thought of the phrases on benches. "In memory of Robert T. Kerr. Walked beaches, talked beaches, lived beaches." And the poem, "Remember me as a scarlet leaf that stops the heart for a moment but brings no grief." In loving memory of Carlo Emmanuele, talked hardware, lived hardware. She could purchase a bench for Carlo. It would mean another few thousand, though, unless the casual employees chipped in.

At the cemetery she stood with the other neighbourhood merchants and Ted and his girlfriend Alicia while the priest anointed the casket and Anthony helped Carlo's wife Joan to throw the ritual first handful of dirt. Joan stood back from the grave accepting the hugs and handshakes of the mourners, the only sign of shock her granite eyes which never actually focussed on anyone but were poised in their sockets precipitously, as if disgorged from a crater into which they might roll back any moment. The passing trough had left the sky the grey of an oyster, with the oyster's flaccid texture and its wet stench. The sharp narrow heels of the women punched holes in the pliable earth beneath the slippery grass. When Shinny looked up she saw golden arches over the hedges meant to screen the cemetery from the cars whizzing by on 33rd Avenue. Had it not been seriously disrespectful, she would have laughed. But she knew what this was, the icy flow down the back of her knees, her eyes squeezed shut, neck tendons in knots as the curtain slammed back, metal rings clanging, fabric swinging. She had breathed the air of the city all these years, but in her mouth today it tasted poisonous. The wind swept through the cemetery exhaust fumes and the scorched odour of strained electricity on the bus lines, rotting vegetables and animal waste from overturned cans in alleys, unwashed bodies huddled in doorways. Corrosive substances and paint from the body shops on East Hastings, cloying emissions from Roger's Sugar. Decay. No wonder rage had flamed in Eberhard Stuibel's terror as he realized the inevitable. What rights had death over a man who was on the brink of enormous wealth?

Money lost, people lost. Did it all come down to what could be said about you when you were gone? A dutiful daughter, a responsible mother, a loving grandmother, a store clerk. She knew what she knew, but today what she knew and who she was seemed too small for the size of the world. Her place a vest pocket, her being no more significant than the ticking piece inside that marked time. She raised her eyes again, having forgotten that she wouldn't find peace or inspiration, only the big McDonald's sign against a rheumy sky. It was better in church, where the organ music had provided the bass line that accompanied the weeping. The traffic noise just seemed to mock everyone's sorrow.

People were heading back to their cars. Anthony had one arm over Joan's shoulder, the other over his wife Adriana's. From where Shinny stood the three appeared a construction, each a beam supporting the other as they hobbled towards the limousine that would transport them to the Italian Cultural Centre for the funeral meal: elaborate antipastos, pastas and sausage and chicken in red sauce and some kind of fish, veal parmigiana, special crusty breads, foccacia, spicy olives, salads with rad-dichio, wine. Shinny had attended Emmanuele family gather-ings in the past. The food was always terrific.

She hurried over to hug Joan, then returned to the grave to whisper goodbye to the bronze, rose-blanketed casket that would be tactfully lowered into the ground after the family left. The other mourners followed Joan, Anthony and Adriana toward the next step in the ritual. Their sure sense of culture, their religion guided them in every crisis. They had no doubts about what to do, but Shinny was not one of them and she daw-dled, reading inscriptions on gravemarkers, most of them sim-ple, names and dates that passed through her mind without registering. She waited beside one of the cemetery's remaining cedars for the procession of cars to pass by before continuing on to her Pony. Grief had not staunched hunger but she shied from the prospect of joining the family at the Italian Cultural Centre. McDonald's beckoned from the next block. If she went inside and sat at one of the colourful checkerboard-sized tables, where no one knew her or all that had befallen her, she might convince herself that the carnival never ended and her pass was good for unlimited rides.

Anthony reopened with a heart heavy as if it were pumping the marine glue he kept in the bonding agent section of the store instead of blood. "What are we gonna do?" he sniffed, a man who didn't care if people saw tears in his eyes, which was fortunate since the tears stood in his eyes like water in a plugged sink for days after the funeral. He jabbed at his face with a wadded handkerchief as he worked, shuffling merchandise from shelf to shelf, accomplishing little. Then, as cells gradually multiply to create scar tissue over a wound, the demands of the business began occupying more of Anthony's attention. Christmas less than a month away. Not the apex for A and C it was for some retailers, but busy all the same, an opportunity to sell the espresso outfits and cappuccino machines, the hand-painted pasta bowls and novelty items—battery-operated slippers to warm the feet, chia pets, a new line of garlic presses in the shape of garden vegetables, a device for drying home-grown herbs. Tortilla warmers. Digital calendars for the first year of the new millennium. Two thousand, two thousand, two thousand.

Anthony had been planning a street party, but now, instead of celebrating, he would be grieving the brother who had not lived to see the start of the new millennium. "It should have been me," he complained spontaneously now and then, and no matter what they had been talking about beforehand, Shinny understood immediately what Anthony meant. That Carlo should be last born, first gone tore at Anthony. Moreover, they were short-handed. Anthony would have to do the paperwork himself or hire someone to do it. Anger presently evicted his tears. "He deserted me!" he shouted at the keyboard Carlo's fingers had skittered over so naturally. He ripped the plug out of the computer and hurled the keyboard against the stack of unsold insulation batting where it chuffed softly before clattering onto the linoleum floor.

"Typical grief reaction," said Lawreen. She and Shinny were talking on the phone because their overloaded schedules had prevented them from getting together the last couple of weeks. Ted, the most experienced of the part-time help, could not work full-time until his college term ended in mid-December, meaning Shinny had to put in extra hours to make up for Carlo's absence. The Blakes were juggling the demands of a TV series, plus two jobs, but Lawreen had good news: her boss was going to give her a three-month leave of absence starting in January so that she could spend shooting days with Mariah on the set. "And I'm going to do more with Matthew, too. I've signed him up at my gym. We'll go together."

"Good. He's been on his own too much." She was asking for it from Lawreen, Shinny knew.

"He'd rather be home by himself than at daycare, Mother. Ask him."

"I have to go, Lawreen, I have a customer." She clicked the phone off before Lawreen could reply because Andrew had just walked into the store with his nephew. They paused at the door, where Andrew shook the rain off his umbrella and set it into the black plastic bucket that served as the store's umbrella stand.

Shinny straightened her back, placed her big hands shoulder-width apart on the counter.

"Hiya, Shinny. Hear from your daughter yet?"

"Mail takes so long. I will. She's pretty good about writing."

"A great girl. I hope it works out for her." Shinny did not know Andrew well enough to determine whether he was being polite, for her sake, or if he really meant it. If he had been as interested in Elfie as Shinny sensed, wouldn't he hope it didn't work out for her? Ty edged a birdbath-sized, hand-painted pasta platter onto the counter. "Wedding present," Andrew explained. "This is a tad spendy, my lad. Can you find something else?"

Shinny reached under the counter for a sucker. "You're getting tall, Ty. Too tall for candy?"

His slick green rain jacket brought out the jade of his eyes. She had to know. "Ty, we have some nice coffee mugs that might fit your budget. Down that aisle over there."

Jas had come over to show Anthony the fine points of the computer program Carlo had installed; the store was otherwise empty.

"Ty has really beautiful eyes. Did your brother have green eyes?" Fragile as a glass bulb, her nerves were filaments he could illumine with a simple word.

"Green eyes? Nope. Those are exact copies of Jeanette's. The hair is alike though, look." He opened his wallet to the miniature album, which contained a studio portrait of his dark-haired brother and strawberry blonde Jeanette, with two-year-old Ty between them.

"Ooh."

"What?"

"Nothing. I just thought he'd be a redhead like you. A good-looking man, such a shame." It wasn't him! It wasn't Elfie's father! Even though she had seen him just the one night, she remembered enough to know that the man in the picture, Andrew's departed brother, Ty's lost father, Eric, WAS NOT ELFIE'S FATHER!

"That's a good choice, Ty." A mug with the image of a cat face, the whiskers three-dimensional. "But you better get one for Keith, too." Andrew pulled a twenty out of his wallet, smiled as he handed it over. If Ty's father was not also Elfie's father, as Shinny knew for certain now that he was not, then Andrew could not be Elfie's uncle. It would not have been incest.

Shinny made change automatically; should she feel guilty about this? Would Andrew have been better for Elfie? Twenty years older? No. But solid and probably not as egotistical as Brendan. Oh, Elfie.

"Here you go." She poured change from her hand into his. A hand larger than hers with hair growing low on the wrist and the backs of the fingers, a thumbnail purple from having been caught in a car door or hit with a misaimed hammer blow. The pale skin on the underside of his arm. "Anything else?" His brown tweed snap-brim hat framed his brows nicely, and his eyes, his slightly bulbous nose. She liked the way his smile revealed his small teeth, thin to the point of being opaque. The teeth suggested innocence, a sincerity that appealed to her. But this was ridiculous, he wanted Elfie, not her, and if she pursued him Elfie was bound to think that Shinny had sent her back to Europe because she wanted Andrew for herself! Ridiculous! Embarrassing! Where did these urges come from? It couldn't be biological, for she was far too old to reproduce. Didn't the body—including the heart—ever get it?

"Nothing else today, right, Ty?"

"Okay then, I'll see you. Maybe at the park, but don't worry. I won't get in your way," Shinny assured him.

He lowered his head when he laughed, as if it shamed him to remember his near collisions with Shinnan women. "I'm not worried. You take care, eh? And if I don't run into you before then—not literally—have a good Christmas." He leaned over the counter and kissed her cheek and she wished he would just hold still for those smooth cheeks of his felt as good as she had imagined they would. Of course he pulled back. "Happy New Year, too!"

"You too! And you, Ty!"

All that worry for nothing. Yet the carroty-haired man with the green eyes and his brothers, sisters—whatever relations he had—were out there somewhere, with the potential to enter her life unexpectedly as the streams that flowed through underground volcanic pipes into the river she had rafted. Maybe now that he was safely unknown again, maybe this would be the time to tell Elfie. A letter would be easier than a heart to heart. A letter would give Elfie time to absorb the news before reacting to it. Shinny began to compose one on the spot. *Dear Elfie, there is something I've been meaning to tell you . . .*

But it was five-thirty, time to close. She cashed out and dimmed the store lights and carried the register tray back to Anthony, whom she found weeping at the computer.

"I can't do this," he confessed. "This is not me."

"Didn't Jas help?"

"Sure he did. I can do it when he's here. You think we ought to merge? A and C's hardware and samosas?"

"Anthony."

"It shoulda been me."

"Oh Anthony." Shinny set the register tray on the desk, put her arm around Anthony's meaty shoulders and hugged him. He let his head fall onto her chest, she patted his upper arm.

"Maybe I should learn. I've been wanting some kind of change. I could take a course. What do you think?" His head was heavy on her and she liked the warmth of it though she had a distasteful view of dandruff cluttering the part in his hair. She was about to bring her other hand round to pat his shoulder, but he had moved his face so that it nuzzled directly into her breasts, not much for breasts—Adriana had the pillowy kind Anthony was used to—but sensitive all the same. She eased away. "What do you think, Anth?"

"I don't know, Shinny." He grabbed the picture of Carlo and Joan with Elfie between them and held it with both hands. "I don't know," he repeated, to the picture. "Maybe I should just pack it in. Those big stores. It's just a matter of time, eh, Shinny?"

"You're not supposed to make any major decisions right after a death," Shinny cautioned.

"Oh no? If not then, when?"

"Do you still have that wine, Anthony? Come on, let's drink a glass to Carlo. Let's remember him before we forget. It can happen."

"Never."

"I agree, but you never know." She fetched the coffee mugs from the bathroom.

The apartment was cold when she got home, though she had left the temperature dial turned to eighteen degrees. Would he really sell out? It was possible. Today had been a bad day, he might change his mind, but tonight she felt that she should be looking for a new job. She had worked in hardware for over eight years; wouldn't one of those super hardware stores love someone with her experience?

The weather had turned colder; the rain emulsified into shredded white ribbons of sleet. She turned the thermostat to 25, hung her wet trenchcoat over the shower-curtain rail. How would she manage if she lost her job? Fifteen thousand just gone! Fifteen thousand could have lasted her the better part of a year. Damn!

"Tina?"

"Shinny, hi. What's up?"

"Oh, Anthony. You could have predicted it, poor guy. He doesn't know if he wants to keep the store."

"Really?" Tina's voice crimped through the line, the sound of someone talking with the phone clamped between her shoulder and her ear.

"Is this a bad time to talk?"

"We're actually going out for dinner, Shinny. Scott is going to babysit Homey so I was just getting him dressed for bed. Can I talk to you later?"

"Tomorrow. Call me tomorrow, or I'll call you. Have fun."

She would try Smokey but Oona might answer and ask her advice about the baby, as if Shinny were her mother—everyone's mother—and not a woman who had been Smokey's lover just as Oona was now. Too bad. Smokey had always listened sympathetically to Shinny's problems, even if he seldom could solve them.

"Annette?"

"Mom, hi! What's up? "

"Oh nothing, just wondered how you were. Have you thought about what you want to do for Christmas?"

"Not really. Do you want to come down?"

"I was thinking you might want to come up here. I'd cook. We could have Lawreen and Ken and the kids over."

"Do you know how hard it is to leave a herd of fifty goats, Mom? I mean Greg is here, but it's a lot of work, and Dad has the new baby. I think he and Oona want me to cook for them, or at least help. Why don't you come down?"

"I'll think about it." Three girls, three different lives. "One of my bosses died, Carlo. I guess you never knew him, but he was the one who was so nice to Elfie."

"Oh I'm sorry, Mom. That's really too bad. Have you told Elfie?"

"Carlo's cousin told her. I wrote. To tell you the truth, after the summer she had I didn't want to hit her with any bad news, but I know she knows."

"Are you okay, Mom?"

"Just a little sad. He was a nice guy. Could mean changes at work."

"Why don't you come down, or wait until after Christmas. We're going to have a humongous millennium party. Everybody's coming."

"Yep. There's going to be a lot of those. Well, say hi to Greg."

"Bye, Mom. Take care. Sorry about your boss." Annette, gone since she was seventeen, physically strong, spiritually adventurous, more like her dad than her mom, she felt, which was why she had moved down to California as a teenager, to live with him.

"It's nothing against you, Mom. It's not like I don't love you, you know?" Her mass of brown hair, her stocky body, still beautiful then, as teenage girls are beautiful with promise, her habit of beaming a smile meant to put a positive stamp on whatever she said, however hurtful it might be.

The steely skeleton of the new development across the street sparkled with collected rain in the light of passing cars. Shinny still felt something was missing when she looked out, but it couldn't be the vacant lot because the lot was no longer vacant. What? Then she remembered. For not the first time since Elfie left, she had passed through the lobby without stopping to check her mailbox. She took the stairs because she wanted to avoid Deke or Jackie or any other co-op neighbours. Then, standing in the cage of her walker, gazing soulfully out the entrance, yet hesitating—as of course she would—was Mrs. Ferishenko, dressed for the weather in her fur coat.

Back upstairs in her warmer apartment, Shinny piled the donation-seeking letters from charities—so many of those at this time of year—to one side and re-examined the postcard from Elfie she had read on the way up. An image of Raphael's Madonna and child on the front, and on the back, only *Grazie Grazie, Grazie, Grazie.* She closed her eyes and whispered a *grazie* of her own, convinced that she had done the right thing.

The envelopes with the rising sun logo she set to the side, not having the stomach just now to learn whether she had lost any more money. She would save them for last, or maybe put off opening them until tomorrow. It would be good if she were richer this month than last, because if Anthony shut down the store she was going to need every penny she had, but it would only depress her to find the opposite.

Finally, there was a letter from Glen, his third since their aborted visit in late September. Instead of handwriting, he printed neat letters that filled most of the space between the pale blue lines on the white paper he used.

Dear Shinny,

I thought I ought to report to you that my shoulder has healed completely. I threw out the mess of stuff they gave me at the hospital up there and just slathered the sore spot with arnica, mostly external applications though I drank many pots of arnica tea also. So now I am my own best advertisement for herbal healing, if I don't count you and the success we had in reducing your poison oak rash.

He wrote the *g*'s but she heard his voice dropping them.

This is the quiet time of year on the farm. I read, I plan, I play with figures, trying to invent ways of financing all my plans. I have decided that I'm going to go independent this year, which means that I will be growing a variety of medicinal herbs instead of devoting my fields to echinacea for the big outfit down here. Do you remember those sample plots I showed you? I have a product to market now and I plan to spend some time this winter visiting wholesalers and retailers in the Northwest. If I can get a few standing orders I ought to be able to make it through my first year, though as a kind of insurance, I've signed on with the State extension branch to do some survey work. Nita and her kids have been thinking of exotic names for our stuff but I would rather keep it simple, Riverbend Botanicals. I intend to let Nita fool with the computer graphics for a basic label, she enjoys a change from housework and kidwork.

Well, that's the news from this neighborhood and though I've been wrapped up in it heavily since our visit in the fall, I have also been thinking we ought to try a proper visit—maybe we ought to call it a date. Am I being too presumptuous?

Good word. Presumptuous.

She picked up the phone again, glad now and liquid with the undersea sensation Glen inspired. She had never known a Glen. A Glen, a Dale, none of those nature names. Not a River, not a Storm, not a Forest. "Is Glen home? Glen, is this you?"

"Shinny?"

"I just got your letter."

"It is nice to hear from you on a quiet night like this, a little snow coming down."

"Here too. Not snow, but quiet." I needed to talk to somebody, she wanted to say. I miss you.

"How are you, Shinny?"

She lied and said "Fine," and then she qualified her answer. "Mostly fine. Getting used to all the changes, my daughter back in Italy, then one of my bosses died of a heart attack. I thought people settled into quiet routines as they got older."

"That is still quite a ways off, Shinny, unless you're much older than you look." Then he said it, so easy for him, it seemed. Well, she reminded herself, he had married a woman and stayed with her for over twenty-five years. "I miss you."

She heard Leonora's lilting aria, the melody she had waltzed to in Glen's imaginary arms. "You do?"

Juggling their work hours so that one of them could chaperone Mariah on the set of "Cuties," the sitcom in which she played an up-and-coming child star, left Ken and Lawreen even less time for Matthew. Lawreen consoled herself with the knowledge that it would all be different in the new century, when her leave of absence began. Until then Mattie could stay home by himself after school, and keep busy with the chores she subconsciously gave him as punishment for her own shortcomings. Put the breakfast dishes into the dishwasher, make his bed, do his homework, set the table for dinner. Mariah's character did not appear in every episode, but the weeks that she was written in, she and Lawreen, or she and Ken, returned home late, usually not hungry because they had eaten on the set, and it was only Matthew, and whichever parent had gone to work as usual, who sat down at the table Mattie habitually set for four.

Tonight would be different altogether because it was reporting week at school and Lawreen had booked a seven o'clock appointment with Mattie's teacher, Mr. Fong. Then a long-standing client of Ken's needed help with an emergency audit. Ken could not refuse him.

"Will you go with him, Mom? He'd love you to anyway, you know that."

"Sure I'll go. I'll pick him up after work and we'll get a hamburger."

But when Shinny met Matthew at the condo, he said he wasn't hungry. "I think I'm sick, Grandma. Maybe we better cancel."

Shinny laid her cheek against his: no fever. Asked him to stick out his tongue. Nothing. She aimed a flashlight down his throat, which looked the normal watermelon colour. Report card jitters.

"Tell you what, Mattie. We'll get through this and then I'll bring you home and make you toast and tea if you're still feeling bad, or pick up some popsicles. Popsicles are good on a sick stomach. If you're feeling better we can get our burgers after the meeting, okay?"

Matthew slumped on a dining room chair. His baggy jeans and oversized sweatshirt masked the consequences of all the snacks he had eaten the last month as he did his homework, watched TV, opened the drapes now and then to see if Lawreen or Ken were coming up the walk. Or anyone else. He had not expected the house to swell as if his presence alone acted on it like a splinter under the skin.

"I might barf right there."

"Come on, Mattie." Shinny prised his spongy hand from his chin and urged him towards the door. He carefully removed his anorak from a hanger in the closet, replaced the hanger, slowly zipped the coat, scanned the shoes and boots on the rubber mat and chose the hiking boots it would take longest to lace.

"Come on, Matt. We're going to be late."

Shinny had not visited Sir Alexander McKenzie Elementary since last year's Christmas pageant. A large brick school recently earthquake-upgraded, it smelled of fifty-year-old chalk dust and the history of glue, of pencil shavings, enough lead granules at the bottom of pencil sharpners to alert the toxic waste police, spilled ink, dried apple cores and wet wool: no single odour equalled the stronger fake-pine scented cleaning solution with which the school janitors had laved every horizontal surface to prepare for this week's parental landings. Matthew had wanted his dad to accompany him to the three-way report-card conference. Ken seldom delved: if Matthew said everything was okay, then as far as Ken was concerned, everything was okay.

Mr. Fong continued to write his conference notes until Shinny and Matthew came within a few metres of his desk. Then he shot up smiling and extended his hand, cool and slick as a plastic bag in Shinny's larger swampy one. Why am I nervous, she asked herself. It had to be the old days, a note from the teacher requesting a meeting to discuss some difficulty with one of the girls, usually Annette: having to explain her situation as a single mother, enduring the skeptical, often downright judgmental expressions some teachers did not try hard enough to disguise. But that was over. She was just filling in here, a substitute parent like a substitute teacher: it's not my fault, she could say, with a shrug. Then she felt guilty for abandoning Matthew, even psychologically, even for the space of that short thought.

"Matthew's mom is involved with my granddaughter, who's in a TV series. Dad had a work emergency. But I'm glad it worked out that way, Mr. Fong, because I'd love to talk with you about my grandson's schoolwork."

Self-portraits the children had painted decorated the corkboard that stretched across the front of the classroom behind the teacher's desk. Rectangles that made a mosaic of faces, some small in relation to the background, yet pivotal as the centres of flowers: round or oblong faces with circular or almond-shaped eyes and smiling or expressionless mouths. Some young artists had matched background to eye colour. Others had incorporated an understanding of perspective: noses poking out of shadows that gave them dimension; chins continued from an obvious facial bone structure instead of being indicated with a sideways C.

"Thank you for coming, Mrs. Shinnan. I'm happy to meet you. Matthew has shared news of his sister's accomplishments. I believe he even made her part of his family history project, right, Matthew? You must all be very proud of her."

Matthew kept his hand over his mouth, the vomit could spurt up any time.

"And Matthew, too, of course, who is doing very well, as you see." He opened a cardboard file folder of Matthew's work: the report card lay on top and Matthew could see As and Bs. Maybe it would be all right.

"My only complaint, Matthew, as you know, is that . . ." Matthew sweated as Mr. Fong scrunched his shoulders together, making himself small. "My only complaint, Matthew, is that you're so . . . quiet," he whispered.

"I'd like you to speak up more in class, Matthew." This sincerely, with his eyes opened to their maximum circumference. "But he's a good listener and he has good study habits." Shinny restrained herself from hugging Mattie, knowing it would embarrass him. Mr. Fong flipped through the assignments Matthew had offered as evidence of his work until he found the black duotang cover in which Mattie had gathered his family history papers. "He also did a wonderful job on his millennium project. It looks like the whole family cooperated."

"Well, Grandma, mostly," Matthew said.

"An interesting family story, too."

"He worked hard on it, I know. He's the one who deserves the credit."

With his upper lip sucked right into his mouth, Matthew held his breath as if he were inching along the narrowest of paths, between a boulder and a precipice. He didn't want to look down because his body would follow his eyes and he would crash at the bottom but he didn't want to scrape himself on the rock, either. One step, slide the other foot behind, a second step. The same suspense in his body as when he hung over the river by Glen's farm. Each hair on his head felt like a straw through which sweat spouted up and trickled in lines down his neck. Then he noticed Mr. Fong reach for the stack of track program forms. "We're encouraging the kids to participate in the Heart Foundation's run for your life program. It's designed for students who don't participate in any of the team sports, eh, Matthew?"

He'd sign up. Sure. He'd sign up for anything if they could just leave.

"Do you have time, Mattie? Do you want to?"

"Sounds good."

Shinny wondered if she should have cancelled this meeting because Mattie did look pale, except for his mouth area, which was red from his nervous biting and licking.

"Just get your parents to sign the form." He turned to Shinny. "It's an honour system. Each participant agrees to run ten kilo-metres a week. When they reach one hundred kilometres they get to choose a prize donated by the Heart Foundation. Things like fanny packs, T-shirts, you know."

Shinny took the form and folded it as she stood. "Well thank you, Mr. Fong. My daughter and son-in-law will be proud to hear Matthew is doing so well."

Mr. Fong checked his watch: seven fifteen, right on schedule, but the next student had not yet arrived. He watched Mattie show his grandmother the round table at the back of the room where he regularly sat; they examined Matthew's self-portrait, in which he was smiling and his teeth were straight.

"Oh, Mrs. Shinnan?"

Matthew suddenly had to pee. "Grandma?"

"Just a minute, Mattie. Yes?"

"We're planning a bit of a ceremony around the millennium project. It would be terrific if you could talk a bit about your father's role in the war. We don't have any other submarine spies in the class. Unless all that material is still classified."

"*My* father?"

"Grandma, I really have to go to the bathroom."

"Go ahead, Mattie. I'll just finish talking to Mr. Fong."

Mattie couldn't let her do that: if they started talking she'd find out everything. If he could get her out of here right now he could convince her that the submarine story was just a mistake: Mr. Fong had her mixed up with somebody else.

"Grandma?"

"Go ahead, Matt."

"It's my stomach." He held his hands over where he imagined his intestines to be, forced a burp. Shinny looked from him to Mr. Fong.

"We'll talk another time, Mrs. Shinnan. My next customer is here anyway."

Christy Teagan, with both parents, the mom carrying a baby, pushed past Matthew.

Shinny inspected the hall decorations alongside the boy's washroom. Charts of all kinds depicting the history of the last hundred years, the major achievements in science, in the arts. Cut-out magazine pictures illustrated the charts, a Model-A Ford to the left of the advancement in transportation chart, the Challenger space shuttle on the right; Alexander Graham Bell and his primitive telephone to a shot of a computer lab; some-one in a white coat beneath a headline heralding the discovery of penicillin, to the famous picture of the cloned sheep Dolly. Century reviews much like this in tone had dominated the TV magazine shows until recently, when the emphasis switched to the future. What would the next hundred years be like? The optimists were predicting a new, more enlightened age, the pes-simists cataclysm. The same discussions occurred whenever a comet streaked close to earth. Signs, signs, everyone always looking for signs that their lives were about to change in significant ways. Shinny winced, remembering the halo she thought she had seen around Carter Biggs. Yet some perfectly respectable people were publicly weighing the potential effects of harmonic convergence.

Matthew was taking a long time. The first five minutes passed quickly, the next five slugged along as Shinny paced, keeping an eye on the door of the bathroom. More charts displayed examples of the school millennium project. She looked for evidence of Matt's family history but could find nothing she recognized. One picture showed a woman in an old-fashioned bathing suit holding a medal; someone's great-grandmother had been an Olympic swimmer. Nothing so glamorous in their family; it was no wonder Mattie made up a story about a submarine spy. Okay. She understood the impulse, but this was school: she could not allow Matthew to think it was okay to blatantly lie about the past, to invent a more interesting story just because he did not like the facts.

It was not until later as she tossed in her bed, troubled on Mattie's account, that Shinny realized she too could be accused of altering the past for her own purposes. It was a thought unwelcome as the notice of a fine for a parking ticket you've forgotten. Okay, superficial similarities, maybe, but deep down the two cases were hardly comparable, she told herself as she kicked off the covers and flipped her pillow to the cool side. Mattie's relatively harmless fiction would affect neither the living nor the dead, while the whole point of Shinny's story had been to erect a screen between Elfie and the injurious truth. If it came to a choice between hurting or lying, Shinny would lie every time. Especially with stakes as high as they were: Carlo's death had left her in no doubt about priorities. Matthew might make the same choice when he grew old enough to understand, but this was different and Matthew must have known he was wrong, she suspected, because he avoided her for as long as he could.

Finally, a boy younger than Matt, in a Spiderman T-shirt, came along and pushed at the bathroom door.

"Little boy? My grandson's in there, Matthew Webster. Will you ask if he's all right? He's been in there a long time and he might be sick."

The boy agreed with a nod, and when he returned, holding the waist of his jeans steady while he finished zipping his fly, he told her that Mattie was okay. "He says he'll be out in a minute. I think he's a little sick but he says he's okay."

Not sick so much as stuck. It would be easy enough to convince her that he had made up the story for fun, because of the sailor uniform, if she'd just leave the rest of the stuff alone. He felt just as he felt about the wallet, bound by fact. Grandma was the real live daughter of the man he described as a submarine spy, though the man was really a cripple who couldn't work much, which kept their family poor. The sick feeling came from trying to reconcile those stories.

He stepped out wincing, his hand over his mouth. If she thought he was sick she might forget to ask about the submarine spy.

"Can we go home?"

She had planned on treating him to ice cream. Instead they drove the few blocks to the condo. Almost seven forty-five and no one home yet.

"I'll make you some tea, Mattie. You go get into bed."

Matthew hunkered under the covers, still dressed, and pulled the cord that shut off the light. If Mom and Dad and Mariah came home just now the house would fill with their presence, their voices, the urgency of their needs, and he could hide out here unnoticed. He reached under the bed for a box of chocolate-covered raisins, a new box, which helped to quiet his rumbling stomach. The ceiling sparkled with lights from his stick-on stars. Perseus, Cassiopeia. He had copied those constellations from the encyclopedia but he didn't have enough stars to form any other whole constellation. The remaining stars floated solo or in minor constellations of his own design.

"Are you going to sleep already, Mattie?"

"I'm pretty tired."

"Here's some of that tea that settles your stomach."

"Okay, Gran. Thanks. Thanks for coming with me, too."

"I was glad to, honey. You're doing so well." She could simply decline the teacher's invitation. Lawreen and Ken would never have to know. Soon all this millennium business would be over and the past would settle into the usual recesses until Remembrance Day or some other anniversary released it again for a day or so.

"Matt?

"Yeah, Grandma?"

"Remember this summer when we were camping and playing pretend, and we made up stories and you changed them however you wanted?"

She wouldn't be mean about it. At least there was that. If his mom had found him out, she would have yelled at him. Matthew, how could you embarrass me like that? "I remember."

"You must know, Matt, that playing pretend and doing a history project for school are different."

"I know that."

"I guess you thought it would be cool to have a submarine spy for a great-grandfather. Well, it would have been, and let me tell you there were plenty of times I wished he was somebody else too." Because he got fat. From the handsome man in the photograph he turned into a large, wheezy cripple who smelled like cigarettes and sweat. Pain preoccupied him, though her mother was always trying to come up with ways to relieve it, like the suggestions from that book Shinny gave Matthew: "Be sure your socks are snug inside your shoe to avoid pressure sores."

Shinny supposed no one would want to hear about the real Joseph Shinnan, but she would not continue the hoax and speak at the ceremony. "Sip on the tea, Matt, it will help your stomach."

Mattie said okay but he didn't want to move. Shinny's big hand anchored the quilt over his chest in a comforting manner.

The electric baseboard heater ticked on. The stars were losing their light and when they dimmed completely the room would be darker than night in the city.

"Are you going to tell Mom?"

"I guess you don't want me to, eh?" Lawreen would be angry, Shinny knew, and demand that Mattie tell Mr. Fong the truth, rewrite his essay, and that would serve as punishment for lying.

"What are you going to do if I don't? Are you going to tell Mr. Fong yourself? That you misunderstood me? He was a sailor, so I suppose it isn't an absolute lie, more stretching the truth."

Matthew whispered in the dark. "Do you think I could just leave it, Grandma? Nobody really cares, not him, not Great-Grandma. All those people are dead. Does it make any difference?" His whisper thinned to a squeak so that she thought he might cry. Then they both heard the door opening downstairs.

"Let's think about it and we'll talk on the weekend. But I'm not going to participate in that ceremony. I can tell you that for sure."

"We could say you're going to be out of town, or sick."

"See, Matthew? It never stops at one lie."

The tension had exhausted him so that he didn't remain awake for long after his grandmother left the room. But in those few minutes he imagined the people who would open the millennium box a hundred years from now. Somebody had to think of them. They would have no way of knowing what was invented, what was fact. If he told the sad, boring truth, they probably wouldn't even read it.

Cara Mama.

I think of how miserable I was in Vancouver. All the things I could have done to thank Carlo for all he did for us. I meant to, Mama. Do good intentions count?

Brendan has written a little air for me, which we are going to record on tape and send to Joan. We went to church with Marietta and Luigi, and we lit candles for him. I feel almost guilty for being so happy again, Mama. But I love it here, and Cremona! We really feel there might be a future for us there. Brendan might even be able to get a job. About him and that cellist, last summer? Well the one time I did talk to Carlo he made a joke of it. Said Brendan was only doing the 'when in Rome thing'; said to get married, and that way, at least, I'd always be sure he came back to me because that's another 'when in Rome' thing. So I think Carlo must be smiling now that we really have decided to get married. We want to have a small wedding. Marietta will help with the arrangements, but you have to come, Mama, and Smokey, if he can get away, and Joan. Maybe you could even bring Mattie.

*It must be so different at work. I know you're going to miss him,
Mama. Me, too*... His eyes that looked so much like a happy ter-
rier's, his unique voice, and his obvious affection for her. He and
Joan had seen her perform in more concerts that her own father
had.

Elfie finished her coffee and stared out the window at the
rain. Not so different than Vancouver would be this time of year,
late fall. But here was Brendan pushing through the door, the
peak of his ball cap dripping across a frown that softened when
he saw her at the corner table. He pulled her violin case out
from beneath his rain-streaked trenchcoat, which meant it was
time to be going. *Pronto, pronto*, he said, then stalled her
progress with a kiss. She folded the airmail letter and stowed it
in her shoulder bag. Even if she were to post it today, Mom
would not receive the letter for weeks. Between the Italian and
Canadian postal services, it was impossible to know when it
would reach her. Maybe she would just phone instead. Mama,
guess what? We're getting married!

Following the instructions he found in her note on the door of
the co-op, Glen walked up the Robertson Street slope to the
Drive. Wet snow dribbled from the sky and clotted on the grass
of the small yards in front of bungalows plastered with light-
coloured stucco, their trim painted lavender or turquoise, hulk-
ing old-timers and newer buildings designed to look like
old-timers. Shinny, who was listening for him, nevertheless
jumped when she heard his rap on the door. She unlocked it and
let him into the store, which was lit in selected areas after hours
to discourage both customers and thieves.

"I'm sorry, Glen." He looked good. His glasses, the jutting
chin that suggested he was ready for whatever should happen
next. Greying hair, well, of course: at fifty or more, whose hair
was not greying? Those large soft earlobes.

"My boss Anthony is falling apart. I had to sit with him until his wife came to take him home, then I locked up for a minute to run home myself and put the note on my door. But I'm almost finished here."

She was wearing her work clothes and she hadn't bathed yet, though her hair was at its post-hairdresser best and she had grabbed a lipstick in that quick dash home. A splash of water on her face in the closet-sized bathroom off the storeroom, some lip colour dotted on her cheekbones and rubbed in with toilet tissue, to rosy her complexion. She had planned a rerun of their September date. Foccacia and chorizo for hors d'oeuvres, clean sheets just in case, though he would have to make the first move. It had been too long for her to risk being turned down. Now she couldn't leave the store until she finished the receipts, and she was doing them by hand because she didn't trust herself on the computer. If she made a mistake, hit the wrong button and destroyed all the accounting files, who would help her out of it?

"You could sit at Anthony's desk and wait, or take a walk? You might even find something you like in the store and if you do I'll let you use my discount."

He was shorter than she remembered but taller than Anthony as he stood in front of the counter she had moved behind automatically. Wearing a navy blue duffel coat with barrel-shaped wooden toggles that he fingered as he stood smiling at her. She saw hair sprouting from a gully in his cheek. Had he been thinking of her as he shaved and dressed for the trip? Carlo, face half-lathered: what had he been thinking when his heart constricted that final time? Of love? Of money? Of hardware?

"I will be just fine, Shinny. You go ahead and do whatever it is you have to do." When he turned she saw the squared off hairline that divulged his recent visit to the barber. They might have been having their hair cut at the same time in establishments separated by a hundred miles and an international border. Shinny had sat in the high swivel chair avoiding the image of herself under the relentless lights, brooding about both love and money, the potential of one, the uncertainty of the other, the capacity for hope in people.

Was it too late for her and Glen? The sudden memory of Carlo getting his last glance of himself in the mirror before he fell put hope in perspective. To be stricken in his bathroom! Toothpaste goo undoubtedly clinging to the sides of the sink, perhaps a line of black mildew around the seam between the tub and the wall. The smell of urine or deodorant. The toilet of his that stubbornly ran though he repeatedly brought parts home from the store to try and fix it. "Get a new one," Anthony had counselled. "You give up too easily, Tony, that's your problem," Carlo had replied. Would you say the same of me, Shinny wondered, already beginning another conversation with the dead. Sure, I could fall in love and kid myself that it would last forever, that I would last forever, but what would I see when I took off the blinders? If only life's concerns would swirl away, romance flood in. But there always seemed to be something or someone demanding attention, lapping at her feet, tugging at her hem, whispering in her ear like the echoes of the sea in a conch shell. Hadn't that always been the way?

"Glen?" A nice name. Glen, a mountain glen.

"Yes?"

"You can take this flashlight to help you see better."

In the office she finished balancing the cash and writing out the accounts, and stacked invoices that had to be paid in a pile right in the centre of Carlo's desk. She or Anthony would have to deal with them tomorrow, or hire an accountant, which was what Carlo would no doubt recommend. Carlo liked to pay on time. It had been important to him to be considered honourable, reliable: no wonder so many people attended his funeral.

"They'll understand," she told him. Here was another dead one to talk to. So many over there now, on the other side. She was tired, hungry, anxious for the evening to begin yet also apprehensive because she didn't know if she had the energy to catch up. She collapsed against the back of the desk chair and it bobbed and she drifted. Over there. She imagined the far shore of a river wide as the Fraser, people arrayed on a dazzling plain, poised attentively as the bank of volunteer telephone answerers on public TV pledge nights.

Glen came in and perched on the edge of the desk, facing her. "I'm just about there."

"It's all right, you can take your time. I don't intend to go anywhere without you."

"Carlo, at Elfie's going away party," she said, pointing at the picture on the desk. "He was our paperwork man. He knew everything." She glanced at the shelf of damaged goods, boxes containing jumbled plumbing parts, tools with broken handles, remnant lengths of cord and chain spilling out. "The place is really falling to pieces without him."

She was worried about losing her job, grieving for her lost boss. Brushing at her nose with the knuckle of her forefinger, casting her eyes in every direction but his. Was she having second thoughts? He moved to the back of her chair and placed his hands on her shoulders, which lifted and fell with her sigh. His thumbs slanted up and pressed the cables on the back of her neck, tentatively at first, and then, as he saw that she liked it, more deeply.

She felt clipped hairs grinding into her skin. Can I do this?

He was out of the habit of courting. Unattached women in the town came around after Louise died, bringing meals or inviting him over on the pretext of comforting him in his grief. There was a space and candidates eager to fill it the first two years. In the three since, his reputation as a resigned widower had erected a collar around him. He travelled for a few weeks each winter, stopping first in Bend to visit Evan and get to know his grandchildren, then winding south, visiting farms. Once he met a friendly woman in need in a tavern and let her seduce him after he slipped into the men's room for condoms from the machine. In that he felt like the high school boy he had been.

He liked Shinny and he thought he could love her. She had taken a step away from her family into the larger world, faltered, and fate had placed her near his farm. Then it was sheer empathy, and curiosity about the reasons behind her great embarrassment, as if the poison were her fault. A responsible woman. The absolute sincerity of her deep brown eyes. An honest woman. They had touched one another in aid.

The overhead fluorescent light flattened colours and when she raised her face he saw the weariness she felt.

To date someone who lived a hundred miles away, across the border with another country, could be a foolish thing to do, but why else had they bumped up against one another like this, both alone, over fifty?

His eyes roamed from the sympathy cards lying open on Anthony's side of the desk, to the framed pictures on the wall, of the brothers, individually and together, of the small staff of the store, including Shinny, with her hair long and springy, so that he didn't recognize her, to a poster advertising Eveready batteries.

With his hands still on her shoulders, he bent forward and kissed the bone above her ear and she melted a little before she remembered and intentionally lowered the temperature. She raised her hand, intending to take his and squeeze it: It's just that I'm so tired. But he took it and pulled so that she spun around on her chair and the miasma of sadness began to dissolve as clear blue desire burned through. Well yes. Pulled her up. Over her shoulder he saw the dangling cord that controlled the light above the desk, reached for it and yanked, and as accommodating darkness replaced the glare she fit herself against him, her big hands moving up to his flattened-out shoulder blades at the same moment as his arms crossed her back. His head craned around and down, nudging her face up from his chest, his lips across the facial landscape his mind had explored all these weeks.

Soft-hard, softness pressing on softness and her opening, the sea-anemone sensation again but responding to actual, not just the possibility of touch. Lips opening here and there, tongues meeting and regret for the coffee dregs she had drunk, the bitter taste that must be her mouth yet him not seeming to mind as they separated for an instant before he hove back onto her and their bodies swayed and pushed and his head came over her shoulder to move his mouth over her ear—mmm—her throat. She swallowed.

His hand found the space where her shirt had slipped out of the waistband of her pants, moved underneath and caressed the berms along her spine, hesitated, until her snuggling assent permitted him to continue up to her breasts. The phone signal fluttered, soft beeping sounds that were less startling than a ring.

"Leave it," Glen whispered.

She waited through the third ring when the machine intercepted the call, heard the worn recording of Carlo's voice inform the caller that A and C Hardware was closed for the day and would reopen at nine-thirty every day but Sunday. Anthony had not let her replace the recording. Not yet, he kept saying. It's all we have. The gentle, squeezed tones tore at her heart, as always. But who was calling after hours? Adriana? One of the girls? Nothing, no voice, only an audible sniff, a swallow. Joan?

It had to be Joan dialling to reach Carlo's voice, and her call deflated the mood. Shinny pulled back. It was too dark to discern Glen's exact expression, but light enough to see that his hair was mussed and that at some point he had removed his glasses. She laid her palm on his cheek.

"We should go back to my place."

He nodded as he leaned in, helpless not to, and slanted his head so that their noses would not keep their lips from meeting. A harder kiss that forced through the catch in her throat as she thought of Joan. Do it, do it. Do it before it's too late. Carlo would approve, might even smile at the teenage urgency that had them simultaneously think of the packages of insulation and throw them on the floor, enough to make a serviceable pallet between the desk and the shelves. Smile for sure at the farty sounds the batting made as they fell on it and Shinny helped Glen with the buttons of her blouse, anticipating the cool-hot sweep of his tongue on her nipples. Too long since she had felt that. As he moved onto her Shinny's eyes flew open and she saw the malfunctioning blender she had to send back to the distributor, catalogues, tools—including a long-handled screw driver that could stab them if it fell the wrong way. "This is silly," she breathed, her being divided into the equal parts of a quartet, yet each in a contrasting key. Would the police who patrolled the block and looked into the stores, just to check, look into A and C's window and notice the shelves shaking? Or was it still too early, it not being eight o'clock yet, on a winter's night in December, hardly anyone out?

Downtown Vancouver at noon bustled with office workers and shoppers and out-of-season tourists looking for deals in the city hotels. Unusual for Shinny to be downtown this time of day during the work week, but Anthony could not face the trip to his accountant's office himself. He wanted Shinny to go, but not for long: if she was away for more than a couple of hours he might edge back into panic. He no longer joked, he fretted, and not in the endearing mother-hen fashion Carlo used to fret. Anthony was fighting his urge to give up and the battle, combined with grief, forged the kind of anxiety that makes a person testy. The smallest frustrations provoked explosions.

It was a relief to escape his wearing presence for more than her usual lunch hour, but Shinny regretted having to hurry because she seldom got downtown. She parked in the basement of Eaton's and found an exit to the street, past the art gallery hung with banners advertising an exhibit of major British Columbia art from the century just ended. Fairy lights twinkled white in the bare branches of the trees along Georgia Street. She crossed Georgia at Howe on her way to the Marine Building, past Cathedral Place and the Brussels Chocolate shop. Then she spotted him, Carter Biggs, waiting to cross from the west side of Burrard: brown trench coat, beige shirt, brown tie, his brown suit, his brown hair. She thought it was him, yet it seemed as unlikely to see Carter Biggs here on an ordinary Vancouver street as it would have been to see Clint Eastwood or the Prime Minister or the President of the United States. Was it Carter Biggs himself or only a man who resembled him? When the light changed, she did not join the crowd of pedestrians heading west, but waited in place until he reached her side of the street.

"Mr. Biggs?"

A middle-aged woman whose platinum hair was covered with a dark purple, opaque scarf, aging skin, dark eyes, wearing a purple jacket and dark pants, duck shoes, peach lipstick. He paused before it registered that she knew his name.

"I've been trying to call you." His silvery-blond eyebrows gathered in tucks. "You're Carter Biggs, aren't you?" Before he could deny it she continued. He had to be Carter Biggs.

"I guess you don't remember me. We met at the trade and convention centre but that was almost a year ago now."

The traffic control light turned green and pedestrians and cars moved west again down Georgia towards Stanley Park and the Lions Gate bridge. Carter Biggs *tch*d impatiently: he would have to wait for the next light to cross and she was still talking.

Humiliating that he should not even remember her when she had thought back then he was reading her mind. "You gave me a pin." Up close she saw that his teeth were capped, his neatly trimmed beard shone and his skin did too, a light sheen of oil that smelled of apricot and almond. Perhaps the spotlight bouncing off his gleaming skin and beard had produced the halo that night. She had definitely seen something. "You wrote me that letter, about the possibilities like stars in the northern sky. I'm one of the people who lost money in your Futures Fund."

The light changed yet again and traffic roared up the Burrard slope through the intersection, but not before a driver turning west had completed his turn. The loud, flat thunk of metal on metal froze all motion for a second or two. Shinny glanced over and Carter Biggs stepped towards the curb. She grabbed the belt of his trench coat.

"Hey, wait a minute," he said.

"I'm sorry, but please don't go. I've been trying to reach you." This was not quite true: she had thought of calling, but she could not condense her feelings into words that would make sense to him. Didn't everyone dream of being rich? She and the girls used to buy lottery tickets once a week and tune into the Saturday night TV draw to watch the little balls tumble out the plastic tube. Hoping to see their numbers roll up, expecting to see their numbers actually, and comforting each other with philosophical phrases when they didn't. Then she did get rich, and now a good portion of that money was gone. So fast it left her breathless, exposed, as if the wind had ripped off most of the shingles in a single gust.

The massing crowd edged them back onto Christ Church Cathedral's grass apron, a corner of which had been worn through to mud by short-cutting pedestrians. Shinny stepped on a head of ornamental kale, moved her foot to the side. For Carter Biggs to understand, she would have to explain who she was.

"I've never lost so much. I never had that much to lose."

Irritated, he wrenched away. "You're out of line, lady. You should be talking to your broker."

Of course, he never was speaking directly to her, Shinny realized. Jas had been showing her all a computer could do and she knew now that modern business technology could make a form letter appear personal by simply adding a person's name to the standard salutation. She knew it and denied it in the same second because it was hard for her to confess to that degree of naïveté, even to herself. Over fifty and still a believer! Yet she had the pin to prove that there had been some personal contact.

The crowd had started moving again and Carter Biggs joined the flow.

"I just wanted to ask . . ." She followed him along the street, through the side entrance of Cathedral Place, into the high-ceilinged lobby where he stopped and swung around to answer her.

"I never said it was a sure thing. I emphasized that our new fund was a high-risk fund. You have to have guts to play that game. Did you sell your units?"

"I haven't had the nerve to do anything."

"Good. That fund is depleted, I'll admit, but it isn't empty and I still believe in Esperanza."

He meant his nod to end the conversation. He even smiled, if curtly, as he turned towards the bank of elevators, and, spotting one which was open, its green arrow pointing up, jogged inside. Before the doors slid closed Shinny impulsively stepped in too. Carter kept his eyes on the grey speckled floor tiles. He pressed the number of the highest floor, and the elevator shot up. In the startling ambiance—mirrors on three sides and an encircling brass rail at mid-height—Shinny did not recognize her own reflection and half-consciously tugged the purple scarf off, which helped.

"You talked about fear that night and I thought it was the fear of getting rich you were talking about, not the fear of losing everything. Isn't that what you meant?"

The elevator reached its destination and the door slid open to reveal a softly lit blue-grey expanse of textured wall with the brushed brass symbol of a company whose name she did not recognize instead of the rising sun logo of Vistagrande she expected to see. She had wondered about that logo, too: was it a rising or a setting sun?

"Can we talk in your office? I'll just take a minute."

He hesitated. The door began to slide closed.

"Aren't you getting out?"

He sighed, the brushed brass sides of the doors met and sealed.

"Which floor is your office on, then?"

He stroked his beard. "My office is in Toronto."

"You were trying to lose me?"

He pressed the G button and the elevator dropped. Shinny put her hand over her stomach. In the light of the recessed fixtures, his irises had a distinct topaz cast, like a cat she once had, and the expression in them—it amazed her to notice—was defensive as a cat's caught inside the neighbour's house. He thought she wanted to hurt him? Like disgruntled ex-post office employees in the States who return to their former work-place with a machine gun and open fire on their former work-mates? Did she look to him like the kind of woman who packed a gun?

"I just wanted to ask you what I should do," she assured him, and with the words in the air for her to hear she realized how foolish it had been to ever think he could counsel her: it would have been smarter to go out and buy a copy of the *I Ching* Smokey took with him when he finally left for good.

"Listen," said Carter Biggs. He began to repeat the advice he offered to clients over the phone and through radio and TV interviews, glancing from the burning sincerity of Shinny's gaze to the mirrored image of himself. There were all these clients who clung to him, he the fan on display, they the ribbons whipping on his mechanical gale. "At this point it's only a paper loss. And the lower price of the units means you have a good oppor-tunity to buy. If I were you, I wouldn't stop now, I'd invest even more. It would be the best way of honouring Eberhard. Don't lose heart. He never did. It takes courage."

The doors sighed open again and Carter Biggs patted her arm and she asked, tried to ask, if he had known Eberhard well enough to decide if that's for sure what the man would have wanted. Weren't some ventures just not worth the risk? But Carter Biggs was striding through the lobby to the street and her question was drowned out by approaching police and ambulance sirens. Two vehicles arriving at once, red lights spinning.

"Go for it," he called over his shoulder, seizing the opportunity to sprint across Georgia, where traffic had been forced to a stop by the accident.

"Hey!"

The snow line sharply cuts the north shore mountains in half. Wisps of cloud, not yet burned away by the sun, play around the peaks of the Lion's Range. There's enough wind to coax wavelets, which occasionally break out white on the starched deep blue of Burrard Inlet. The canning shed is brilliant, the bench damp—it never really dries out in winter—but Shinny has come prepared with a plastic garbage bag to spread out and sit on. Gulls balance on a shaded log still frosty. The wind cuts up but there is warmth in the sun. The occasional raven flaps airily overhead. January tenth already and this is the first time in the new century Shinny has come to the bench to clean up and commune with Mom. In her mind she sees the lips tighten, the chin dimple, the head turn. Mom, on the other side, a shadow on the dazzling plain, but forgiving. Shinny has brought her flannel cloth and some brass polish she picked up at the store. Take A Load Off, In Memory of Elfriede (nee Vanderclag) Shinnan. Maybe too simple, as Lawreen thought. But what else could she have said: Look before you leap? Make a lemon out of lemonade? The plaque on the newest bench in this park has a catchier phrase, the Teress Family's Magical Memory Bench. Lips part, eyes crinkle. See how beautiful, Mom? And in winter it stays much cleaner. It's too cold down here for junkies and prostitutes. There's hardly any garbage.

She reads the names on the sides of the big, boxy containers. Evergreen. Hyundai. It's possible her Pony arrived at this dock, in one of those containers, though it seemed a strange way to ship a car. Maersk. Lots of those. Hanjin.

She had meant to get down here on New Year's Day but she stayed with Mattie instead while Ken and Lawreen and Mariah attended an open house at the studio. Mattie was feverish and he slept for most of the day. The big snow kept Glen at Riverbend, to shovel roofs, and it was hard getting around, which is why, when she left Mattie, she didn't drive to the park but straight home, using the most well-travelled streets.

Carlo's death, Glen, Christmas. She had lost track of Mattie, and New Year's Day, which he had been looking forward to all year, as all the kids were, he passed in bed instead of celebrating and hanging all the new calendars, setting watches and computers to 2000, as he had planned to do.

She made a special tray for them, their first meal of the new century, with turkey soup and Portuguese buns, a fruit salad made with fresh kiwi and banana, frozen berries and the little marshmallows he liked. She mixed orange juice with soda water and trickled in some juice from a bottle of maraschino cherries. Carried it up.

"Mattie? It's Grandma. Happy New Year, honey. Can I come in?"

"Mm?" He feigned grogginess, sleep, because he was hoping to avoid Grandma and everyone else until that capsule, with his stories, was safely buried in the earth. He imagined them stewing in a pot for one hundred years after which time they could be safely consumed. It was supposed to happen today but a lot of activities had been cancelled on account of the weather. He would have to wait here, in torture, until he knew. Though he had not given her the go-ahead, Grandma came in anyway.

"You feel okay, honey? Let me feel your head." Her big hand cool on his skin, rough with callouses, not soft, like his mother's. "Well, you don't seem to be running a fever. Stick out your tongue. Mmm, yes. Looks like something's going on in there, but I bet it isn't contagious." She kissed his cheek. "See what I brought? We have to celebrate. This is your century. People my age won't see much of it. It's your turn now."

She piled pillows at his back and helped him up, smoothed his hair, smoothed the blankets. Placed the tray on his lap and sat on the edge of the bed. He reached across the bunched steam from the soup and fished a marshmallow out of the salad.

"This reminds me of last summer when I had poison oak. You know there's still a kind of scar from that." She held up the back of her right hand where a blot of faded brick mingled with pale brown spots, the horizontal wrinkles, the bulging vertical veins. "Glen invited us back. Kids cross-country ski down there, Mattie, and he said he could fix you up with a pair. You and David could go together, if you were careful. Wouldn't want you to try any stunts like last time."

Mattie saw Shinny's head in miniature with white hair around it like frosting on a cake and her raisin eyes. "Grandma?" She had this dreamy smile.

"Hmm?"

"This might not really be it, but if it is, Happy New Century, Grandma."

"You too, Mattie. Especially you. It's your century and I'm glad for you."

The buns were still warm and Grandma had buttered one. Matt bit off small pieces, took a long time to chew. Crumbs fell on his dark green sheets. Shinny speared a slice of kiwi. Narrowing his eyes, as if looking through his scope, made it seem to Mattie that Shinny sat on a rumpled bed far away. A nice, light-haired lady wearing a red sweater with a big rolled collar. When she pursed her lips, crepe-paper creases formed in the space between her nose and her mouth. He blinked and she moved further back. Already they lived in their own countries, where she believed one thing and Matthew knew that what she believed was a fantasy. When Mr. Fong asked the children what they had learned from their projects Matthew kept his hand down, because he didn't think Mr. Fong wanted to hear what he'd really learned, which was that if you're able to convince someone of a lie it gives you power over them. The people who opened the capsule a hundred years from now and read his family story would have no reason to think it was not entirely true. Shinny believed his story was false in only that one part about her father. Matthew knew the full extent of the falsehood, which set him apart from every other person in the world.

A confusing thought. The pieces of it didn't exactly come together in his mind so that he absolutely understood, but the distance he had created between himself and his grandmother, not to mention the rest of humanity, pained him as tangibly as stomach cramps. He saw himself floating through southern seas, balanced precariously on an iceberg chip, and the journey made him hungry.

Shinny ascribed Mattie's reticence to illness and decided it would be best if he slept. Downstairs, she dialled Glen's number, but no one answered. She imagined him standing on the roof of his house, shoving off snow. He would have to have boots with good treads on them; he better have. Another catastrophe might finish their delicate join, unless this was to be the pattern for them, passion like a fish occasionally leaping above the calm waters of mutual comfort. Maybe Elvis had been right after all, maybe there was a natural progression from want to need to love.

Please, Mom, she whispers now. Just this one more chance. The puff of her breath mingles with the atmosphere too quickly for her to discern its singularity for more than an instant.

"Hark go the bells, sweet silver bells, all seem to say, throw cares away." The radio stations stopped playing Christmas music weeks ago, but the carol of the bells continues to chime in her head. Ding dong, ding dong. Only a paper loss, said Carter Biggs. Low prices are good opportunities to buy. Ding dong, ding dong. He said she had to have courage and a truly courageous person would chuck the entire business, she suspects; content herself with all she has. This waffling identifies her as either a coward or a smart cookie, something else she can't decide.

Cold seeps through the plastic bag from the sodden slab of cedar. Shinny stands, then sits back down, reluctant to leave in spite of her discomfort. She will bring Glen here if it doesn't snow before Thursday, when he said he would come. If it does snow he will have to postpone his visit and stay at the farm to shovel roofs again. Until planting time nears he will drive up whenever he can, he promised, and then it will be her turn. She closes her eyes to better revisit the sensation of them both waking at the same moment in the middle of the night, amazed and grateful, soon wildly laughing at the memory of their frantic coupling at the store. Then she remembers who's listening to her thoughts and blushes, just as if her mother had actually caught them. A tug blares notice of the freighter it is piloting out towards the open Strait, and the gulls lift off the black silhouettes of their claws on the frosty log to scream soulfully after it.